I0819038

K'WAN
TROUBLEMAN

K'wan is the bestselling author of *Animal*, *Welfare Wifeys*, *Section 8*, *Gutter*, *Still Hood*, *Hood Rat*, *Eve*, *Hoodlum*, *Street Dreams*, *Road Dawgz*, and *Gangsta*. *Animal* was chosen as one of the five Best Books of 2012 by *Library Journal*. K'wan has also been featured in *Time*, *King*, and *New York Press*, and on MTV and BET best-seller lists.

ALSO BY K'WAN

Black Godfather: The Black Death

Passion for the Heist

False Idols: A Reluctant King Novel

Promise Kept

Promise Broken

The Reluctant King

Animal 5: Executioner's Song

Black Lotus 2: The Vow

Wrath

Lawless

The Diamond Empire

Hoodlum 2: The Good Son

Animal 4.5

Diamonds and Pearl

The Fix 3

Animal 4: Last Rites

No Shade: A Hood Rat Novel

The Fix 2

Animal 3: Revelations

Ghetto Bastard: The Beginning

Black Lotus

The Fix

Animal 2: The Omen

Animal

Eviction Notice: A Hood Rat Novel

Welfare Wifeys: A Hood Rat Novel

Section 8: A Hood Rat Novel

Gutter

Still Hood: A Hood Rat Novel

Blow

Eve

Hood Rat

Hoodlum

Street Dreams

Road Dawgz

Gangsta

TROUBLEMAN

AUWA
MCD / FARRAR, STRAUS AND GIROUX
NEW YORK

TROUBLEMAN

A NOVEL

K'WAN

AUWA
MCD / Farrar, Straus and Giroux
120 Broadway, New York 10271

EU Representative: Macmillan Publishers Ireland Ltd, 1st Floor,
The Liffey Trust Centre, 117–126 Sheriff Street Upper, Dublin 1, D01 YC43

Printed in the United States of America
First edition, 2026

Title-page art by d1sk / Shutterstock.com.

Library of Congress Control Number: 2026010102
ISBN: 978-0-374-39425-7

Designed by Gretchen Achilles

10 9 8 7 6 5 4 3 2 1

For Marvin . . .

We're still trying to figure out what's going on?

CONTENTS

PROLOGUE

Have you ever found yourself surrounded by people but it was so quiet that you could hear a pin drop? Like something had occurred to where everyone who had witnessed it was stunned to silence? That's how this story starts, with something so heinous that no one uttered a word after it happened, but it would be talked about for years to come.

He stood before the hotel window gazing out. The room was on the twelfth floor and gave him a view of the city. Sometimes he forgot how beautiful the City of Brotherly Love could be, mostly because he rarely got to see it from such heights. Most of his time was spent in the mud, wallowing with the pigs who dwelled there. A strong wind came through what remained of the shattered window glass, causing his leather trench coat to flap in the breeze like a superhero cape. Fitting, because that's how he felt at that moment, like a superhero who had just clobbered a villain. It was said that the glass they used in those high-end hotels was damn near indestructible, even able to stop bullets. He had punched holes in that story—and the window.

A young girl sat huddled in the corner. She was brown-skinned and maybe seventeen years old. Her arms and legs were covered in what looked like cigarette burns, and one of her eyes was swollen shut. She had taken a hell of a beating. With her good eye, she watched him standing in front of the broken window, seemingly fearful that he would now turn his rage on her. It had been so long since he had seen her that he doubted she even remembered who he was. He wanted to explain to her who she was to him, and how he had ended up there, but there would be no time for all that.

Behind him, he heard banging at the door and someone shout, "Police!" He remained at the broken window, looking out into the night. A few ticks later, a master key clicked open the hotel room door lock. This was followed by the sounds of several sets of footfalls on the carpet. Somewhere behind him a police radio squawked. He went to his knees and placed his hands on his head. He was all too familiar with the procedure. Someone grabbed his hands and twisted them behind his back with more force than necessary. He could feel the officer's hands trembling while he put the cuffs on him. *The nervous rookie,* he thought to himself. He didn't fault the young man. He'd probably have been extra cautious too encountering a six-six behemoth in the middle of a situation that was certain to make the front page of the *Inquirer*.

Once he was secure, the cop who had placed him in handcuffs stepped into view. To his surprise it was a woman, a Black woman. Brown if we were being technical—her skin was the color of unprocessed chocolate. Micro braids, pulled back into a ponytail that hung down her back from under her patrolwoman's cap. Her brown eyes bore into him as if she was trying to figure out if he was on drugs or had just taken leave of his senses. Toussaint was indeed blasted out of his mind, fresh off a bender, but even sober the result would've been the same. She moved to the broken window and cautiously peeked out.

While she was looking out, her partner appeared next to him. This cop was white and had two stripes on the sleeve of his blue shirt. He looked into the face of the man they were taking into custody and it was clear that he recognized him immediately—and was suddenly confused as to what exactly was going on. He opened his mouth to ask a question and that was when they heard the shriek come from his partner. She barely made it to the hotel room's wastebasket before she started throwing up.

Curious, the white cop with the stripes went to the window and peered out to see what had rattled his partner. Twelve stories below was the mangled, naked body of a young Latino man. A Chevy Trailblazer had spared him from hitting the concrete, but not his life. He was dead, but his would not be the only life snatched away that night. The white cop turned to the kneeling Black man, all the color having drained from his face. "What the hell did you do this time, Trouble?"

The man looked up at him with eyes as hard as his combat-worn knuckles and replied, "What needed to be done."

PART I

•

I BE TROUBLE

1

1,825 DAYS LATER

Outside 30th Street Station, in line with the Ubers and taxis picking up and dropping off travelers, sat a pearl-colored Lexus ES. In the driver's seat, smoking a blunt, sat a young man everyone called Jay-Jay. He was Chinese, handsome, in his early twenties, and acted like his brain held the wisdom of the ages. Jay-Jay, like most kids, thought that he knew it all, and would be quick to try and convince you as much. What Jay-Jay may have lacked in knowledge, he was sure he made up for in finesse.

It was a dreary day in the City of Brotherly Love. The rain had been coming down nonstop since the wee hours. It was eleven in the morning, but the heavy overcast made it look closer to midnight. The darkness hanging over the city was a sign of things to come.

The thump of an AR-Ab cut played from the car's stereo, rattling the windows. Jay-Jay sang the lyrics with so much passion you'd have thought he'd been the one moving coke on Allegheny Avenue instead of the notorious Philly rapper. It was way too early in the day to be bumping that kind of music at such a high decibel, but Jay-Jay didn't care. Ab's music spoke to everything Jay-Jay aspired to be in life. Jay-Jay considered himself a gangster and wanted the world to know it.

While singing along, Jay-Jay's fingers drummed impatiently on the steering wheel of the Lexus. He checked his watch and saw that it was after eleven. The person he was waiting for was supposed to arrive at 10:00 a.m., but he had seen no sign of him or the bus. "Fucking Greyhounds never on time," he muttered to himself. Had this been any one else Jay-Jay would've pulled off and left them to find their own way, but this passenger was special.

A blonde white girl was standing nearby, hiding from the rain among the pillars that fronted the station, handing out flyers to any traveler with a spare hand. She was cute, Jay-Jay thought. Not fine, but cute. Jay-Jay got her attention and motioned for her to come over, under the pretense of him wanting one of the flyers. The girl sheepishly approached the driver's side, sheltering her head under a handful of flyers. "What you doing out here? Selling Girl Scout cookies?" he asked playfully.

"No, I'm campaigning for Atticus Gallagher. He's running for mayor!" the girl said proudly and handed Jay-Jay one of the flyers.

Jay-Jay looked at the flyer. On it was a picture of a handsome redheaded man dressed in a navy suit and red tie standing in front of the Liberty Bell, posed like a superhero, his blue eyes narrowed and focused. "Shit, you're wasting your time. Everybody knows Sparks is going to wipe the floor with him in this election." He tossed the flyer out the window and onto the ground.

"For as hard as Sparks has been on criminals of color, I'd think you of all people would be planning to vote for someone whose mind isn't stuck in the sixties," the girl shot back.

"First off, lil mama. I ain't colored; I'm Chinese. And second, everybody knows the votes from the ghetto don't get counted, so why even bother?"

The girl opened her mouth to say something, then closed it. It was obvious that the Chinese boy in the flashy car was too ignorant to even grasp what was at stake, so why bother even trying to explain it? She picked up the discarded, soaked flyer and walked away, shaking her head.

"Square bitch." Jay-Jay laughed to himself before relighting his blunt.

It was close to 11:30 when Jay-Jay finally spied the man he had been waiting for. He was moving through the wave of people who had just been dropped off, bumping by the white girl like she wasn't even there. He was hard to miss since he towered over most of the crowd. He was a brutish-looking son of a bitch, standing at about six-six, with shoulders so broad he looked like he was wearing football pads under his cheap, white cotton T-shirt. Jay-Jay sat up straight and tossed the blunt out the window, fanning away the excess smoke. He looked at himself in the mirror to make sure that his pristine Phillies hat was broken at the perfect angle and that his gold chain hung just right. For him, this was more than just a pickup. It was an audition.

The man had broken away from the crowd and was making his way towards where Jay-Jay was parked, green duffel bag slung over his shoulder. He walked down the row of cars, peering into each of them curiously and at a safe distance. He was a few cars down, so Jay-Jay flicked the high beams of the Lexus to get his attention. The man took a few steps in the direction of the car and suddenly paused. It was then that Jay-Jay realized that the windshield was too heavily tinted for the man to see who was behind the wheel. He had been gone for a while but not long enough to dull his street edge that dictated he never approach a car before making a positive ID of whoever was inside. Jay-Jay stepped out into the rain and stood so that the man could see him. He still didn't seem convinced. "It's me, Uncle T! Jay-Jay!"

Toussaint hesitated for a beat before deciding that the man was being truthful about his identity. It had been years since he had seen Jay-Jay, but the boy had his mother's eyes. Jay-Jay, his mom, and his sister were the only people of Asian descent that Toussaint had ever met who had green eyes. It was a genetic quirk passed down from their great-great-grandmother, who was said to have been Irish. "I know that ain't John Junior out here shining like a new penny?" He playfully shielded his eyes as if the image of Jay-Jay in his fancy car and jewelry were blinding him.

Jay-Jay spread his arms so that Toussaint could get a

look at him in all his new fabulousness. "Who but me?" he capped arrogantly.

Toussaint grabbed Jay-Jay in a bear hug and swept him off his feet. Jay-Jay stank of weed, but it was so good to see the face of a loved one, Toussaint didn't even care. That stench coming from Jay-Jay's clothes affirmed what had felt like a dream during his entire ride back to the city. He was home. They must've been quite the spectacle—the behemoth Black man twirling around with the Chinese boy like they were auditioning for the Ice Capades—because people had stopped to watch. Toussaint felt like he was embarrassing Jay-Jay, so he set him back down. "Shit, John Junior, you done grew so much I almost didn't recognize you."

"Can't stay a kid forever. And it's Jay-Jay now."

Toussaint understood what Jay-Jay was saying. He was a man now, who had stepped out of his father's shadow and simply asked that his individuality be acknowledged. "My bad, Jay-Jay."

"Let me get your bag for you."

"Fuck that bag." Toussaint reached inside and pulled out what looked like a book, neatly wrapped in a pillow case, before shoving the bag into the trash can. "It ain't nothing but full of reminders of where I came from. Only thing I need to be reminded of is where I'm going."

Toussaint sat with his seat reclined and the window cracked just a sliver. Not enough to let the rainwater in and risk it damaging the interior of Jay-Jay's fancy car, but just enough to where he could hear and smell the city. He had been born and raised in and around Philadelphia, but it didn't stop him from feeling like a tourist, taking in the sights and sounds for the first time. It was an odd thing how the landmarks that he had passed almost daily and never gave a second look before he went to prison took on new value now.

"This is a nice ride, Jay-Jay." Toussaint ran his hands over the wood-grain dash of the Lexus.

"Sweet, ain't it?" Jay-Jay beamed. "I can get this jawn up to a hundred on the highway and you'd barely notice."

"I'll take your word for it. You must be doing pretty good out here these days to be able to afford such a fancy whip."

"I do okay," Jay-Jay said with a nonchalant shrug. But then he admitted, "It actually isn't mine. A friend of mine let me hold it when I told him I was coming to pick you up."

"You've got some pretty generous friends," Toussaint said. No way he would've let Jay-Jay's young ass borrow his fifty-thousand-dollar automobile.

"Membership has its privileges." Jay-Jay winked. "There was no way we were gonna let the legendary Troubleman get ushered back into town in some old beater. Now that you're home, it'll be nothing but the best."

"I'll settle for some clean sheets and a hot meal."

"We got that on deck. Mom is in the kitchen hooking it up for you as we speak," Jay-Jay informed him.

Toussaint smiled, remembering Sue Wei's cooking. Sue was the head chef in the Chinese restaurant she owned with her husband, but her skills weren't limited to just Asian cuisine. Sue could cook just about anything. One time she had made Toussaint some macaroni that was almost as good as his granny's. "It'll be nice to see your family again. They did a lot for me when I was down."

"Only repaying the kindness you showed us before you went away. My dad has never forgotten how you helped save his business. Never lets us forget either." Jay-Jay chuckled.

Toussaint had first come to know the Wei family many years ago. Their restaurant, Good 4 Yu, was one of the newer ones in Chinatown, having only been open maybe a year or so. Toussaint had stumbled upon their establishment by chance. This was when they were still going by New Wei Chinese. He had been working a case in the neighborhood and was looking for something to eat. He had popped in looking to grab some wings and fries and discovered that New Wei was anything but your typical Chinese restaurant. They had a menu that had everything from traditional Chinese cuisine to soul food. He wasn't sure what to get, so Sue suggested he try their smothered rib combo. Toussaint was skeptical but gave it a shot and was surprised to find that the meal was delicious. From then on, New Wei became his go-to spot whenever he was in the area and sometimes when he wasn't.

The relationship between restaurateurs and patron

developed into a genuine friendship, between Toussaint and John Wei especially. The older man became somewhat of a mentor to Toussaint and helped him through some rough times. So when the opportunity presented itself to return the kindness, Toussaint eagerly rose to it. A dealer named T-Bone had been putting pressure on some of the businesses to pay him a weekly street tax. Those who complied would be left alone, but those who didn't would suffer the consequences. John refused to pay T-Bone's tax. And in the beginning, he was able to hold off, but replacing the windows T-Bone's boys kept busting had started to get expensive. One night, two of T-Bone's boys had even robbed the place at gunpoint. They were wearing masks, but it was no secret who had sent them. Sue urged John to pay, but he refused to cave. For him, it was a matter of pride. The Weis never told Toussaint what they were dealing with, but the streets talked and Troubleman was always listening. A few days later news hit the neighborhood that T-Bone was in the hospital with two broken legs. As the story went, old T-Bone had gotten himself drunk and stepped out in front of a moving car. The problem with that story was that everyone knew that T-Bone didn't drink. When T-Bone was released from the hospital, he found a different neighborhood to terrorize and never bothered the Weis again.

"Tell me something, Toussaint. Did T-Bone really get drunk and step in front of a car that night?" Jay-Jay and Toussaint both knew this question was just a way to warm the big man up and welcome him back home.

Toussaint gave him a knowing smirk. "How would I know?"

There was a long, comfortable pause as they both soaked in their shared past. Finally, Toussaint broke the silence: "So, I know how your parents have been doing, because they wrote me a lot and sent packages while I was in prison. And you look like you're doing all right for yourself. But haven't heard too much about your sister. What's Aimee up to these days?"

"Mostly running dad's pressure up." Jay-Jay shook his head.

"How you mean?" The Aimee who Toussaint remembered was a sweet little, chubby girl, who used to light up like a Christmas tree whenever he would sneak her snack cakes from the corner store. He did this in secret because Sue was always on her about her weight. The only thing Aimee liked more than snacks was computers. While other girls her age were outside jumping rope and chatting about boys, you could find Aimee in her room on her laptop teaching herself how to code. Aimee had always been the less problematic of the Wei children.

"Aimee been on some different shit since she got kicked out of college."

"*Kicked out?* Aimee loved school like Black grandmas love church. What she do that got her the boot?"

"Same thing she's been doing since we were little: minding other people's business." Jay-Jay went on to tell Toussaint the story of Aimee's meteoric rise and fall.

Aimee had always excelled in all things related to academics. She never received anything less than an A in school and graduated high school at the age of sixteen. In one of the letters Toussaint had received from John, the man bragged about how Aimee had received a full academic scholarship to the University of Pennsylvania. By year two, to hear John tell it, she had become the crown jewel of their computer science program. There was no computer system that Aimee couldn't find a way to crack. It was a rare gift, and one that would put her on the short list of potential recruits for the FBI after graduation.

But then Aimee had been accused of hacking into the school's system and went from FBI recruit to their watch list. She had done it to help a friend, Jay-Jay said, Trudy, who had found herself in a spot of financial trouble. Her dad had lost his job and their family was struggling to keep up with tuition. Unlike Aimee, Trudy didn't have the benefit of a full ride. Aimee created a computer worm that allowed her to crack into the school's financial aid system, where she fudged Trudy's parents' tax info. She had designed the worm to die once the deed was done, but it turned out to be unexpectedly resilient. Trudy's account ended up being flagged by the IRS, and when the girl was brought in for questioning, she gave Aimee up. Aimee would've ended up in prison if it hadn't been for the fact that she hadn't actually taken anything. She was, however, expelled from school and given five years of felony probation. As a part of her plea agreement, Aimee was also prohibited from using the internet for six years unless it was for work or school, and even in those instances, her activities would be heavily monitored by Pennsylvania's cybercrimes division.

"Aimee's ass is lucky all she got was a slap on the wrist," Toussaint said when Jay-Jay finished his tale. "So, what's she doing with herself now?"

"She's taking courses at CCP during the day, but at night she's the assistant manager at some fancy club out near King of Prussia."

Community college was a big step down from UPenn, Toussaint knew, and working hospitality was never in Aimee's dreams that he knew about. "Well, it'll be good to see her."

"*If* she shows up. Aimee comes and goes as she pleases. Sometimes disappears for days at a time, hanging out with her punk-ass rich friends."

Toussaint got the impression that it bothered Jay-Jay to talk about the new changes in his sister's life, so he didn't press it. He would draw his own conclusions as to what type of woman Aimee had grown into when he saw her for himself. He let the conversation go and tried to flip the radio on, which only caused Jay-Jay to pull out his phone and get AR-Ab back on. Toussaint fell back into silently busying himself looking out the window and people-watching. In one of the neighborhoods they were passing through, Toussaint spied a familiar piece of graffiti sprayed on a building, a black heart with a silver cross piercing it like a sword. The only reason he even gave it a second look was because he had seen the image before—though not quite as crude—but he couldn't remember where.

"I almost forgot, I got something for you," Jay-Jay announced. He reached into the back seat and grabbed an orange bag with the words BOOST MOBILE etched across the front and handed it to Toussaint.

Toussaint pulled the box from the bag, the latest iPhone. "Thanks, but you didn't have to blow your bread on getting me no phone. I know these things ain't cheap."

"Don't sweat it. I got a homeboy who has a hookup. Can't have you out here with no means of communication. It's already set up for you, and I programmed all our numbers in it," Jay-Jay said proudly. "And I put some good music on that jawn too. Oh and you've got another gift coming soon, but I don't want to spoil that. Me and Aimee did some serious digging for you on that one, *Troubleman.*"

"The radio's good with me. Those cats on Power 99 kept me connected to the city when I was inside." Jay-Jay didn't take the hint, and Toussaint turned to his own new phone, trying to get familiar with the features while Jay-Jay drove through the city. When he looked up, he noticed that they were riding down a familiar strip of Osage Avenue, one of the most notorious blocks in West Philadelphia, but not for the reasons one might think. "Pull over right quick," he told Jay-Jay.

"What you gotta take a leak or something? We'll be somewhere where you can use the bathroom in a few minutes, if you can hold it?" Toussaint's bus arriving late had already put him behind schedule, and Jay-Jay didn't want to make another stop.

"Just pull over, man," Toussaint repeated. With a sigh, Jay-Jay pulled over. Toussaint rummaged through Jay-Jay's cup holder and plucked out a few coins, while the young man watched him in confusion. "Be right back."

"Where you going?"

"To pay my respects."

The minute Toussaint's boots hit the ground, he felt it: that ominous sensation that could be picked up by the human soul when in proximity to something terrible, like a sixth sense warning you that you were in the place you should not be. His feet carried him to an address that he had visited many times over the years: 6221 Osage Avenue. Four decades later the windows of the building were still boarded up, but no amount of wood could hide the ugliness of what had happened here. It was remembered as the MOVE Bombing. Police had shown up to the Cobbs Creek neighborhood in force, with intentions on executing warrants they managed to obtain for several members of the Black revolutionary MOVE organization who were holed up in the building. This led to a standoff that turned violent. When brute force and tear gas hadn't successfully rooted out the MOVE members, someone within the police brass decided that dropping two explosive devices onto the roof of the building would be more effective.

Toussaint had been knee-high to a grasshopper back then, so he couldn't really grasp the severity of what had happened, but it hit home when one of his mother's friends came by the house in tears, hollering about how the police had killed her only child. Toussaint had been outside the door ear-hustling while his mother tried to console her friend. It was then that he had learned about the bombing and the eleven souls that had been lost, nearly half of them children. In the aftermath, they found themselves living in a city divided in half, one half wanting to tear shit up and the other wanting to march and sing "We Shall Overcome," as if that had gotten them anywhere so far. Over time, the bombing faded into memory and became a fable mostly spoken about by people who had lived through the event, but Toussaint never forgot. This is why whenever he was in the area he would stop and pay his respects to the dead. Before leaving, he placed the pennies on the curb. They were so that everyone who had died during the bombing would have the required two coins to pay the Ferryman so that they may be carried into the land of the dead.

"What's so special about that old building?" Jay-Jay asked once Toussaint was back in the car.

Toussaint flashed him a look of utter disappointment. "The fact that you were raised in this city and don't know what this place is speaks to how badly the system has failed your generation."

"So, how was your ride in?" Jay-Jay asked once they were back in traffic.

"Long," Toussaint said with a chuckle, thinking about the scheduled three-and-a-half-hour ride from SCI Rockview, which had stretched into well over four hours.

"That's the damn Greyhound for you." Jay-Jay shook his head, remembering the days of taking the bus up to New York and back to drop off packages. "I don't know why you didn't just let me drive up to the prison to pick you up? I told my dad I was okay with the road trip, but he said you insisted on taking the bus."

"Man, that place is cursed. Even touching that soil as a visitor, you run the risk of whatever bad juju is baked into them walls getting in your spirit." The whole time Toussaint had been locked up, there were only two people whose visits he never refused, his lawyer and John Wei, Jay-Jay's dad. He received his lawyer because he was paying him, and John because he was the one man he knew who was pure of spirit. John was a good man, one of the best Toussaint knew, and he knew his friend couldn't be corrupted by the evil that covered that place like a blanket.

"I've heard stories about that place from some of the homies who did time there. Keep it a buck. Was it as bad as they say?" Jay-Jay wanted to know. He had never done more than a few days in the city lockup but was fascinated by the stories told on the block by the men who had survived state prison and made it home to brag about it.

"Worse," Toussaint said, rubbing his hands together as if he was still trying to wash the blood from them of those who had died in his arms or by his hands.

"*Viral!*" Jay-Jay near-shouted, impressed by Toussaint's intensity. It was slang that Toussaint was unfamiliar with, and he couldn't be sure if it was a good or bad thing, so he didn't respond. He returned to staring out at the city, indicating that he had no more to say on the subject, but Jay-Jay wouldn't let the silence last this time. "You know you've been the talk of the town for the last couple of months, right?"

"Why is that?" Toussaint asked, as if he didn't know his coming home from prison was a big deal.

Jay-Jay glanced at him to see if he was serious or not. "Man, I know they ain't buried you too far under the ground that you done forgot who you are? You the only nigga living who took it to the pigs and the streets and lived to tell the tale! The name Troubleman is on the lips of every street dude with a dream to be more. The hood giving you props!"

"First of all, watch your mouth," Toussaint checked him. "Just because you was raised around Black folks don't give you liberty to say the N-word. Second: What the fuck do I care about receiving props from folks I don't know, will probably never meet, and ain't never put a dollar on my books while I was down?"

"Trouble, all I'm trying to say is—"

"*Toussaint,*" he corrected. "Cool it on that *Troubleman* shit. That's a name for people I done shit to, or have designs on making their lives miserable." "Troubleman" was a nickname he picked up as a kid because he was always a magnet for trouble. Every time you turned around young Toussaint was into something. And it only got worse when he was an adult. "Here comes Trouble," he could hear people call out whenever he stepped on the scene. And yes, his presence was usually followed by something sinister jumping off. Toussaint was such a badass that some of his fellow cops had started referring to him as Troubleman. "Call me Toussaint."

"You got it, *Toussaint.*" Jay-Jay said, sounding halfway disappointed. From the stories he had heard about Trouble when he was growing up, he had expected to be in the presence of a real gangster when he picked him up. The man in his passenger seat, staring out the window like a lost puppy, Jay-Jay couldn't help but wonder what had happened to him in prison.

As if to answer, Toussaint started talking as he watched the city scroll by. "Listen, Jay-Jay, I really do appreciate you showing me love, but I need you to be clear on something. I don't know who you thought you'd be picking up from the station, but I ain't him . . . not anymore. All I am now is a washed-up ex-cop who just did a nice piece of time over a bad decision. That ain't nothing to celebrate."

"*Toussaint*, the hood ain't celebrating you because of the time you done," Jay-Jay protested. "It's why you did it. That pimp you bodied had it coming. Could've easily been my little sister that he had out there selling ass. You did the world a favor when you tossed him out that window. They should've given you a medal for it, instead of time."

"If only the district attorney shared your enthusiasm," Toussaint half joked. They drove for a few blocks more, and Toussaint noticed that Jay-Jay had passed the freeway entrance that would've taken them to Jay-Jay's parents' place, where Toussaint was expected. "You missed your turn," he pointed out.

"Don't worry about it, man. I'm taking the streets. Got a little stop and see my guy right quick before I drop you off."

"C'mon, man. I'm fresh out of prison and been on a bus for the last five hours. I ain't up for running the streets with you all day, Jay-Jay. You can drop me off then go handle your business." Toussaint was tired and hungry, and he did not want to spend his first day out hanging with Jay-Jay and a bunch of kids half his age doing God knew what.

"It'll only take a second," Jay-Jay promised.

Twenty minutes later, Jay-Jay pulled the car to a stop in front of a strip that Toussaint hadn't seen in a while. It was lined with houses that looked like they couldn't have been more than a few years old, with beautiful trees planted outside. This was *not* how Toussaint had remembered it. The last time he had been on this strip it had been to visit a whorehouse at the end of the block. At the time, he had been in the company of his old buddy Leroy "Left-Shoe" Jackson, commander of the tactical unit he had been assigned to. It was Toussaint's first time there, but Left-Shoe was a regular. That was his place, as he liked to call it. Somewhere he could indulge in his vices without judgment. And Left-Shoe had plenty of vices. The girls who worked there loved Left-Shoe and never charged him for pussy. He was their guardian angel of sorts, warning them when busts by vice were coming down and making sure none of the stick-up kids fucked with them. That night he and Toussaint had freaked off with three Puerto Rican broads. It was the first time Toussaint had gotten his dick wet while on the job, but it wouldn't be the last. Back then that area had been a haven for junkies and criminals, but now it was the image of gentrification.

The engine going quiet brought Toussaint back from his trip down memory lane. Jay-Jay had shut the car off and was preparing to get out. "You could've left the car running. I wouldn't have let anything happen to it."

"Man, nobody in this city is dumb enough to fuck with this car," Jay-Jay boasted. "Besides, I want you to come in with me so I can introduce you to some of the guys."

"I'm cool on making new friends, Jay-Jay."

"C'mon, don't do me like that. I've been chatting you up all week and the guys think I'm lying about you being family. Most of these jokers have never met a real-life legend, and it'll make their week for you to pull up on them," Jay-Jay pressed.

Common sense told Toussaint to sit his ass right there and let Jay-Jay go and handle his business. From the car he had picked him up in to the diamonds in his chain, it was obvious that whatever Jay-Jay was into could land him back in prison quick. His good mind said to tell Jay-Jay, "*No*," but his heart took him back to how good it had felt the first time Bo-Deal let him ride shotgun in his Deuce and a Quarter Buick up Market Street. Being tied in with a man of substance gave you credibility, and Jay-Jay was only looking for what Toussaint had been seeking that day he was in Bo-Deal's Buick . . . to be seen. So Toussaint relented to this one ask. "Five minutes. Then I'm gone. With or without you."

2

Toussaint followed Jay-Jay up the driveway to a two-story brick house. It was nice, same as the rest of the houses on the block. The difference, Toussaint noticed, was that this was the only house on the block with security bars over the windows. Jay-Jay tapped the steel-mesh screen door: once, twice, and then once again. He took a step back while he waited for someone to answer. The whole time he was smiling at Toussaint like he'd just found a puppy on the streets and was about to beg his parents to let him adopt it.

One of the first things Toussaint clocked was the camera on the front door. Nothing too crazy: a basic Ring camera that even five years ago you could get from Amazon or any other retailer. But the same couldn't be said for the other two. These were high-end surveillance cameras mounted at the north and south ends of the house; one giving half-a-block scope of the street the house sat on and the other giving a wide shot of the avenue. There was definitely some shit going on inside this place that Toussaint had no business being in the middle of. Trouble, maybe, but not Toussaint. "Whose house did you say this was again?"

"Chill, Toussaint. These guys are cool."

A few beats later, the door to the home came open

and a big-boned Hispanic woman filled the archway. She wasn't fat, but if she didn't curb her diet she might be in a few years' time. Her dark hair was pulled back into a ponytail and held in place by a red bandana. "You're late," she greeted Jay-Jay.

"Had to stop and pick my uncle up from the bus station." Jay-Jay nodded at Toussaint.

"This is your uncle?" She eyeballed the Black man leerily.

"On his mama's side." Toussaint gave her a wink.

After weighing the lie, Flacka unlocked the mesh door and allowed them to enter. He and Jay-Jay followed her down the long hallway. Toussaint casually observed the place as they walked through. There were a few pictures hanging on the walls, one of a family, a white couple, their two kids, and a dog. It looked like one of the stock photos that came with picture frames when you bought them. To his right, there were several doors leading to what he assumed were bedrooms. One of them was locked from the outside by a thick padlock. He wondered if the lock was to keep prying eyes from seeing whatever was hidden behind the door, or to keep someone from getting out? Toussaint had a bad feeling and wished, not for the first time and not for the last time, that he'd stayed in the car.

The hallway let out into a wide living room, sparsely furnished with a couch, a coffee table, and a large television screen where some show broadcast in Spanish was playing quietly. Flacka escorted them to the kitchen, before excusing herself to the couch to get back to her show. In the kitchen, there were two men sitting around a small table, one Black and one Hispanic. They were drinking beers and scooping small piles of heroin into plastic bags. The sight made Toussaint's mouth go dry. There couldn't have been but a few ounces, but that was more than enough to get Toussaint crossed back into the penitentiary less than twelve hours after being released. He scowled at Jay-Jay, who only smirked like everything was cool. What happened next was a strong hint that everything was anything but cool.

"Who the fuck you brought up in our spot?" the Black man at the table demanded. He was short with a powerful build and holding a 9mm. A red bandana hung from the back right pocket of his sagging jeans.

"Yo, chill with all that, Man-Man!" Jay-Jay threw his hands up nervously, like he was being arrested. All the bravado he had been carrying around with him since he picked Trouble up from the station disappeared when he was staring down the barrel of that pistol.

"Easy with that blower, shorty." Toussaint raised his palms, cursing himself for not staying in the car. Instead, he had let Jay-Jay walk him into some bullshit.

"Jay, what I tell you about bringing strangers to my crib?" The handsome Hispanic man was sitting at the table with his hands folded in front of him. From neck to wrist he was covered in tattoos that told the story of his life. His calm demeanor in the midst of everything going on around him told Toussaint that he was the man in charge.

"Victor, I ain't dumb enough to do something like that. This is my uncle that I was telling you about! Call off your dog, huh? This is the guy I've been telling you jokers about. My uncle, Trouble!" Jay-Jay explained in a shaky voice.

"Trouble?" Victor let the name roll around in his head to see if it set off any bells and then looked straight at Toussaint. "Should I be concerned about letting a man named Trouble into my home?"

"No cause to be concerned on my end. I'm just a passenger on this ride," Toussaint assured him. He understood that Jay-Jay had stuck his hand into the mouth of a crocodile and the only way to ensure he kept all his fingers was to ease it out.

Once some semblance of calm returned to the room, Jay-Jay slipped back into his swagger mode. "Damn, that's cold, bro. I grace you with the presence of a Philadelphia *legend* and you embarrass me by letting your boy pull a gun."

"What's he legendary for?" Man-Man asked.

"Tossing a nigga who rubbed me wrong out of a twelve-story window, for one." Toussaint made sure to look Man-Man in the eyes when he responded. It wasn't a threat. Just a line in the sand.

"Then I guess it's a good thing we're on the first floor, huh?" Jay-Jay quipped, doing a piss-poor job keeping the tensions eased. "My uncle just came home from doing time. I just picked him up at the station." He said it to impress the men, but all it did was put Toussaint in their crosshairs, especially Man-Man's.

"Where you bid at?" Man-Man wanted to know.

"A few places. Rockview most recently," Toussaint replied.

"I just came home from there about a year ago. Maybe that's where I feel like I know you from?" Man-Man suggested.

"I mostly kept to myself. I ain't very sociable." Toussaint wanted to dead the conversation.

"I was expecting to see Spider. I made it clear that I needed to talk to him about something," Victor said to Jay-Jay.

Jay-Jay gave a shrug. "He had some other business to take care of. So he sent me instead."

"More important than the business he's got with me?" Victor's eyes stared coldly at Jay-Jay. "Since Spider's been snuggled up to Fat Eddie, he's been doing some real suspect shit. The streets are talking, and the shit they're saying ain't good. This is why I wanted to speak to Spider face-to-face. Yet he sends you."

"Vic, you know that's above my pay grade. I'm just trying to make a dollar."

"Right, the loyal soldier who does as he is told without question."

"Say, Jay-Jay, how much longer you gonna be?" Toussaint read the room and didn't like the signs. "I still gotta check in with my parole officer."

"We'll be done in a minute, unc. If you're feeling a little anxious, you can go sit with Flacka in the living room while we finish this up," Victor told him.

"If it's all the same to you, I'd like to keep my nephew where I can see him." Something didn't smell right with these boys. Jay-Jay was too green to smell it, but Toussaint had just spent the last few years with larcenous men who carried the same stink.

"What makes you feel like that was a request, *unc*?" Man-Man challenged, his hand inching back towards his gun.

"Young man, I hope your hand is lingering down there because your balls are itching and not because you got designs on pulling that gun a second time." At that range Man-Man would be at a disadvantage if he tried to draw down. Toussaint could land at least two good ones before the gun cleared his waistline. Or so the optimist in him said.

"Everybody, *relax*. We're good here, right, Vic?" Jay-Jay again tried to defuse the situation.

Victor stared at him for a time before responding. "Let me get Spider what I owe him so you can be on your way." Victor got up and went to the kitchen sink. He reached under the cabinet and produced a small toiletry bag, which he tossed on the table.

"Thanks," Jay-Jay picked up the bag. He was standing to leave when Victor stopped him.

"Don't you want to count it?"

"Nah, I trust you, Vic." Jay-Jay had finally picked up on the vibe and was now just as anxious to get out of there as Toussaint was. But Victor wasn't quite done with him.

"I insist. Wouldn't want your boss thinking one of his soldiers shorted him."

Toussaint watched as Jay-Jay reluctantly sat back down. Under Victor's watchful eye, he zipped the bag open and peeked inside. The change in his facial expression told Toussaint that whatever was inside the bag hadn't been what Jay-Jay was expecting to see. "What the hell is this?" he emptied the contents of the bag onto the table. It was full of newspaper clippings. Toussaint could make out a few headlines about a rash of fatal overdoses.

"Exactly what's owed to Spider," Victor said, as if it should've been obvious. "How long did Spider think he could keep pissing on my head and convince me it was raining, pushing that stepped-on shit through Black and Brown hoods?"

"Vic . . . I . . ." Jay-Jay stammered.

Toussaint had seen this movie before and knew that the fix was in long before Man-Man made his move. The moment Man-Man tried to draw his gun, Toussaint fired an elbow breaking his nose, spraying blood all over the kitchen. He then delivered a chop to Man-Man's gun hand, which was still trying to pull the pistol, and caused it to go off. Man-Man howled when the bullet ripped through his foot, shattering it.

Jay-Jay was still sitting at the table like a deer in headlights when Victor stood and drew his own pistol. He let off a shot, which would've creased Jay-Jay's skull had Toussaint not dumped him from the chair a split second before.

Without missing a beat, Toussaint brought one of his size-fourteen boots up and kicked the table sliding across the room and into Victor. Toussaint bounded over the table and caught Victor with a roundhouse kick that knocked him unconscious.

"On your feet, boy!" he barked at Jay-Jay while scooping up Victor's discarded gun. Jay-Jay continued to sit on the floor, staring at the scene around the kitchen in horror while muttering something. Trouble grabbed Jay-Jay by the back of his shirt and pulled him to his feet. "You move or you die. Understand?"

Jay-Jay nodded.

Toussaint and Jay-Jay streaked into the living room, where they were met by Flacka wielding a baseball bat. She swung the bat wildly, at both of the men. Toussaint raised his arm to block a blow aimed at his head, and pain shot through his forearm and up to his shoulder. Ignoring the throbbing in his arm, he clocked Flacka in the mouth with the gun, knocking out several of her teeth. He felt bad about striking the woman, but they were in a kill-or-be-killed situation and his sense of honor had no place.

The television just beyond where they were standing exploded in a spray of glass. Toussaint turned to find Man-Man standing in the kitchen doorway. He was limping from the gunshot wound to his foot, but his trigger-finger was working just fine, even if he couldn't aim for shit.

"I'm gonna dust you muthafuckas!" Man-Man vowed, his voice all nasally because of his broken nose.

Toussaint returned fire, purposely shooting over Man-Man's head. He wasn't trying to hit him, only get the shooter off his back. Man-Man stood between them and the hallway to the front door, cutting off their escape route. They were trapped!

"I don't want to die." Jay-Jay was damn near in tears.

"You must be out of your mind if you think I sat in prison all those years just to die behind your bullshit before I can even get my dick wet!" Toussaint snapped, as he grabbed Jay-Jay by the arm, who screamed as they went crashing through the window.

The ride back was a quiet one. At least on Toussaint's part. He was driving because he didn't trust Jay-Jay's ass behind the wheel. He was still so shaken up by what had happened that it would be just their luck if he ended up crashing or getting them pulled over, which would've probably been worse if the police got a good look at him. His body was covered in scrapes, and glass still lingered in his hair. Had Victor lived on a higher floor then a few scrapes and bruises would've been the least of Toussaint's injuries. "Good thing we're on the first floor" was the only smart thing Jay-Jay had said all day.

Jay-Jay kept offering weak apologies, but Toussaint ignored him. Had he not been family, Toussaint would've left his ass to whatever Victor and Man-Man had had planned for him. The fact that Toussaint saw that double cross coming and Jay-Jay hadn't went to show just how much John Wei's baby boy knew about the game he was trying to play, which was absolutely nothing. What they had done back at the house would come with consequences, this Toussaint was sure of. Victor and Man-Man didn't strike him as the types to let being embarrassed on their home turf slide, especially by the likes of Jay-Jay. They were going to spin behind this, and when they did, Jay-Jay wasn't going to be the only person on their shit list.

Toussaint looked over at Jay-Jay and had to fight the urge to slap him. In the months leading up to Toussaint's release all he could think about was putting his days of being *Trouble* behind him, but thanks to the wannabe gangster, he now found himself knee-deep back in it.

3

It was already dark when Toussaint and Jay-Jay pulled up to his family's restaurant. The rain had turned into a full downpour by the time they turned onto South 6th Street in Chinatown, where Good 4 Yu was located. The rain was just the icing on the cake of an already shitty day.

Most of the lights at the restaurant were out, and the place was empty save for the few employees who looked to be cleaning up after what was supposed to have been Toussaint's welcome-home dinner. Among them was Jay-Jay's mother, Sue Wei. She paced back and forth nervously, occasionally looking down at her phone. Jay-Jay's parents had been blowing him up for the last hour or two, but he didn't answer because he wasn't sure what he was going to say. "You think she's gonna be pissed?" Jay-Jay asked. Toussaint gave him a look that questioned his mental capacity. "About what happened earlier . . ."

"If you're worried about me telling your parents about you almost getting us killed, don't be." Toussaint told him. "I can't imagine how my friend John would react, finding out he raised a damn fool. Fuck were you thinking about taking me to a damn drug deal?"

"It wasn't a drug deal. I don't touch drugs. I'm just a bag man."

"More like a sacrificial lamb," Toussaint said with a snort. "You need to see about getting a job in the restaurant, because you ain't built for the streets."

"You think because Victor and them did some snake shit means I don't know what I'm doing out here?"

"No, the fact that you almost wet your pants when the shots started flying does."

"It wasn't my fault."

"That's always what punks like you say after getting some poor sucker killed behind your bullshit," Toussaint told him before sliding from the car.

When they stepped inside the restaurant, David Ruffin's "Statue of a Fool" was playing softly over their sound system. It summed up how Toussaint was feeling after his near-death experience with Jay-Jay, like a damned fool, but he was trying to let it go. Sue was the first to greet them. A short woman, standing at about five-two including the black hair streaked with gray that she wore in a high bun atop her head. She rushed to Jay-Jay and pulled him into an embrace. You could tell she had been worried. Once she checked him to make sure that he was still in one piece, she whacked him across the back of the head. "Your phone doesn't work anymore? Your father and I were afraid that something happened to you when you didn't pick up our calls."

"Sorry, Ma. My phone went dead," Jay-Jay lied.

Sue narrowed her eyes at him. "As much time as you spend on that thing? You'd have a heart attack if you couldn't play with it. Where have you really been?"

Jay-Jay looked stuck on stupid as he tried to piece together a lie that his mother wouldn't see through. Fortunately, Toussaint was far better at bending the truth. "That was my fault, Auntie Sue. My bus got delayed and I didn't have a phone yet, so I couldn't let anyone know I was running behind. Jay-Jay was waiting on me."

Sue Wei turned to Toussaint as if she was just noticing him. She had been so worried about Jay-Jay that she had almost forgotten the errand they sent him on in the first place. She looked the convict up and down, taking in his ragged appearance and the cuts on his arms. "What happened? Did the bus flip over?" She had seen right through his lie as well. "Because you've just come home and both of you look to be in one piece, I'm not going to light into your ass tonight, but we're going to talk about this in the morning. Welcome home, Troubleman." She hugged Toussaint. Sue had always been hard on Toussaint in public, but beneath the surface she had a soft spot for him.

"It's good to be home, Auntie Sue." Toussaint closed his eyes and took in the warmth of her. It wasn't until he felt Sue's thin arms wrapped around him that his mind was able to accept the fact that he was finally home.

"Unfortunately, you missed the dinner I spent the last

two days cooking for you," Sue said, making no secret of her displeasure with him over it.

"I'll make it up to you, Auntie Sue. Once I'm settled, *I'll* cook dinner for the family!"

"Ha, the last time I let you in my kitchen you almost burned it down," Sue said with a chuckle, thinking back to the time she tried to teach Toussaint how to make Cantonese beef. He'd been a little too generous with her special cooking oil over the open flame and it almost went disastrously. "Quite a few people showed up for you, but you'd know that if you were here."

"Fair enough," Toussaint replied. "But where the hell is John? I'd have thought he'd be the first one lined up to give me shit when I came through that door." He looked around for his old friend but didn't see him anywhere in the restaurant.

"Watch your mouth in my house," Sue warned.

"We're not in the house. We're in the restaurant, Ma," Jay-Jay pointed out.

"You know what I meant. Stop being funny before I give you another whack!" Sue raised her hand as if she were about to backhand Jay-Jay, and he mock-cowered behind Toussaint. "John should be back any minute now. He left to pick up Aimee."

"Cool, I was hoping to bump into baby girl tonight. Ain't seen her in years!" Toussaint said excitedly. "Maybe I should run up to the corner store and get some of those Tastykakes she always liked before she gets here?" he joked, knowing he could at least get a rise out of Jay-Jay by acting like Aimee was still a little girl. But Sue's frown only deepened.

Not even a minute after he had cracked the joke, the front door to Good 4 Yu swung open, bringing the nasty weather in with it. There were three of them: an Asian boy with a pretty face who walked with a slight limp; under a rain slicker and wide-brimmed hat, John Wei; and between them they half carried a young woman in a slinky black dress that was bunched at the hips, showing off the colorful tattoo of a dragon snaking up one of her thighs. When she moved, her legs were like noodles and it took the combined efforts of the two men to keep her from falling. Even at that distance, Toussaint could smell the booze coming off her. Her head lolled up and she whipped the hair from her face, and Toussaint was able to get a good look at her. She looked different than Toussaint remembered, older and more statuesque, noodle legs and all. Had Toussaint passed her on the street he might not have recognized her had it not been for her eyes. Those same jade-green eyes she had inherited from her grandmother. Aimee Wei glared at the lone Black man in the room before a light of recognition went off in her eyes. She smiled at him drunkenly and slurred, "Sorry I missed your party," before throwing up.

4

Toussaint's first day out of prison had gone nothing like he had expected. So far, he had been at the wrong end of a bad drug deal, nearly been murdered, and then spent the remainder of his night helping Sue Wei clean vomit from the floor of the restaurant.

When things finally settled, he tried to get some sleep, but it was no easy task. He was back in his old attic room, the last place he had slept before heading to prison, but he spent most of the night tossing and turning. Every time he managed to drift off into some semblance of sleep, he'd find himself popping back up at the slightest noises. He was so used to sleeping with one eye open inside his cell that he had a hard time adjusting to sleeping in a regular bedroom. This went on until sunrise. When it became obvious that sleep would continue to evade him, he decided to get up and try to work off some of the stress he was feeling.

At the crack of dawn he found himself on the roof of the Wei brownstone, where John had built a makeshift gym. It wasn't much other than a few weights, a Wing Chun wooden dummy, a pull-up bar, and a heavy bag, but it would do. He hit the heavy bag for a while to warm himself up before turning his attention to the wooden dummy. It was roughly six feet in height, with four wooden pegs representing arms and legs. Toussaint danced on the balls of his feet in a tight circle on the black-tarred roof, throwing kicks and punches at the dummy, with each strike ringing through the morning sky like a crack of thunder. Unlike the heavy bag, the wood wouldn't give under the weight of his strikes, so each hit came with a measure of pain. Pain was good. Pain was focus. He kept at it until his body was drenched in sweat and then went harder.

After having been at this for the better part of an hour, his limbs had started to burn and his shins throbbed from kicking the wooden dummy. His chest heaved and he could hear the rattle of his pack-a-day Newport habit in his chest. His body was trying to get him to quit, but the demons he carried with him with the regularity of a wallet wouldn't let him. They were demanding tribute, and his only two choices were to free them or feed them. The last time he'd let them taste freedom he ended up in prison, so he chose the latter. He'd feed them but wouldn't allow them to gorge.

In his head he could hear his former mentor and cellmate, a guy name Harvey Chung, but everyone simply called him Old Man. When Toussaint first arrived in prison he was full of anger and resentment, which often got him into scuffles. Being an ex-cop hadn't helped his situation much either. It seemed like every other week he was having to sit some punk on his pockets for testing him. He was offered protective custody for his own safety, but Toussaint refused. He was never one to duck any smoke from anyone. One incident he had gotten into resulted in a man getting his jaw broken and Toussaint being tossed into the hole for eight weeks. When he got back to population, he was placed in a cell with Chung. Chung wasn't much to look at, a wisp of a man who couldn't have weighed more than 150 pounds soaking wet. But both prisoners and guards showed him a great deal of respect.

Chung was doing life for multiple homicides. As the story went, he had murdered six men. Over what? Toussaint didn't know and felt it would've been rude to ask. Chung seemed to appreciate the younger man's discretion, and over time Chung became a mentor to Toussaint, helping him to channel his anger through meditation and Tai Chi. Chung helped him strengthen both his mind and his body.

Chung was a man of few possessions, but the one thing he cherished the most was a tattered leather-bound book that he carried with him at all times. It was called the Book of Wah Pei. The book was an heirloom passed down over generations from master to student, containing philosophies from great thinkers who had owned it over the years as well as their stories. Also inside the book were diagrams of different fighting styles that were known only to a select few. The book was as sacred to Chung and those who had the honor of carrying it before him as a Bible to a holy man. Since Chung had no students, he chose to teach these lessons to Toussaint.

Toussaint had never been much of a reader, but he became fixated on the book and the knowledge within the pages, especially the fighting techniques. When Toussaint wasn't meditating or working out, he had his nose poked in that book. He would spend hours on end practicing the techniques, and every night Chung would have him demonstrate what he had learned. Toussaint had always been a good fighter, but the Book of Wah Pei transformed him into a living weapon. The only things that Chung ever asked in return for teaching Toussaint the sacred techniques were that he never share the secrets with another soul and that he never use the styles from the book to do harm. They were to be employed in the direst of situations when no other choice was given. Being in a place where you literally had to fight for your survival made it hard for Toussaint to keep his promise, but he managed to finish his prison sentence without killing anyone using the techniques he'd learned.

Close to a year before Toussaint was set to be released, Chung fell ill and passed away. Losing Chung hit Toussaint hard. He had been like a surrogate father to him during his time in prison. Before Chung passed, he gifted Toussaint two things, his leather-bound book and some words of advice: *Learning to channel your anger to bend it to your whims is the only way you'll ever be free of the yoke it has hung around your neck. Be the master and not the slave.*

Up on the roof, Toussaint measured his breathing and

channeled everything he was feeling into his shoulder, then pushed that same energy into his forearm and supercharged his fist before taking a swing. His calloused hand struck the dummy with so much force that it chipped the wood. Toussaint continued to hammer the dummy until his knuckles began to bleed through the boxer's tape he had wrapped around his fists. He probably would've kept going until he had broken one of his hands had he not felt a presence behind him.

When he turned he found Aimee standing in the doorway of the rooftop. She was wrapped in a pink bathrobe, jet-black hair spilling around her face. She was taking short tokes off a thin joint, watching him with hooded jade eyes. She appeared to be sober now, but her skin looked pale and her eyes were red from her long night.

"When I heard the thunder, I thought a storm was coming," Aimee said, hitting the joint. "I didn't see anything in the forecast on my phone."

"Sorry, I hope my workout didn't wake you or your people?" Toussaint asked, starting to unwrap his fists.

"You know they're early risers. They've probably been up for hours prepping the food for the restaurant," Aimee told him. "You're up and at it pretty early. Trouble sleeping?"

"A little." Toussaint slipped the stained wraps into the pocket of his sweatpants.

"You know my mom can whip you up some herbal tea that can help with that," Aimee said, gently brushing a strand of hair from her face. It was a simple gesture, but something about the way she did it made it look provocative. Aimee was a beautiful woman with a face that could stop traffic, but she seemed oblivious to her allure.

"Last time I let your mom give me some of her herbs I was walking around like a zombie for two days," Toussaint recalled. A few years back he had gotten into a dustup with some guys during a drug raid. They busted up his ribs pretty bad, so Sue had given him something for the pain. "I don't like anything that dulls my reflexes. Especially right now. Gotta stay sharp. Sure as hell learned that yesterday with your brother."

"Maybe you should try a little of this? Works for me." Aimee offered him the joint.

"I don't fuck around with that." Toussaint waved her off.

"Why not? It's not like you're a cop anymore." It was an innocent enough question, but the minute she asked she regretted it. "Sorry, I didn't mean . . ."

"It's cool, Aimee. And you're right, I'm not a cop anymore, but I am on parole. Can't have my piss come up dirty."

"My mom has an herb for that too."

"I'll bet she does." Toussaint chuckled. "How you feeling this morning? You were in bad shape last night."

"Too much Don Julio. I hope I didn't embarrass myself too bad?"

"I've seen worse. But since when did you become a party girl?"

"Since I turned eighteen and finally managed to get out

from under my parents' thumbs. You know what they say about keeping your kids too sheltered."

"Yeah, when they finally taste a little freedom, they overdose." Toussaint was familiar. "That contribute to you getting booted out of school?"

"That Jay-Jay runs his mouth like a bitch." Aimee sucked her teeth.

"Wasn't like that. He was just bringing me up to speed on what's been going on in your life. Last time I saw you, you were a little girl playing video games."

"Well, I'm a grown woman now. I still like to play games, just a different kind," Aimee said suggestively.

Toussaint was quick to change the subject. "So, how's the new gig? Jay-Jay told me you're managing some kind of club these days?"

"It's cool. The pay isn't great, but I'm making some great connections. I've got the next few nights off though. Had a fire at the club the other night."

"Anybody hurt?"

"Only that cheap-ass polyester couch my boss bangs the cocktail waitresses on. I warned him that damn thing was a fire hazard, but it took a cigarette that someone didn't properly extinguish to show him the error of his ways," Aimee joked. "I could use the time off anyhow. I have some code I've been working on that I need to finish writing."

"Jay-Jay said as a part of your probation you're banned from using the internet."

"Not banned, *restricted*. There's a difference."

"I don't think the Feds are gonna hear that if they catch you wrong again."

"I'm not the kind of girl who makes the same mistakes twice."

"Let's hope not," Toussaint said seriously. A gust of wind blew across the rooftop and pushed Aimee's robe open a tad, exposing her snake-tattooed thigh. Toussaint felt his mouth moisten. A wicked thought tried to creep into his mind, but he immediately locked it out.

"It's okay."

"Huh?" Toussaint had briefly checked out.

"The way you're looking at me. I see you checking me out."

"Aimee, you're tripping. You're John's baby girl."

"No, I'm a grown-ass woman, not that kid you used to sneak candy to. I've always had the biggest crush on you. You know that, right?"

Toussaint blushed. "Stop it."

"I'm serious. When I was a kid I used to pretend that you were my boyfriend. I would dream about turning eighteen and having my dad arrange a marriage between us like some old-school China shit."

"I don't think John would cosign us hooking up, in dreams or otherwise."

"Then maybe he doesn't have to know," Aimee was suddenly in his personal space. She ran one of her manicured fingers down his muscular chest. She stopped at the fresh scar above his rib cage, and traced a line over it.

"Don't." Toussaint grabbed her by the wrist.

"I'm sorry, does it hurt?"

"Only the memory of how it got there."

The scar had been a parting gift before Toussaint had been released from prison. Towards the end of his bid, after the death of Chung, he'd gotten a new cellmate, a kid named Milton Hodges. Milton was in on a possession charge, but from his appearance Toussaint could tell that on the streets Milton had been a user, not a dealer. Toussaint could remember Milton venting to him one night about how his rich father allowed him to go to jail instead of paying for a lawyer. His father had hoped that prison would do for him what a million dollars spent on rehab stints over the years hadn't been able to: force him to get his shit together. What Daddy-Deep-Pockets hadn't counted on was that it was easier to get drugs in prison than it was on the streets.

It wasn't long before Milton found himself in debt to a crew of Puerto Ricans who moved heroin through the prison. One night, after doing his laps around the yard, Toussaint arrived back at his cell to find three of the guys from the crew collecting on Milton's debt. Drug crews weren't like bill collectors, who called you nonstop when you missed a payment. They took what was owed to them in blood, which is what Milton was in the process of learning. Prison protocol dictated that Toussaint walk away as if he had never seen it. This beef had nothing to do with him. Besides, he was on short time, scheduled to be released in a little over a month and couldn't afford getting himself wrapped up in anything that could threaten that. "Walk away," he said to himself, but he wasn't named Trouble for nothing.

When Toussaint stepped into that cell, he had no intention of getting into a physical confrontation. He simply wanted the gang, and Milton, to take their madness somewhere else. That's not how it played out though. One of the gangbangers accused Toussaint of butting into their business and clocked him on the chin. It was a mistake that he would live to regret. Toussaint gave in to that all-consuming rage that he carried around with him and blacked out whatever happened next. All he remembered after was being face down on the ground, being manhandled by three corrections officers, a homemade knife in his side. While he was in the infirmary being treated, he heard through the grapevine that he'd cracked the skull of one of the gangbangers and broken the arm of another. The third one escaped only because he had run off after stabbing Toussaint from behind. After what he'd done to those boys, Toussaint knew that he had blown his chance at being released, but it turned out he hadn't at all. In a strange turn of events he learned that one of the gangbangers had insulted one of the female sergeants at the prison, so Toussaint had done what she and some of the other COs had been planning to do already. When the incident was written up, it was downplayed as a minor scuffle. Toussaint would spend the remainder of his time in solitary confinement, but he didn't get any extra time.

"So, you gonna keep standing here holding my wrist or act on whatever it is you're thinking?" Aimee gave him a mischievous grin.

"Knock that shit off, Aimee." He released her.

"Toussaint, I don't get you. I'm a beautiful girl, and you're one fine specimen of a man. We can both feel the attraction between us, so why are you afraid to act on it?"

"I only fear two things in this world: God and being locked up again. Me not digging on you has got nothing to do with fear, Aimee. It's about respect. Your old man has been good to me, gave me a place to lay my head when the rest of the world wouldn't piss on me to put a fire out. How would it look if I deflowered his daughter?"

"*Deflowered*? You're a little late for that," Aimee joked, but Toussaint didn't laugh. "I know you have a great deal of respect for my father, but it's not like I'm looking for you to knock me up and make me your lady. I just want to live out my childhood fantasy. How about we have a good time, just this once?"

Toussaint considered it. He hadn't had sex in five years and desperately needed to get his dick out of the dirt, but Aimee wouldn't be the one holding the shovel. "Sorry kid," he said, touching her cheek softly, "but you're gonna have to find somewhere else to get your kicks."

5

After his rooftop workout, et cetera, Toussaint felt the need for a long, cold shower, and it had little to do with him being sweaty. He couldn't believe that Aimee had come at him that way. What was even harder to believe was that for a split second he had considered entertaining her. Aimee had grown into a strikingly beautiful young woman, and he could only imagine what those green eyes would look like while she was on top of him, but she was still John Wei's little girl. The fact that it had even crossed his mind—and kept crossing his mind—made him feel like a dirty old man. He needed to get in between some thighs before he did something stupid.

From the roof, Toussaint retreated to his apartment. Well, calling it an apartment might've been a stretch. It was a small bedroom and kitchenette with a bathroom that sat on the top floor of the Weis' brownstone. It was a downgrade from the townhome he'd owned in Cherry Hill before his arrest, but it was clean, out of the way, and rodent free. Which was more than he could say about Rockview. He peeled off his sweaty clothes and jumped into the shower, trying not to think about Aimee.

After the shower, Toussaint stood in the bathroom and

took stock of himself. He was in his forties but didn't look it. This was partially thanks to good genes, but mostly because he was a man who believed in taking care of himself. Even while he was in prison he remained conscious of what he put into his body, aside from the cigarettes, and made sure to get regular workouts in. He pinched the bit of fat on his stomach, once a six-pack but now somewhere around a four-and-a-half.

After applying oil to his salt-and-pepper-flaked beard, he brushed his hair. The gray hadn't migrated there. At least not yet, and he hoped it wouldn't happen anytime soon. The top of his tapered fade was still dark and wavy, a gift from his late mother. She had been a native of Ethiopia, and she remained one of the most beautiful women Toussaint had ever seen. She busted her ass to make sure that he and his siblings were provided for, even during the dark periods of her life. While in prison he had often found himself thinking of her and what she could've been had his father not dragged her down the rabbit hole of addiction before he abandoned them.

Wrapped in a towel, he stepped from the bathroom and went to the small closet that held what was left of his wardrobe. It was roughly one-quarter of what it had been before he went away, but there were a few nice pieces and a couple of pairs of shoes that had cost him a few dollars. Not too shabby, but a downgrade from the arsenal of fine silks and leathers that had filled the walk-in closet of his former town house. Most of that stuff had been lost when

Tisha, his then-fiancée, double-crossed him. She had stuck with Toussaint through the trial, playing the role of the true ride-or-die chick, but the moment he got sentenced, she was in the wind. She sold his town house and damn near everything else he owned and ran off with some young dude that she had been fucking behind his back. Toussaint had been so focused on the job that he had neglected his woman, and her running off was the price for that mistake. In Tisha's defense, she hadn't been the only one who was unfaithful in the relationship. Toussaint was nailing broads left and right on her watch. Tisha was just better at hiding it.

Still, it took Toussaint around twenty minutes to select just the right outfit from his limited collection. Back in the day his buddies would often tease that he took longer to get ready than a woman. And they weren't wrong. Toussaint was very particular about his appearance. As a child, he had been relentlessly teased about the way he dressed. Everything he owned had either been a hand-me-down or purchased at the Goodwill. This is partially why he started hustling when he was a teen. A lot of his friends back then had vices that consisted of drinking, getting high, or tricking off on women. Toussaint's vice was clothes. His money went into things that made him look good.

The outfit he settled on was a bone-white cotton shirt, dark jeans, and a tan cashmere sport coat. He carefully laid his outfit on his twin-size bed and sprayed everything down with Febreze. The clothes were freshly cleaned, but what Toussaint had learned since renting from the Weis was though the rent he paid living above the Chinese restaurant was cheap, the downside was that his clothes always smelled like fried chicken.

He slipped into the sport coat and looked at himself in the full-length mirror that hung on the back of his closet door. It was a little snug around the shoulders, but otherwise it still fit him as good as when he'd bought it. It was one of the few pieces from his original wardrobe that he had been able to hold on to over the years. He felt something in the breast pocket and reached inside to see what piece of his past the jacket had been holding on to all this time. Inside he found three loose hundred-dollar bills folded around a business card. Toussaint unrolled them, running his thumb over each bill as he did so. They still felt as fresh as the day Left-Shoe had placed them in his hand. The business card they had been hiding was to a massage parlor, which he was sure wasn't around anymore, but he wished that it was. The two things he'd found in his pocket forced a smile to his face, as memories of the night he had last worn that jacket came back to him. It had been a night to remember . . . or forget, depending on which side of those hundred-dollar bills you were on. He stuffed the items back into the pocket and turned to the mirror. "Even the most broken things can be repaired," he affirmed, before snatching up the cloth-wrapped book he had brought home from prison and heading out to start his day.

The sun was out and the birds were chirping. These were all the makings of what was sure to be a beautiful day. Toussaint was ready to tackle whatever the world would throw at him and overcome it. He was in a great mood but found it darkened a bit when he stepped outside and found a cluster of young men at the foot of the stairs leading to the brownstone entrance. They were throwing dice against the stairs, passing blunts around, and yapping loudly like it was nine at night instead of nine in the morning. There were about four of them, with Jay-Jay's ass right in the center of the action. He was shaking the dice in his hand, whispering sweetly to them about what he would do with his winnings. After his promise, he kissed the back of his hand for luck and prepared to throw the dice. He froze when he saw Toussaint glaring at him from the top of the steps, but the momentum caused one of the dice to pop from his hand and bounce off the bottom step.

"What the fuck, Jay-Jay? I told you about them funny-ass rolls. All three gotta hit for it to count!" one of the two Black dudes in their quartet barked at him.

"That shit don't count, man. I was about to hold the bones out of respect to let the OG pass," Jay-Jay said, picking up the die and moving to the side to let Toussaint descend the stairs.

Toussaint came down the last few steps and intentionally stood in the path of where they had been throwing the dice. He made eye contact with each of the assembled young men, so they could get a good look into his soul and see what he was about. He then turned to Jay-Jay. "Showing respect to me is wise, but showing respect to your parents is honorable. Why you out here making your parents' place of business hot, Jay?"

"It's all good, *Trouble*. Ain't nothing but a friendly game. We ain't making the *jawn* hot," Jay-Jay said in his best Philly drawl.

"Tell that to the police when they roll up and roust y'all. And what did I tell you about that Trouble shit?"

"My bad, Toussaint," Jay-Jay corrected himself.

Toussaint noticed the other Asian boy with them. He was perched on an e-bike, with a blunt cupped in his hand trying to keep Toussaint from seeing it. "You ain't gotta hide it, Charlie. I'm not on the job anymore." Charlie Tang was Jay-Jay's best friend and literal partner in crime. "Why don't you boys move this party somewhere else? Preferably off this block?"

"C'mon, fellas. Let's hit the bodega. I need to get another roll-up anyhow," Jay-Jay announced. He was about to lead the boys around the corner, but Toussaint stopped him.

"Let me rap with you for a second, Jay." This wasn't a request.

"I'll catch up with you guys in a second," Jay-Jay called to his boys.

"What's wrong with you, kid?" Toussaint asked Jay-Jay

once his crew had gone. "It's bad enough you almost got yourself killed and now you're trying to get knocked? Out here smoking and shooting dice." He shook his head.

"Police ain't stunting me for no little bit of weed. It's legal now," Jay-Jay answered.

"In Pennsylvania? Medicinally, not recreationally. Somehow, I doubt you took the time to do it the right way and apply for a card. And fuck the weed, I'm talking about these shady-ass cats you're out here keeping time with."

"You know me and Charlie been down since grade school," Jay-Jay said. "He's harmless."

"He might be, but what about those other two? Especially the one holding the pistol?" Toussaint was speaking about the Black kid who had been with him. He could tell by the way that his hoodie was hanging on one side that he was carrying something in the pocket that was heavier than a phone.

"Damn, you don't miss nothing, do you?"

"At all," Toussaint confirmed. "You hear anything about that business from yesterday?"

"Nah, it's quiet," Jay-Jay said with a shrug. "I think you're worried over nothing. Victor and them ain't got the balls to spin the block behind this. They know who I'm with."

"They didn't seem to care too much who you were with when they tried to pop your little ass. Maybe it's best you keep a low profile for a time? At least until we're sure this thing has blown over."

"Whatever you say, man." Jay-Jay frowned. "But you gotta stop trying to play me like I'm slow out here," Jay-Jay told him.

"Then stop acting like it," Toussaint snapped. Jay-Jay looked like he wanted to say something slick, but thought better of it and walked away. Toussaint watched him round the corner and shook his head. Toussaint had seen scenarios like the one Jay-Jay was setting himself up for play out a million times when he was still working the streets. They never ended well. Jay-Jay, like so many other kids his age, had to burn his hands before he believed that fire was hot.

After the pointless chat with Jay-Jay, Toussaint strolled next door to the restaurant. Now that it was daytime, he could really take in the renovations the Weis had done to the place. They had remade it into a posh Asian-fusion joint, which stood out among the more traditional Chinese-owned establishments. From the looks of things, the Weis had invested quite a bit of money into the place to try and keep up with the gentrification happening all over the City of Brotherly Love, even if it hadn't quite transformed Chinatown yet. Over the years Good 4 Yu had become a staple of South Philly, a hole-in-the-wall spot that visitors and transplants loved to come through and discover the chicken-and-gravy combo with the fried rice, much like Toussaint once had. But things were looking different now.

Nevertheless, when Toussaint stepped inside the restaurant he was met by the familiar smells of Mrs. Wei's spices.

It was still early, so Good 4 Yu wasn't officially open for business yet, but Mrs. Wei liked to come in early to do her prep. Near the front, wiping down tables, Toussaint encountered the boy he had seen helping John bring Aimee inside the night before. His name was Tommy Lung, a relative of the Wei family, but Toussaint couldn't remember from which side. He had never met the boy in person prior to the night before, but John had written about him in letters to Toussaint when he had come to stay with the family. When Tommy noticed Toussaint, he greeted him with a warm smile.

"Good morning, Mr. Batiste," Tommy greeted him in his singsong voice. His long black hair was pulled back into a ponytail, showing off his girlish face. His cheeks were a ruddy shade of rose, and Toussaint thought he might be wearing lipstick or lip gloss. Tommy was a *sweet* boy, in every sense of the word, which was part of the reason the Weis had brought him to America, as John had told him in one of their letters. One night while out with friends in Beijing, a group of homophobes had tried to use Tommy's head as a kickball. Their intent had been to kill him, but through the grace of God, Tommy had survived the attack. He spent three weeks in the hospital recovering from his injuries and still bore the scars on his forehead from where they had to place staples in his cracked skull to hold it together. In his home country, Tommy had to hide who he was, but in America he was free to walk in his truth.

"Hey, Tommy. I'm good, and Toussaint is fine. You calling me Mr. Batiste makes me feel like an old man."

"Sorry . . . *Toussaint.*" Tommy corrected himself.

"Much better." Toussaint gave him a nod of approval. "Where are your aunt and uncle?"

"Auntie is in the kitchen, prepping the food and uncle John is—" he was saying when they heard shouting from the back, followed by a loud crash.

Toussaint rushed across the dining room and slid over the take-out counter like an action hero, with Tommy on his heels. He was moving so fast that he almost collided with Sue, who was washing chicken in the stainless steel sink. "No running in my kitchen!" she shouted after the men as they passed.

From the storeroom, where they kept the nonperishables and other goods, Toussaint heard more shouting. It sounded like Mr. Wei was in there fighting for his life. Toussaint's first thought was that the bullshit he and Jay-Jay had gotten into had blown back on the family, and he expected to find Victor or maybe that lunatic Man-Man in the back kicking John's ass, so he was taken aback by what he saw when he entered the storeroom.

It was a large space, part of the renovations the Weis had done during their expansion. There were tall shelves lined with food and spice containers and boxes stacked just about everywhere. There was broken glass on the floor and one of the smaller shelves had been knocked over. It took Toussaint a second to find Mr. Wei in the maze. He was at the far end of the room with his back to Toussaint. A baseball bat rested on his shoulder while his eyes darted around the room wildly.

"What's the word, OG?" Toussaint asked, also looking around the room for whoever Mr. Wei was into it with.

"Shhhh!" John hissed over his shoulder, still focused on an enemy that only he could seem to see. He was zeroed in on the corner of the storeroom where they kept bags of rice stacked. Toussaint thought the man was losing it until a fat, black rat darted out from behind the rice bags. Mr. Wei chased the rat around the storeroom, cursing at it the whole time. For a minute it looked like he had the rat cornered, when the rat got himself caught up in the nook where boxes of cheap Walmart glasses were stacked. The Weis kept those for the church crowd who came in once per month when Good 4 Yu hosted their brunches. He swung that bat with everything he had, only to miss the rat completely and fall on his ass from the momentum. He did, however, manage to break at least a half dozen of the glasses in the process. That rat had escaped, leaving John sitting on his ass in a pile of broken glass, even more frustrated than he had been when he started out.

"You okay, John?" Toussaint asked, stifling his laugh. He extended his hand to help the older man.

"Do I look okay?" John swatted his hand away. With a little effort he managed to get to his feet on his own. John Wei was a slight man, weighing no more than 150 pounds on a good day. He wore what was left of his balding black hair in a comb-over that Toussaint had been begging him to cut since he had known him, but John refused. He was old-school and set in his ways. "I almost had him had you all not come in here making all that noise and distracting me!" he fumed.

"Looks like he had you," Sue Wei offered from the doorway, where she had been watching the whole thing with a comical smirk on her face.

"Instead of standing there making light of my struggle you should've helped me," John told her.

"I tried to help you when I offered to call the exterminator," Sue countered.

"Do you know what that would do to our sales? People see that van parked outside and they're gonna start talking like Good 4 Yu is dirty. We're barely holding on as it is while competing against these cafés that keep popping up in the neighborhood and that damn Korean barbecue spot down the street. They don't even use flour to batter their wings!" He threw his hands up in frustration. "No, I'll hunt Ben down myself." He called it Ben because that had been the title of one of his favorite Michael Jackson songs when he was a young man. Back then he didn't know a lot of English, so he had no idea what Mike was saying while he was crooning, but it was beautiful to him. So beautiful, he sung it to his wife at their wedding. One of his American-born cousins had been the one to inform him that the song was actually an ode to a rat.

"And who is expected to clean up the messes of your

little hunting parties?" Sue Wei motioned towards the scattered glass and overturned shelves.

"Woman, did Jane complain to Tarzan about who was going to clean the lion he hunted down for dinner?" John asked sarcastically. He had been raised on American television shows, so damn near everything that came out of his mouth was a quote or reference to an old American song or TV show.

"Jane had meat to clean. All you bring me is broken glass." Sue was no docile Asian wife. She gave just as good as she got and didn't tolerate bullshit from anyone, including her husband.

John was gearing himself up for one of his legendary responses that would likely lead to them arguing for the next couple of hours when Tommy stepped in. "I'll take care of it."

Sue wanted to argue that her husband had made the mess so it should be on him to clean it up, but she let it go. Her eyes softened and she placed a hand on Tommy's cheek. "You're a sweet boy, nephew."

Tommy blushed. "Anything for my family." He went off to retrieve one of the push brooms to begin cleaning up the broken glass.

"You baby that boy any more and he's going to need to start wearing a diaper," John told his wife after Tommy had gone.

"He's been through a lot," Sue Wei reasoned.

"And he'll go through more. Make sure he's built for

it," John replied. Sue rattled off something in Mandarin, and John gave her a sharp retort in their native language. They went back and forth like this for nearly a minute, before Sue went back into the kitchen to finish cleaning the chicken that would be served that day.

"Walk with me, Toussaint," John Wei said. "I have something to show you."

6

Toussaint and John Wei walked out of the restaurant and cut down the small alley that separated the restaurant and the brownstone. The alley led to an open yard behind the brownstone, where a covered carport sat. The space was cluttered with junk, old restaurant equipment, the kids' old bikes, and tons of other items that John had been promising his wife he would get rid of since before Toussaint went to prison. John was something of a hoarder, reluctant to let go of remnants of his past.

John gave a cautious look around to make sure that no one was watching before plunging his hand into a pot of dirt, which used to hold a plant. From beneath the soil he retrieved a pack of cigarettes. "America has made my family soft," he complained to Toussaint after firing up the cigarette.

"I thought that was always a plan? To create a softer life for our families than the ones we had to endure. At least, that's what you were always preaching to me."

"There's a difference between a soft life and a soft spirit," John countered. "Part of the reason that me and my wife decided to leave all that we had built behind in China and come to America was that we didn't want our children to grow up only seeing shades of gray, as we had. We wanted to raise our family in a place full of colors, where they were afforded the opportunities to be whatever it was that they wanted to be in this world and not what the government mandated they had to be."

"How'd that work out for you?" Toussaint joked.

"Don't be an asshole, Toussaint. My baby girl flushed her education down the toilet and my son spends his days throwing stones at the penitentiary. How do you think it worked out?"

"Relax, John. I was just trying to lighten the mood."

"You know what would lighten my mood? A stiff drink and a few pulls off whatever that is Aimee smokes on the roof and thinks we can't smell. How about it? You wanna join me for some day drinking?" John asked hopefully.

Toussaint looked down at his watch. It was only 9:30 a.m. "Normally, there's no one I'd rather get shit-faced with before noon, but I can't today. I gotta go see my parole officer."

"Ah," John offered as if he was only just remembering that Toussaint was fresh out of prison. "What does she look like?"

"No clue. I haven't met her yet."

"I remember meeting Aimee's probation officer. I thought she would be some shriveled old white broad, but she was actually a cute Puerto Rican. Had a nice shape on her too," John said with a sly smile, recalling how he had been ogling the young woman in the tight dress. "Maybe you'll luck up and land a nice-looking officer too. Maybe slip her a little of that Troubleman on the side?" he joked.

"I doubt it. Lord knows I need to get my dick out of the dirt, but I'll probably end up paying for my first shot of pussy. Hooking up with some nice square broad ain't really in the cards for me right now. I'm carrying so much baggage and don't want my karma rubbing off on anybody."

"Just don't let yourself die a lonely old man."

"I'm not lonely. I've got you guys. You're my family, aren't you?"

"Of course we are. I don't have to tell you how much my family loves you, Toussaint. You've always been like the son I wished I'd had." John paused. "Instead I was cursed with that idiot namesake of mine."

"That's cold, John."

"But is it not true?" John let the question linger for a time before continuing. "Don't get me wrong, I love my son. He is the heir to whatever it is that I leave behind, but let's just say I'm less than optimistic about the future of my family."

"Jay-Jay isn't a bad kid. Just misguided." Toussaint spoke truthfully.

"Oh, I know that. He has the purest of hearts. Sadly, this is what makes him the family's biggest liability," John said with a heavy heart.

Toussaint reflected on what the old man had just laid at his feet. "Jay will be fine. I'll talk to him, John."

"To say that which I haven't already said?" John wanted

to know. "But let me not get off topic. This is about you, Trouble." When John called him by his street name, Toussaint knew that he was about to hang something heavy on him. "Do you remember when we first met?"

"How could I forget?" Toussaint smirked remembering how high T-Bone had flown into the air when he pushed him out in front of that car.

"You were a man, a confident man . . . cocky even. You always walked with your head held high and your chest poked out. I hoped you would come back from prison as that man again. Your debt to society has been paid, Toussaint, and it's okay to find your happy. Unyoke yourself from all that weight you're carrying around." John patted Toussaint on the shoulder compassionately.

John sounded just like his old cellie. He used to say the same thing to Toussaint, about unyoking himself. Thinking back to his old mentor reminded him of why he had come looking for John in the first place. "Oh, speaking of being happy, I got something that might put a smile on that sour face of *yours*." He extended the clothbound parcel.

"What's that?" John looked at it suspiciously. Toussaint smiled and motioned for him to open it. When John unwrapped the cloth and saw what was hiding inside, his breath caught in his throat. "My God—" he gasped. "Is this authentic?" He turned the book over, using the cloth to hold it, for fear of the dirt on his fingers damaging it.

"The real deal."

"I always thought this was a myth. How did you manage to come into possession of it?" John asked, eyes still on the relic. "Did you kill somebody for it?"

"A gift from a friend," Toussaint told him "My cellmate for a while."

"Whoever this friend of yours was must've been clueless about what this was or he surely wouldn't have given it to some random guy he met in prison," John said.

"He knew exactly what it was, which is why he gave it to me. I was hoping you could put it some place safe for me?"

"Hell, for this I'll kick Sue out of our bedroom and sleep with it every night," John joked. "I've got to go to the bank this week. I'll lock it away in my safe-deposit box. I'll keep it safe."

"Appreciate it."

"Well, since we're exchanging gifts, I've got something for you too." He winked and walked back to the covered garage. There was a tarp covering what Toussaint assumed was one of John's reclamation projects. The elder Wei had a thing for cars. He had been an engineer back in China, and the itch to fix broken things had followed him to the States. Over the years, John had gotten his hands on several junked cars, which he attempted to restore but never got around to finishing. Toussaint braced himself for whatever decayed monstrosity was lurking under the tarp. Then John snatched the tarp away.

Hidden in John's yard was not another of his half-ass

rebuilt cars, but a 1987 matte black Chevy Monte Carlo. It sat on eighteen-inch tires with five-star red rims. It was a thing of beauty, and one he knew intimately. Toussaint ran his hand over the hood of the car and stopped at the dent on the side of the right front bumper. It was barely noticeable to the naked eye, but Toussaint knew that it was there. He'd been behind the wheel drunk one night and tapped a fire hydrant while trying to park it. It had broken Toussaint's heart when he had to tell Tisha to sell his baby. He would never have parted with it had he not needed the money to pay his lawyer. Toussaint opened the driver's side door and slid behind the wheel. Being in the car again made him feel like he had just hooked up with an older lover and hit it again for the first time after several years. It was familiar, but after being away from it for so long it felt new. "How?"

"It wasn't easy," John admitted. "Tisha had sold it to some guy in New York, who flipped it and sold it to somebody in South Carolina. But I had the VIN, and Aimee tracked it down on her computer. I gotta tell you, the last owner was reluctant to part with it, but I made him an offer that he couldn't refuse. Fire it up." John handed Toussaint the key.

Trying to keep his hands from shaking with excitement, Toussaint put the key in the ignition and turned it. The car sputtered two or three times before the engine finally turned over. "Yes," he whispered to the car, running his hand over the dashboard. He was so happy to be back in his baby's embrace that it took a minute for him to realize that there was something not quite right with the car. For the most part, it was still in the condition that he'd left it in, but something was off. Then he realized what it was. "They ripped out my tunes?" He looked to the space in the center console that his CD player once occupied to find it replaced by a ten-inch HD screen.

"Yeah, but Jay-Jay upgraded you. You can play your music using Bluetooth now. You play your music through your phone. Jay-Jay said he's already made you a playlist. Let me show you." John extended his hand for Toussaint's phone.

Toussaint handed him the cell and watched as John tapped the screen as if he had done it a hundred times before. The car speakers made a beeping noise, and the next thing Toussaint knew, he found himself embraced by Heatwave's "Always and Forever."

"See, no more carrying around that CD case you refused to get rid of," John joked.

"Thank you, John. I love it. But I hope you didn't get into no trouble trying to get this car back?"

"Not at all. But I may be catering this guy's family reunions for the next five years for free. You want to pay me back? Do something with this second chance at life you've been given. Go out, find yourself a good woman, and make some babies. Find your happiness, Troubleman," John capped before heading back towards the restaurant.

Toussaint stood there for a while letting John's words

sink in. *Find your happiness . . .* Even before he'd gone to prison, life had begun to harden Toussaint. He was glad to be out of prison for damn sure, but Philly had hardly been his happy place when they put him away. Everything and everyone he allowed himself to love had abandoned him. From his father walking out on them, to his brother being murdered, to his estranged sister. Even the rotten skank who had robbed him when he got sentenced; they had all left him. John wanted Toussaint to find love, but in truth, he was afraid to. Toussaint's life had been filled with pain, so that's what he held on to. Pain was familiar, and it would never disappoint you. Love was a different story. Happiness? Toussaint wouldn't even know where to begin looking. But no question this beautiful car made him feel like he was going to get there a whole lot quicker.

Toussaint pulled the Monte Carlo out of the alley and onto the street. The thing shook like a hooker in church, definitely in need of a tune-up, but it felt good to be reunited with something familiar. Something that was his and his alone. Marvin Gaye's "Trouble Man" beat through his speakers. No matter how he felt about the moniker, the seductive opening was the perfect way to roll out.

One hand gripped the wheel while the other played with the iPhone Jay-Jay had gifted him, and he remembered the kid's awkward patter in the car yesterday before things had gone sideways. He felt a new wave of affection for the young man. Didn't quite wipe out the anger, but yes, this was family. He snapped out of the reverie when he saw that he was running late for his appointment with his new parole officer. The last thing he wanted to do was start off on the wrong foot by not showing up at his scheduled time. You only got one chance to make a first impression. He revved the V8 and got ready to impress.

He had just reached the corner of the block where Good 4 Yu sat when something unfolding on the other side of the avenue caught his attention. Jay-Jay's boys were hanging out in front of the grocery store while Jay-Jay himself was leaning into the window of a cherry-red BMW X5. The windows were heavily tinted so as to hide the identity of the driver, but from the way Jay-Jay kept poking his head up and looking around, Toussaint knew the boy was up to no good. Toussaint was already behind schedule and really didn't have time to save Jay-Jay from himself again. But even as all of yesterday's annoyance flooded back, he also knew he didn't have a choice. As he slow-rolled past the X5, Jay-Jay opened the back door to enter the vehicle, and Toussaint, staring him down to let him know he still had his eyes on him, caught a glimpse of the driver's face. A face that he remembered from his past, and seeing him again, with Jay-Jay no less, made his blood boil. He had slammed the brakes and was up out of the Monte Carlo almost before it had stopped moving, his hand preventing the BMW's door from closing before Jay-Jay could shut it. "Get out of the car, Jay-Jay."

"What? Why?" Jay-Jay didn't understand.

"Because I told you to. Now," Toussaint insisted.

"Say, Trouble, why don't you be cool?" the driver asked. He was an Asian man in his early thirties, with spiked blond hair. The large tattoo of a tarantula on his neck was one of at least a dozen that marked his body. In his mouth he sported a ridiculous-looking set of diamond and gold teeth.

"Was I talking to you, Aaron?" Toussaint growled.

"Aaron?" Jay-Jay chuckled. "I always thought your mama named you Spider."

"As in the same *Spider* who sent you on that dummy mission last night?" Toussaint made the connection. He'd only ever known him as Aaron. Spider must've been the moniker he took on while Toussaint was away.

"It's cool, Toussaint," Jay-Jay tried to assure him. "Spider is handling that for us."

"Yeah, I'm handling that. Victor and Man-Man won't be a problem after tonight. So why don't you relax, old timer?" Spider added.

"Aaron—Spider—or whatever insect you're calling yourself these days, this is a family issue. I suggest you mind your business," Toussaint warned.

"Jay-Jay is my business, so I suggest you watch all that aggression when you're speaking to me." Spider matched his tone. "Now, close my door so I can finish hollering at my man."

Toussaint ignored Spider, continuing to hold the door

open while waiting for Jay-Jay to get out. Jay-Jay wasn't moving fast enough for Toussaint, so Toussaint grabbed him by the arm and started pulling him out. Spider gave a nod to his friend in the passenger seat, a stout man with a bald head covered in tattoos who Toussaint had managed to completely ignore so far. The bald man stepped from the car and stood to his full height, which was an inch or so taller than Toussaint. He stood with the passenger door open, glaring at Toussaint from behind dark sunglasses. "Old head, you need to take your hands off the lil homie."

"Look, I don't want any trouble. I'll get the boy and you two can go on about your day," Toussaint tried.

"Maybe you're not hearing me." The big man placed an aggressive hand on Toussaint's shoulder. "I said let—" He never got any further.

Toussaint chopped him in the throat with the back of his hand, causing him to gag. He followed with a knee to the balls, doubling him over. While he was stooped Toussaint slammed the car door against his head. Twice. The bald man collapsed in the space between the passenger seat and the door. About that time, Spider's hand was inching beneath his seat. Toussaint's cold eyes landing on him gave Spider pause. "Spider, you know exactly who I am and what's gonna happen next if you reach for whatever you got stashed in there, right?" Spider wisely put his hand on his lap, knowing not to test Toussaint. "Let's go." He dragged Jay-Jay from the car.

"You know you can't just go around putting your hands on people like that, Troubleman. These streets are dangerous and you ain't got that badge to hide behind anymore," Spider called after him.

"I ain't hard to find, Spider, but when you come . . . you better come heavy," Toussaint capped over his shoulder.

"Toussaint, what the hell was that all about? Why'd you wanna embarrass me in front of my friends like that?" Jay-Jay was hot. "I'm not some little kid for you to protect no more. You just lookin' for *trouble*, aren't you?"

"Dudes like Spider ain't got no friends. He's a piece of shit who makes his money turning naïve kids like you. He'd sooner feed you to the dogs than risk getting his own ass bit. Or didn't them bullets flying at your ass teach you that?"

"You got it wrong, man," Jay-Jay argued.

"No, you got it wrong, putting your trust in that guy. I don't know who Aaron has convinced you he is, but I know his true nature." Their paths had crossed a few times back when Toussaint was still a cop. In those days, Aaron was a petty smack dealer, and he happened to work for the man Toussaint had tossed out of that hotel window. After Toussaint had gotten locked up, he had gotten wind that Aaron—*Spider*—had picked up where his old boss had left off and was running girls of his own.

Jay-Jay just glared at him, still wearing a sour impression.

"Look, I'm sorry if I came down a little hard on you, but

I'm just trying to look out. You don't want to get tied up with a man like Spider, get me?"

"I guess," Jay-Jay said.

Toussaint wasn't convinced, but now he really didn't have time to argue. "I gotta go, kid. We'll talk about this more later, but remember what I said about staying away from Spider," he warned before he slid behind the wheel of the Monte Carlo.

7

Toussaint burned the road up in an attempt to make it to his parole officer's office at the appointed time. He was a stickler for punctuality, even when it didn't affect his freedom. Generally the ride would've taken him roughly twenty-something minutes, give or take, but an accident on Market Street had traffic backed up. He arrived at the Adult Department of Probation way behind schedule. He skipped the elevator and ran up the four flights of stairs to where the parole office was located. He checked in at the reception area and searched for somewhere to sit and wait for his name to be called. The waiting area wasn't crowded, but it wasn't empty either. A few men sat around waiting to see one of the parole officers who had offices on that floor. None of them looked happy to be there. Toussaint took a seat in the corner, near a guy who was wearing a nervous expression on his face. Toussaint knew that look. That was a man who feared that he was about to be violated and sent back to prison.

The man tried to chat Toussaint up. He was likely just talking out of nervousness, but Toussaint didn't entertain him. He was there to handle business and not make friends, so he busied himself with an old copy of *Sports Illustrated* he'd found on one of the waiting room tables, hoping the man would catch the hint.

"Edwards!" someone called from the back, causing the chatty man to almost jump out of his skin. He got up and walked in the direction the voice came from, head down and shoulders slumped.

Yeah, he's definitely getting violated, Toussaint thought.

A few minutes later he heard his own name called. "Batiste!" He got up, smoothed his clothes, and walked towards the glass doors that separated the offices from the waiting area. A brief conversation with the guard at the door directed him to where he needed to be. Mrs. Richards's office was at the end of the hall. When he reached the door marked D. RICHARDS, he found it ajar and he could hear a woman's voice inside talking to someone on the phone. Toussaint tapped on the door twice before stepping through. Inside, he found an older white woman sitting behind a desk, almost hidden in the maze of files stacked on top of it. She was blonde, wearing a man's suit. She reminded him of Meryl Streep in the film *The Devil Wears Prada*. Her lips were painted a shade of cranberry that popped against her pale skin. Not at all what he had expected.

He stood waiting for her to finish the call.

"Have a seat, Mr. Batiste," she said, motioning to the empty chair opposite hers. For a time she didn't say anything, only studied him with her cold blue eyes. The silence made him uncomfortable, which he reasoned was her intent.

"Nice to meet you, Mrs. Richards." Toussaint took it upon himself to break the silence. He extended his hand in greeting, but she didn't take it. Only continued to study him.

"Mrs. Richards won't be joining us today. I'm Ellen Gould, the supervisor here," she introduced herself.

"Oh . . . okay, I was under the impression that I would be meeting with Mrs. Richards, not her supervisor. Is everything okay?" When you were on paper—parole or probation—one position you never wanted to find yourself in was sitting across from a supervisor. It was never a good sign.

Mrs. Gould rested her chin on her knuckles and gazed at him. "I don't know. Is it?" She let the question linger until Toussaint looked uncomfortable. "Relax, Mr. Batiste. You're not in any trouble. I told Mrs. Richards to take an early lunch so that you and I could get to know each other a little. You're quite infamous in this city."

"That right?"

"Don't be so modest, Mr. Batiste. There aren't many people in Philly who don't know Troubleman. Your exploits are legendary." Mrs. Gould glided quietly over *Troubleman* but drew out the word *le-gen-dar-y*. "I just wanted to take in your measure for myself."

"So what do you think?" he asked.

"I don't know just yet." Mrs. Gould pulled a folder from the pile on Mrs. Richards's desk. It was Toussaint's. She flipped through the pages. "It says you were arrested for murder. The charges were reduced to involuntary manslaughter. Seven to fifteen years in state prison, served five. I'm not a religious woman, but if I were I'd say that the Lord has smiled favorably on you."

"It's complicated," Toussaint mumbled.

"How so? You intentionally tossed a man from a window . . . a fellow officer at that. Most men, cop or not, would've never seen the light of day again, if they were fortunate enough to survive the trial. Yet, here you sit. Either your lawyer was a magician, or as the kids say, you nibbled at the cheese?"

Toussaint's fist balled so tight that his knuckles audibly cracked. Had it been anyone else, man or woman, Toussaint would've knocked them on their ass for insinuating that he was a rat. He guessed that she knew this too and was trying to provoke him into doing something stupid. He didn't trust whatever would come out of his mouth so he remained silent.

"*Extenuating circumstances,*" Mrs. Gould read from one of the many notes in the file. "Funny, your file doesn't say exactly what those circumstances were. Would you care to elaborate?"

"Not really." Toussaint didn't care to discuss with Mrs. Gould or anyone else circumstances surrounding his crime. The thing that had pushed him over the edge that night and why the courts had shown him mercy. Those who knew *knew*. And those who didn't could kiss his ass.

Mrs. Gould stared at him for a time, as if he might change his mind and start spilling his guts. He wouldn't, this was clear. "A man who plays his hand close to his chest. I can respect that." She nodded approvingly before going back to the interview. "Have you managed to find gainful employment yet?"

"Yeah, it's like I told my counselor before I was released, I've got a job working at a restaurant. I believe you guys have confirmed this with my boss, John Wei, already?"

"Yes, we've been in contact with Mr. Wei. However, I wouldn't call fixing pipes and taking out the trash for that Chinese restaurant *gainful employment*."

"I was under the impression that Mrs. Richards didn't have a problem with it," Toussaint pointed out.

"Well, I'm not Mrs. Richards. As a part of your parole, you need to be working someplace where you can produce a pay stub and show that you can support yourself. I doubt that cleaning grease vats can provide you with a respectable living wage. I'm going to need you to find a real job. Are we clear?"

"Sure. I'll get right on it," Toussaint told her halfheartedly. He was an ex-con, an ex-cop, and a notorious convicted killer in his forties—not exactly the king of the job market. The look on her face told him that she knew he was full of shit.

"Let me ask you something, Mr. Batiste. Have you ever heard the name Ezekiel Darkhart?"

Toussaint thought on it. He knew he'd seen or heard the name before but couldn't recall where. "Can't say that I'm familiar."

"Mr. Darkhart transplanted to this city from New York while you were away on vacation. He's only been here a short time but is doing some really remarkable things for Philadelphia," Mrs. Gould told him.

"Good for him," Toussaint said, not understanding why any of this should matter to him.

"It'll be good for you, too, if you play your cards right. I have it on good authority that Mr. Darkhart is currently in need of a man with your particular skill set."

"Skill set?" He looked at her curiously.

Mrs. Gould measured her words before answering. "I've spoken to people familiar with you, and they all tell me the same thing: that you are both an efficient and discreet man when it comes to handling sensitive matters."

"Don't know who you've talked to, but if they say so." Toussaint shrugged.

Mrs. Gould removed one of her business cards from her purse and scribbled down a phone number on the back of it before sliding it across the table to Toussaint. "Give him a call tonight. You might find yourself interested in what he has to say."

"Right." Toussaint took the card and slipped it into the inside pocket of his sport coat. He had every intention of throwing it away as soon as he left the building. "Anything else?"

"No, we're done." Mrs. Gould closed his folder and returned it to the pile on the desk. Toussaint rose to his feet and prepared to leave. "And don't forget, Mr. Batiste. I expect you to have some job leads by the time we meet next week."

"Next week? The conditions of my release only require me to report once per month."

"Well, consider those conditions changed. Maybe after you've spoken to Mr. Darkhart we can revisit this conversation. Until then, see you in a week."

"A'ight." Toussaint turned to leave.

"Oh, one more thing, Mr. Batiste." Mrs. Gould stopped him. She produced a small plastic container and slid it across the desk to him. "I need you to drop a urine."

"No problem. Can you point me to the rest room?"

"It's out of order, so we'll have to improvise," she told him, sitting back in the chair with her arms folded. Toussaint stood there with a confused expression on his face. "It's like I told you, Mr. Batiste; your exploits are quite legendary and I want to take in the entire measure of you for myself."

"Dirty bitch!" Toussaint cursed once he had exited the building. He knew from when he walked into Mrs. Richards's office and saw the blue-eyed white woman that things were about to go left. But he didn't expect to be put on display after being shook down. That was essentially what she was doing by *suggesting* that Toussaint go and see this Darkhart character about a job. Who the hell was this Ezekiel Darkhart, and why was a supervisor at the Department of Probation such a big fan? A quick Google search could answer at least one of his questions.

Toussaint pulled his phone from his pocket and powered it on. He had turned it off when he went inside the building to meet with his parole officer. No sooner than the screen came to life, several notifications popped up. John had left him two voicemails and had sent several texts. He was about to open the text app when the phone started ringing. "SNOTTY SISTER" Jay-Jay had programmed the phone to say. "Yeah?"

Aimee sounded frantic. When he was able to make sense of what she was saying, the color drained from his face. "Okay . . . okay. Just try and keep your mom calm. I'll be right there."

8

Toussaint made it from the parole office back to Chinatown in record time, running more than one red light to do it. The whole time he never thought about what getting stopped for a traffic infraction might mean to his freedom—he hadn't even had a chance to renew his license yet. All he could hear was Aimee's frantic voice in his head.

The Monte Carlo screeched to a halt in front of the Wei brownstone. He found Aimee sitting on the front steps, foot tapping nervously. Her green eyes were rimmed red from crying, and she was trying to suck the life out of the joint pinched between her lips. When she spotted him getting out of the car, she tossed the joint and moved to meet him. Before he could even ask what happened, she threw herself into his arms and began to sob. "It's okay. I'm here now." He rubbed her back comfortingly.

"They took him! They snatched my brother!" Aimee managed to get out in between sobs.

"Who? Spider?" Toussaint questioned. He'd known from the moment he saw Jay-Jay with Spider that things would go bad.

"The cops!"

Toussaint held her at arm's length. "*What?*" He hadn't

expected that. "Tell me what happened and don't leave out any details."

He listened intently as Aimee recounted the morning's events. Everything kicked off about an hour or two after Toussaint had left. The Wei elders had opened the restaurant for business and since Aimee didn't have to work, they asked her to help for the day. Aimee had hated working in the family restaurant since she was a little girl but agreed to help out. However, there was no way in hell that she was going to spend the next few hours sweating out her hair in the kitchen and dodging grease splatter without smoking first. She ducked across the street to where Jay-Jay and his boys loved to loiter. His friends were out there, but she didn't see her brother. From the store, she grabbed some rolling papers and a lotto ticket before heading back. It was when she bent the corner that she spied Jay-Jay and his friend Charlie Tang climbing out of the back of Spider's red BMW.

Jay and Charlie went into the brownstone and locked themselves in Jay-Jay's room, while Aimee went up to the roof to smoke. Aimee was halfway through her joint when she heard police sirens coming from downstairs. Police presence was a regular thing, so she didn't pay it much mind. But as the sirens got louder, she peered over the rooftop to see who from the neighborhood was about to get locked up. She was shocked that the cops had converged on her brownstone. Several officers stormed the building. By the time Aimee got downstairs, the police had Jay-Jay in cuffs and were dragging him kicking and screaming down the stairs, while her parents futilely tried to stop them.

"What did they charge him with?" Toussaint asked, his mind already ticking through the list of petty crimes that Jay-Jay might've been guilty of. If last night was any indication of what kinds of things Jay-Jay was into, it was likely possession. He was prepared for that, but not for what Aimee was about to reveal.

"Murder."

"*What?*" Toussaint asked in disbelief. The boy Toussaint had watched almost shit himself in the face of danger might've been a lot of things, but he was no murderer. This Toussaint could say with certainty. He didn't have it in him. "Who is he supposed to have killed?"

"Some prostitute."

At the mention of a dead prostitute, Toussaint immediately thought of Spider. A dead girl showing up and Spider being in the mix felt way too familiar to him. Toussaint had seen this movie before and knew how it was written to end for Jay-Jay. He couldn't let that happen. Not on his watch. "Where are your parents?"

"Mom is upstairs. She's been a wreck since this whole thing jumped off. Tommy is sitting with her. My dad went down to the precinct after they took Jay-Jay."

"Where'd they take him? First or Seventeenth district?"

Aimee thought on it. "I think the Seventeenth."

"Hmm . . ." was Toussaint's only response to Aimee.

Considering where Good 4 Yu was located, the First District would've made the most sense. Taking him to the Seventeenth meant that there was something more afoot. There were good and bad cops working both, but the Seventeenth was where a cop could take a man if he wanted to make his life difficult by getting him lost in the shuffle. Toussaint had personally dropped more than his fair share of perps off at the Seventeenth, let them get swallowed among misfiled paperwork long enough to convince them to play along at whatever he was angling towards. He'd been brought there too. "Where's Charlie?"

"I don't know. I didn't see him when the cops brought Jay-Jay out, and when I went to check Jay-Jay's bedroom, he wasn't there. The little snake probably slithered down the fire escape."

That was telling. Only guilty or frightened men ran. Charlie was probably both. He was also the most logical person to fill in the blanks as to what was really going on.

"Jay-Jay can't go to prison," Aimee continued. "He's not built for it. Especially for a murder I'm sure he didn't do."

"Calm down, Jay-Jay isn't going to prison. He's no killer. This has to be a misunderstanding. I'll see if I can sort it out." Toussaint assured her. The cop side of his brain that had been asleep for so long was now wide awake and processing the necessary information.

"How? You're not a cop anymore, Toussaint," Aimee reminded him.

"That's probably the one thing in all this that still works in our favor." Toussaint told her, before getting back into his car and pulling off.

Less than twenty minutes later, Toussaint was pulling his Monte Carlo into an empty space in the parking lot of the yoga studio on 20th and Federal. He sat in the idling car for a while, staring at the building across the street. He had mixed feelings about being there. The first time Toussaint had set foot in the Seventeenth, he had been wearing a badge. The last time, he had been wearing handcuffs.

Toussaint took a deep breath before killing the engine and getting out. He headed across the street and paused on the steps of the precinct for a beat, flooded with memories of the night he had been arrested. The arresting officers had taken the disgraced cop to the Seventeenth and put him on display for all to see. He'd been left in a holding cell for two days and deprived of food, even a phone call. He had been going solely off water from the rusty fountain in the holding cell. That first day Toussaint was too full of whiskey, cocaine, and rage to comprehend the magnitude of what he had done. It wasn't until the drugs and alcohol had worked their way out of his system that the realization set in. He had killed a man . . . a fellow officer no less. Had he had to do it all over again, maybe he would've just kicked his ass and turned him in, but seeing that little girl all beaten up in the hotel room caused Toussaint to snap. That split-second decision had ruined his life.

He composed himself before going inside, head held high and chest poked out. He would not give his former brothers and sisters in blue the satisfaction of the great shame that filled him at the moment. He had been one of the good guys, a proud cop who would've laid down his life for the same fraternity he had betrayed when he crossed the line between cop and criminal. A few of the officers coming and going spared him curious glances but no one said anything to him. Most of the group on shift at the time were probably too young to know his face, but he was certain they would know his name if someone spoke it.

He heard John before he saw him. He found his friend at the tall desk, giving the sergeant on duty hell. "I want to see my son! You have no right to keep me from him!"

"Sir, if you don't calm down, I'm going to make sure the next time you see your son is when I have you placed in the holding cell with him," the brunette with the sergeant's bars on her arm threatened.

"You think you can threaten me? I did nothing wrong! I'm an American citizen and I know my rights!" John slapped his hand on the desk, loud enough to draw the attention of every officer in the room. John was about to make a bad situation worse, so Toussaint stepped in.

"Take it easy, John. The lady is just doing her job."

John's eyes lit up when he saw his friend. "I'm so glad

you're here. These people took my Jay-Jay and won't tell me anything. I demand to know what's going on!" His voice was raised again.

"Easy," Toussaint told John before turning his attention to the sergeant. She was a pretty brown-skinned woman who wore her hair in a short pixie cut that looked good on her round face. She looked familiar to Toussaint, and he was struggling to remember if they had history together. When he realized that there was an awkward silence hanging between them, he found his voice. "Ma'am, you'll have to excuse my friend. His son has been arrested, so I'm sure you can understand why he's a little upset, right?"

"Doesn't give him the right to come in here showing his ass," the sergeant said, glaring down at John.

"My apologies. We're just trying to find out why his boy has been arrested. The name is John Wei Jr. Should've come in about an hour or so ago," Toussaint told her.

"And who might you be?" the sergeant asked, giving him a suspicious look. She too felt like she had seen him somewhere before.

"I know damn well that ain't the Troubleman up in my house," a voice Toussaint hadn't heard in many years called from behind him. He'd know that voice anywhere, and every time he heard it, he smiled. He turned, expecting to see a familiar face and found himself unprepared to greet the stranger standing before him.

"Jackson?" During Toussaint's time as a detective with the Philadelphia Police Department he had learned both the joys and effectiveness that came with using force on unruly perps. His teacher had been Leroy "Left-Shoe" Jackson. They called him Left-Shoe because he kept his foot in the asses of criminals. Toussaint had barely been a detective for a year when he got word that he had been assigned to Detective Leroy Jackson's unit, a special task force that handled the more volatile crimes in the city. They had nicknamed them the Dirty Birds because they didn't mind getting their hands soiled to make a case. Toussaint had done some things that he wasn't proud of when he was part of the unit, but he had also done a lot of good in the city.

Over the years Toussaint and Jackson's relationship had grown from a professional to a personal one. He learned a lot from Jackson not just about the job but about life. It was after they had become close that Toussaint learned that him being assigned to Jackson's unit had been at the commander's personal request. He saw something in the young detective and wanted him on the team. The last time Toussaint had seen Detective Leroy Jackson, he had been a handsome older man who wore his hair in long dreadlocks and carried three guns. Two the department knew about, and a third for Dirty Bird business. Leroy had been an outlaw with a reputation for doing stellar police work and slinging heavy dick to women foolish enough to become infatuated with him. Left-Shoe Jackson had been an Adonis and a superhero. The balding old man standing in front of him was neither.

"Jesus, I know I dropped a few pounds, but do I look

that bad?" Jackson flashed two rows full of crooked teeth that were in dire need of a cleaning. All of his dreads had fallen out, and the dark, Teddy Pendergrass beard that had made him the object of so many women's desires was now snow white and thinning. "Show your vet some love." He hobbled towards Toussaint, trying to mask the severity of his limp, and pulled him into a genuine hug.

Toussaint awkwardly wrapped his arms around his old mentor. Leroy was so frail that Toussaint feared he would break his ribs if he squeezed too tight. "Sorry, Leroy. You caught me off guard. I didn't expect to see you is all."

"I get that a lot. You go a few rounds with brain cancer and people start counting you out." Jackson tapped the surgical scar on his bald head. "I'm glad to see you free, Trouble. You look good."

"So do you," Toussaint lied.

"Lil nigga, don't bullshit me. I know I look like exactly what I've been through. The years may have been kinder to you than me." Jackson patted Toussaint on one of his boulder-like shoulders, good-naturedly.

"What's with the uniform?" Toussaint asked. "I thought by now you'd have been sipping frozen drinks on a beach with a chick half your age?" Jackson had already had twenty years on the job under his belt when Toussaint first met him. He thought surely he would have been retired by then.

"Shit, I need the insurance coverage. No way I could

cover my medical bills on the bullshit coverage they give us with our pensions. So they got me on modified duty," Leroy said with sigh.

"Never thought I'd see the day when Left-Shoe Jackson would be behind a desk," Toussaint teased him.

"Neither did I, but sometimes you gotta do what you gotta do to get by," Jackson said honestly. "Enough about me. What you doing here?"

"Just trying to sort out a misunderstanding." Toussaint cut his eyes at the desk sergeant, who had been watching the exchange.

Jackson looked to the sergeant. "Dobbs, I know you ain't out here giving my man Toussaint no shit?"

"*Toussaint*? As in *Toussaint Batiste*? I thought that was you!" Dobbs said when it finally hit her.

"We know each other?" Toussaint asked, hoping that she wasn't some girl from his past that he had slept with and neglected to call back. She turned out to be something far worse.

"No, but we've met. I was one of your arresting officers," Sergeant Dobbs announced.

It took a minute before it finally hit Toussaint. She had gained a bit of weight and now wore her hair short, but as he studied her, he did remember her face. She had been the rookie cop who had thrown up into the hotel wastebasket on the night of his arrest.

"To this day I have never seen anything like that on the

job, and I hope I can make it to retirement without having to ever see anything close to it again," Sergeant Dobbs picked up.

"C'mon, Dobbs. The man has paid his debt to society. Ain't no need in going down memory lane," Jackson cut in.

"It's cool, Leroy. I know I ain't the most well-loved man in this city," Toussaint told his old mentor before turning back to Dobbs. "So, being that you were there to get a first-hand look at my work, I guess you got me pegged as some kind of Judas? Seeing how I killed one of my own?" May as well get it out of the way.

"I'd be lying if I said that I didn't feel that way in the beginning. That was before I found out what that bastard was out there doing to those girls," Sergeant Dobbs said with disgust. "My daughter is about that girl's age now . . . the one you saved that night. God knows how I would've reacted if someone tried some shit like that with her." She shook her head sadly. "Instead of giving you time they should've given you a commendation." She raised her hand and saluted him as if he was still one of them.

For a moment, Toussaint felt the same surge of pride in his chest that he had felt every time he put on the badge before they took it away from him. "Thanks," he said modestly.

"Toussaint, you a good man who caught a bad break," Jackson assured him. "Hell, you ain't did nothing that none of us wouldn't have done had the shoe been on the other foot. People talking about protecting these babies, but you really put yourself out there and handled business!" He slapped Toussaint on the back. "For as many of these two-faced muthafuckas wearing the badge who claims to hate you for what you've done, there are some of us who respect the move."

Toussaint smiled, because it felt like the right thing to do at the time, but in his heart, he took no joy from the murder he had committed. This isn't to say that the man wasn't deserving, but that's not who Toussaint was. He had killed in the line of duty before, but what he had committed that night was cold-blooded murder.

"You know, I've always felt some type of way about being the one to arrest you. At least after I got the real scoop on ol' boy. I always said that if we ever saw each other again, I'd tell you this and try and make up for it," Sergeant Dobbs said sincerely.

"Thank you, Sergeant Dobbs."

"You can call me Natasha," she told him. "Maybe one of these days I can treat you to dinner? It won't make up for the years I helped them snatch away from you, but it's a start." She produced a business card and scribbled her personal number on it before handing it to Toussaint.

That was an opening. They both knew it. He doubted that her dinner invitation had much to do with making amends. He had seen the look in her eyes on the faces of many women. It was hunger. "I appreciate it, Natasha, but how would it look to some of your comrades to be seen in the company of a convicted cop killer?" He tried to give her an out.

"How about you let me be the judge of that?" Sergeant Dobbs shot back.

She was challenging him, daring him to buck so that she could break him like ranchers did wild horses. Natasha was fine, thick, and gainfully employed. She checked all the boxes. Toussaint could see the two of them fucking up some sheets, but behind all her slick talk he knew that Natasha was a good girl. He could smell it on her. Why was it that good girls were always attracted to bad men? Against his better judgment, he accepted her card.

"All right now, y'all cut that shit out on my watch," Jackson interjected. He too had seen that look in the presence of the Troubleman and knew how it would end for Dobbs if she wasn't careful. Toussaint had been one of his closest friends, but Jackson knew he was ravenous when it came to the opposite sex.

"Jackson, why don't you mind your business? I'm only offering him a meal," Sergeant Dobbs said, rolling her eyes. Jackson was always playing guard dog when it came to her. She had been like a play-niece to him since they had met.

"I hear you. Just be mindful that you don't find yourself the main course," Jackson warned. He knew that Dobbs didn't appreciate him cockblocking, but he was trying to save her from getting in over her head. In the course of their chat, they had started to draw the attentions of some of the officers who were on duty. By now, word had gotten around that Trouble was in the building. "Say, Trouble. Give a few ticks with Dobbs. I'll meet you outside."

"No more waiting! I need to know what's going on with my son!" John was getting irritated again.

Toussaint picked up on what John didn't. His presence there had the potential to make whatever Jay-Jay had gotten himself caught up in worse. "C'mon, let's go get a coffee." He gently took John by the arm and steered him out of the precinct.

Toussaint leaned against the hood of his car while watching John pace back and forth and ramble angrily. He would finish one cigarette and immediately light another. "Jay-Jay is no killer. You know that, don't you, Toussaint?" he demanded.

"I know, John," Toussaint assured him. "I know. As soon as we have all the facts, we'll get it sorted out."

"Damn the facts! Maybe if they won't listen to reason, I'll rescue my son by myself!" John dipped his hand into his pocket and came up holding a small .22. "One way or another, the people responsible for what's happening to my boy will pay."

"Are you out of your fucking mind? Put that damn thing away!" Toussaint barked, looking around to make sure no one had seen John with the gun. He'd had that rusty old gun for longer than Toussaint had known him. He wasn't even sure if the gun worked, but brandishing it outside the precinct would be enough for some overzealous cop to pump both him and John full of bullets. "You can't help Jay-Jay if you're dead or in prison. I told you that I would handle this, so let me do my thing."

John mumbled something before putting the gun back into his pocket. "I wish I shared your optimism. Jay-Jay is a second-generation immigrant with a bunch of petty crimes on his rap sheet. Even if he didn't do it, how hard do you think it'll be to convince a jury that he did? These are the types of things I constantly warn my children about, but they've become so comfortable living this Western life that they've developed a false sense of security in this country. You watch the news like I do, and this is just the kind of case that the government can use to strengthen their arguments about immigrants being sent back to where they belong. My son, in his attempt to fit in, could jeopardize everything Sue and I have worked so hard to build here in America."

"John, you're going too far down the rabbit hole with this. Both your kids were born here, and you and Sue have papers. You're citizens. They can't fuck with you or your business behind this."

"Can't they?" John asked. Something about the look he gave Toussaint when he posed the question told him that there was still quite a bit to this story that he didn't know. "In America, I'm looked at as just another man who isn't from here, trying to live off the fat of the land. In China, I was a man of means . . . a man of respect! The weight of my name would've been enough to make these bullshit charges go away as well as the people who levied them against my son."

The statement caused Toussaint to give John a look. It wasn't what he said, but how he said it. For as long as he had known John Wei, he had always been a man of peace. He was the most nonconfrontational person Toussaint knew, so it threw him to hear John speaking in this way. John sounded like someone who was working himself up to do something out of character.

Just then Leroy emerged from the Seventeenth. He was clutching something to him and looking around suspiciously as if he were afraid someone were going to try and steal whatever it was. He wore an expression that told Toussaint whatever news he was about to deliver wasn't good.

"Where is my son? Are they going to let me see him?" John picked up on where he had left off with his rant inside the precinct.

"Trouble, let me have a word with you. In private." Leroy cut a glance at John.

"Sure." Toussaint walked off with Leroy so that they could speak freely. Their journey took them just out of earshot of John, and they settled in the doorway of the yoga joint. "If you don't want his old man to hear then it must be bad."

"Bad?" Leroy snorted. "This shit is catastrophic." He handed Toussaint the folder he had smuggled out of the precinct.

Toussaint opened the folder and flipped through the pages. They had Jay-Jay for murder, this much he had already learned from Aimee, but that wasn't all. Apparently, they were also trying to tie Jay-Jay in with a gang who called themselves the White Snakes, traffickers and drug dealers who were becoming notorious in the city over the last few years. They'd been under investigation for a while now, but things really ramped up two weeks prior when a girl who had been seen in their company was found dead in a vacant apartment, along with another unidentified woman. One girl had been strangled and the other stabbed to death. Vickie Sparks had been the name of the girl who had been found strangled. Toussaint remembered watching the press conference about it on television not long before his release. In *Kill-a-delphia,* bodies of young girls were found more regularly than Toussaint was comfortable with, and hardly anybody batted an eye, let alone thought it was worthy of a press conference. That's because none of those girls had been the daughter of one of the most powerful men in the city.

Back when Toussaint was still a cop, Davis Sparks had been an ambitious young district attorney, carrying water for his predecessor, Thomas Hackman. In the time Toussaint had been gone, Davis's star had begun to rise and he was now sitting at the top of the food chain as the district attorney for the Northern District. Sparks had built his career by waging a war against the opioid epidemic that had been ripping the city apart. He recommended the stiffest sentences possible for those arrested for moving opioids, sending a clear message to all the dealers that their bullshit wouldn't be tolerated on his watch. This made him extremely popular among the citizens of Philadelphia and had prompted him to throw his name in the hat for the upcoming mayoral election. Rumor had it that he stood a damn good chance of winning too.

Since his daughter's death, Sparks had doubled down on his war against drugs. He had unleashed a rain of hellfire on drug dealers and promised that things would only get worse until the person who had killed his daughter was brought to justice. And now Jay-Jay found himself the sacrificial lamb in all this. There was no doubt in Toussaint's mind that the grieving father would bring down the full weight of the Pennsylvania judicial system on poor Jay-Jay's head, and he could likely spend the rest of his young life in state prison.

"How'd they come to finger Jay-Jay for this?" Toussaint asked.

"Anonymous tip," Jackson told him. "Somebody says that Jay-Jay was seen in the company of the victim on the night of her murder. When the cops raided the brownstone they found an earring that belonged to the girl in his room. This doesn't look good for your boy, Trouble."

"Tell me about it." Toussaint huffed. He closed the folder and handed it back to Leroy. "Thanks for your help with this."

"Don't mention it . . . I mean that *literally*. This business that boy is tied into is above my pay grade. I could lose my pension for even showing you what was in this file," Jackson told him.

"I've known where your bones were buried for years, Leroy, and ain't never crossed you into no bullshit. Even when turning on you could've shaved some time off my sentence," Toussaint reminded him. When he'd gotten arrested, the district attorney had offered to let him go without serving any time if he agreed to testify against the Dirty Birds and Detective Jackson. Toussaint wouldn't cooperate against his former unit. He did have something to leverage against the DA that was almost as damning as what the Dirty Birds were into, and that was part of the reason he had received the light sentence that people loved to talk about. But he had never turned on the Dirty Birds, and he needed Leroy to remember that.

"I didn't mean it like that, Trouble. I know they tried to put the screws to you about us. I also know that you stood tall. I never expected anything less, and I'll always be grateful for that. You did me a good turn and I'm trying to do you one, by telling you to forget everything you read in that file and leave them Chinese folks to sort out their own beefs," Leroy warned.

Toussaint looked over his shoulder at John, sitting on the hood of his car and firing up yet another cigarette. He was a father in distress, watching his kid go through something and feeling powerless to do anything about it. That was a feeling Toussaint knew too well. "If only I could."

9

The ride from the Seventeenth back to the brownstone was a quiet one, with each man lost in his own thoughts. John had calmed some, but Toussaint could tell that he was still upset. Any man would be in his position. Toussaint had promised him that he would get in the streets and see what he could find out that would help Jay-Jay. John wanted to ride with him, but Toussaint had managed to convince him that the best place for him would be at home with his family. John was in an emotional state, and down the rabbit hole that Toussaint was about to descend, emotions had no place. Reluctantly, John agreed and left Toussaint to his investigation.

The first tree he would shake was Charlie Tang. Aimee had told him where Charlie lived. She had picked Jay-Jay up from there once. Aimee didn't know the exact address, only the street and that the house was painted blue. Toussaint knew that finding Charlie at the first place the police were likely to look for him was a long shot, but it was currently the only lead that he had to go on.

During the ride over, he thought about the dead girls found by the police, Vickie Sparks in particular. What was the daughter of one of the most powerful men in the city doing hanging around with a bunch of Chinese gangsters? It could've very well been a simple case of another suburban white girl who had been caught in the wrong hood at the wrong time, but the death of Vickie Sparks didn't feel quite that cut and dry. One thing about the case that kept tugging at him was where Vickie's body had been discovered. Why hadn't they taken greater effort disposing of her corpse? High as her profile was, whoever had killed her had to know what kind of alarm it would raise to find the DA's daughter dead in some random dope house. Maybe they had panicked after the deed, or a more sinister theory was that having the bodies found had been their intent? What if this wasn't just a murder, but a message?

Aimee had pointed him out west, to a less-than-friendly neighborhood, one that Toussaint had mostly stayed away from even back when he wore the badge. Left-Shoe had his hands in the pockets of several dealers who slung drugs over that way, so the Dirty Birds had been on the block. But not so much that Toussaint felt like he was coming home. The block was comprised of about half a dozen rundown tenement-style buildings on each side, all in various states of disrepair, some looking like they should've been torn down a long time ago. If this was where Charlie lived, it was no wonder he spent so much time at the Weis'. Toussaint rode through the block slow. He needed to get the lay of the jungle before venturing out into it. That was a tactic Leroy had taught him. *Worst mistake a rookie can make is preparing himself to wrestle with a cat and finding himself locking-ass with a tiger.*

Toussaint parked around the corner. He didn't think that Charlie knew his car but didn't want to run the risk of him seeing it and getting spooked into bolting. He opened his glove box and withdrew a Taser and a set of brass knuckles, both gifts from Aimee because she didn't want him wandering the streets without something to protect himself. Neither gave him the comfort of the .45 he had carried when he was on the job, but they would have to do. He kept his head down when he bent the corner and started making his way up the block, but his eyes were constantly on the move. He could feel the eyes of the residents on him as he walked. Most of them were Asian, but there were a few faces of other ethnicities sprinkled in.

When he'd set out, he'd assumed that a blue-painted house would be easy enough to spot, but several of them on the block were painted shades of blue. No way he was going to go house to house like some sort of salesman, so he needed to figure out a better way to determine which house was Charlie's. Across the street, on the front porch of a house that looked like it might have been blue at one time, before the paint had stared to fade, three sets of eyes watched him. There were two guys and a girl. The guys looked rough and unkempt, but the girl was relatively well put together. She was an Asian woman with dyed blonde hair, sporting tight jeans and an Eagles sweatshirt. He took note of her because her observation of him went beyond curious and leaned more towards expectant. As if she knew his presence on the block would bring about something outside the norm. What did she know that he didn't? With no other real plan, he decided to walk over and ask.

Toussaint had just reached the foot of the stairs when one of the men broke off to meet him. He was a thin Latino man with long, dark hair that looked like it hadn't been washed in a while. "You lost, amigo?"

"Nah, I ain't lost. Looking for a friend," Toussaint said.

"Dressed like that?" The man studied Toussaint's outfit. "You ain't got no friends in this neighborhood. You're either a cop or you looking to get high. Which one is it, vato?"

Had Toussaint been thinking about it he would've changed out of the suit jacket and shoes into something that would've helped him to better blend in before going on his little search mission. "I ain't no cop. It's like I said, I'm looking for somebody. His name is Charlie, maybe you know him?" Toussaint decided a little direct honesty might serve him better in this situation than trying to make up some half-ass story.

"Never heard of him."

It was a lie. Toussaint had seen the recognition flash in his eyes when he heard the name. Toussaint didn't have the time to play with the young man, and his first instinct was to slap the information he needed out of him, but he had to remind himself that he wasn't a cop anymore . . . His Dirty Bird days were behind him. Instead, he flashed his detective skills. "Really? Because I could've sworn that was his bike." He nodded towards a green e-bike resting against the porch railing. It was the same bike he had seen Charlie riding earlier . . . or so he assumed. The city was lousy with them these days, so there was no way to know for sure if that was the same bike he'd seen with Charlie. It was a bluff, but it yielded results.

"Beat it, pig. He already told you we've never heard of Charlie Tang!" the blonde girl barked. Toussaint had hit a nerve.

"I never gave you a last name," Toussaint pointed out.

One of the guys who had been on the porch with them, a stout Chinese man with a shaved head, stood and descended the stairs. He stood directly in front of Toussaint. "You hard of hearing? We don't know no Charlie Tang or Charlie Kelly or Charlie Chaplin. Get your Black ass out from around here before something bad happens to you." Being that the man speaking only stood about five-eight, he had to look up at Toussaint when he levied the threat. He was a small man, but the wooden baseball bat in his hand gave him the presence of a giant. While he was telling Toussaint what he was going to do to him, he kept cutting his eyes at the blonde. It was as if he wanted to make sure that she was watching the spectacle. He probably didn't really want any smoke. He was showing out to impress the girl.

"Check this out," Toussaint began in an icy tone. "You

ain't the first young dude I seen ready to leap off the deep end over a shorty." He looked at the blonde. "No matter how many times this movie gets rerun, it never ends well for the wannabe hero."

"What the fuck is that supposed to mean?" Bat Man's grip tightened on the bat.

Toussaint slipped his hand into his pocket before answering. "Meaning, this is your opportunity to decide if that puppy love you think you're in is worth the world of hurt that's gonna come with it." It wasn't a threat, but a warning from someone who had also once been a slave to a great shot of pussy and understood how it could mess with a man's head. It had been his hope that Bat Man would heed the warning and rethink whatever he was planning. He didn't.

Toussaint saw Bat Man's right shoulder tense and he instantly moved in the opposite direction. The bat missed his skull by an inch, but the momentum pulled Bat Man off balance and left him exposed. This was about the time Toussaint's hand came out of his pocket, brass knuckles secured around his fist. Toussaint cracked Bat Man in the jaw with enough force to nearly knock it from its hinges. He was asleep before he hit the ground.

From the corner of his eye Toussaint caught a glint of steel. The Latino kid thrust a knife at Toussaint's spleen, but missed his target, opening up a cut on Toussaint's side. Toussaint ignored the burning and delivered a roundhouse to the back of the kid's head, dazing him. He followed this with a palm to the chest. The kid paused and gasped when he felt his heart skip a beat. Toussaint slipped behind the dazed young man and put him in a reverse headlock. He squirmed as he felt the viselike muscles in Toussaint's forearm begin to constrict. He howled as the bones in his neck started to crack. Toussaint hadn't wanted to hurt anyone, only to talk and gather information, but they had forced him into survival mode and now all bets were off. He would've surely snapped the kid's neck had a gun not fired right behind him.

When the dust settled, Toussaint didn't find himself in the waiting room of the afterlife, waiting for the receptionist to point him to the escalator that would take him to hell. Instead, he was sitting on a plastic-covered couch in the middle of a living room that looked like it had been plucked from a Sears catalog that dated back to the late nineties. On the glass coffee table in front of him was a hot cup of untouched green tea. Leaning against the doorframe that separated the living room and kitchen was the blonde Asian girl. Toussaint had learned that her name was Coco. Coco clicked her gum, while giving him a look that clearly said he didn't belong there. He was inclined to agree with her. Unfortunately, the choice hadn't been either of theirs. It had been at the insistence of the owner of the home. Toussaint would've declined the invitation had he not been at gunpoint at the time.

When Toussaint heard the gunshot, he had turned expecting to see another of Coco's associates from the stoop, but instead he found the woman who was currently sitting across from him on a love seat, also covered in plastic. If he had to guess, he would say that she was in her sixties, give or take, with snow-white hair that she wore in a messy bun atop her head. Her legs were crossed at the ankles, beneath her floral duster. In a lot of ways, the old woman reminded him of Mrs. Wei, except she had more grit to her. This was a woman who had seen and done some things in her life, including firing her .38—which was resting on her lap—at him. Well, her firing *at* him was an exaggeration. She'd clapped in his general direction to get his attention. She now had it. One of her feet shook impatiently inside one of her Jesus sandals. It was a nervous tic. He knew this because it hadn't started until she had gotten off the phone, verifying who he was with Sue Wei. Apparently, the two of them had history.

"You sure you no want me look at that?" the old woman asked in a heavy accent. She was referring to the cut in Toussaint's side. After getting off to a rocky start, he had learned that her name was Betty Tang, but everyone called her Nan. She was respected in the neighborhood. Toussaint could tell from the way she lit into the guys who had attacked him and how they both stood with their heads hung the whole time, like children being chastised by their mother.

"No, I'm fine," Toussaint lied. "Thank you." He was

pressing the rag that Nan had given him against the cut so he didn't ruin her couch. It had stopped bleeding, but he would still have to go to the ER to get it properly cleaned and stitched up.

"Had you tell us Mr. Wei had sent you, we have no trouble," Nan told him, sipping from her tea cup. The .38 that had introduced them was resting on her lap.

"He didn't exactly *send* me. I'm just trying to help his kid out of a jam is all," Toussaint said honestly.

"I go along with what you need, if I can. You just be sure tell *dage* I no give trouble," Old Nan said.

"*Dage*?" Toussaint questioned. He had picked up a bit of Chinese here and there from the Weis and then spending so much time with Chung while in prison, but this was a term he wasn't familiar with.

Old Nan bit her bottom lip. She was trying to find the words in English that the Black man in her living room would best understand. "*Boss man,*" Coco translated when she tired of watching her grandmother struggle to overcome the language barrier between them. "In America it means like . . ." she thought on it, "OG or a person who the streets respect."

"I see," Toussaint said, trying to picture John Wei as anything other than a straightforward, hardworking man who wanted nothing more than to feed his family. He was sitting there and going over the pieces of the puzzle in his mind when he noticed Nan and Coco staring at him curiously, as he hadn't said anything for a few beats. "It's like I told you earlier," he picked up, "your grandson and Jay-Jay are caught up in some really bad shi . . ." He caught himself. ". . . stuff."

"Son," Nan corrected.

"Say again?"

"Charlie no my grandson. Shamefully, he come directly from the source," Old Nan clarified, touching her stomach.

Toussaint glanced at Coco, who he had already learned was Old Nan's granddaughter. She and Charlie looked to be about the same age, so he was a bit thrown to discover that Charlie was her uncle and not her brother. He turned back to Nan. "I didn't mean to imply—" he began, but she waved him silent.

"Happen more often than not. You see Coco my granddaughter and Charlie so close in age. You shocked? I shocked too. I done with make baby long years ago, my womb no active"—she dusted her hands together as if there were crumbs on them—"but my young friend on side sperm still very active. This how Charlie surprise us, six months before my daughter-in-law give birth Coco." She cackled.

"Grandma!" Coco was embarrassed to hear about her grandmother's exploits with a younger man.

"You don't like? Don't listen. This my truth. Only truth for Mr. Batiste." Old Nan flashed him a smile wide enough to show off the silver fillings in her back teeth.

"I appreciate that, but I'm more interested in finding out where your son has gotten off to rather than how he got here," Toussaint said respectfully. "Jay-Jay Wei is in jail for something I don't believe he did and Charlie can help me prove this."

"So, that's what this is? You want barter my son's life in exchange for Jay-Jay's?" Nan accused.

"I'm not trying to barter anything. I'm trying to help!" Toussaint stressed. "I have reason to believe that both those boys' lives might be in danger. I won't know how bad this thing is until I speak to Charlie."

"Wish I could help. Charlie come and go as he please. In fact, I haven't seen him in weeks." Nan said with a fold of her arms. She was lying. They both knew it, but Nan was intent on standing on business.

"Mrs. Tang—"

"My granddaughter will see you out, Mr. Batiste," Old Nan dismissed him in her suddenly precise English. What little warmth she had shown him when she offered the cup of tea, she was once again the hard-as-nails old woman who had introduced herself with that .38.

There was nothing else to be gained from Old Nan. He stood and smoothed his bloody sport coat. "Thank you for your time," he said politely, while following the blonde granddaughter to the front door. "Your grandma is a tough old bird," he said once he and Coco were outside.

"If you'd survived some of the things that old woman has, you'd be a little hard too," Coco told him.

"And here I thought it was hereditary, since none of y'all hardheaded asses wanna let me help Charlie," Toussaint told her.

"Fuck you! Who do you think you are coming in here and passing judgment on us?" Coco got in his face.

"Somebody that's trying to keep your people alive!" Toussaint shot back. "I know you and your grandma think you're protecting Charlie by not telling me where he's holed up. I get it, because I would do the same for my family. I ain't mad at you for that, but make no mistake that you ain't doing him no favors. Charlie is into some bad shit. If it's as bad as I think, there won't be a rock you or your grandmother can hide him under where these people won't dig him up. If I find him first, at least he's got a chance."

"A chance at what? Putting my grandma's health or house at risk again?" Coco questioned. "You think this is the first time somebody has come around here looking for Charlie over some bullshit he's gotten into? All Nan does is clean up his messes or make excuses for her baby boy. My uncle is a fucking cancer, always has been. Maybe the cops getting hold of him and sitting his ass down for a few months will get him out of our hair for a while and allow my grandma a little peace for once," Coco spat. She clearly wasn't a fan of her uncle.

"Oh, they'll sit him down all right. Likely in an unmarked patch of dirt and leave your grandmother to spend the rest of her days wondering what happened to him. That's going to be a heartbreaker for your ass. But I hope you and Grandma Tang keep that same energy when it happens," Toussaint said before stepping off the porch.

He'd made it halfway down the block to the Monte Carlo when he heard Coco's voice.

"Blue Skies!" Coco called after him. Toussaint paused and gave her a questioning look. "It's a lounge on 10th Street. That's usually where you can find Charlie. Fat Eddie runs the joint. I'm sure I don't have to tell you who he is?"

Toussaint searched his mental Rolodex. He'd heard the name Fat Eddie over the wire a few times while he was in prison. Supposedly Fat Eddie was now the man in charge in the city. "Might've heard the name, but can't say we've ever met."

"For your sake, you might want to keep it that way. Fat Eddie doesn't fuck around," Coco warned. "And please don't tell anyone you got that information from me."

"Of course not. You're doing the right thing for your uncle. I hope you know that."

"I could give a shit about what happens to Charlie. This is about Nan. If she's going to lose him either way, I'd rather it be to prison than the grave. At least this way, when she visits he can talk back."

10

Toussaint drove across Market. The sun had recently set on the City of Brotherly Love and the nighttime streets were starting to come alive. He was sunk low in the driver's seat, one hand on the wheel and his body in a gangster lean. Marvin Gaye's "What's Going On" knocked through his speakers. The casual observer would've probably looked at Toussaint and thought he was on some cool shit, but his posture was due to the fact that his side was killing him. His next stop after leaving Nan's should've been the ER to get his side stitched up, but his injury could wait. Jay-Jay couldn't.

When he pulled back up at the Weis', he found Sue Wei fast asleep. According to Aimee, they feared she was on the verge of some type of breakdown over what was going on with Jay-Jay, so John had given her one of her own herbal teas to help her sleep. Toussaint inquired about the whereabouts of her father—he had some new information that he had obtained from the Tangs and wanted to share it with John. They weren't any closer to solving the case, but maybe what Toussaint had discovered would help to ease John's mind for the time being. Aimee said she had no clue where her father was. After helping him put her mother to bed, she had gone down to help Tommy close the restaurant for the evening. In light of everything going on, there was no way they could continue operating through dinner. When she came back to check on her parents, her father and his car were nowhere to be found. She had called his cell phone several times, but John had failed to answer. Toussaint could tell she was worried about him, and rightfully so. He assured her that he would handle it. It was yet another promise that he had made that day that he wasn't confident he would be able to keep.

He gave Aimee the overview of his visit with Nan and Coco before quizzing her on what she might've known about the social club where Charlie was rumored to spend time, Blue Skies. According to Aimee, it was a hangout for gangsters located on the north side of the city. She warned him that the hardest of men kept time in that place and you had to know someone to get in as they were distrustful of outsiders. It would be tricky for Toussaint to gain entry, but not impossible. He still knew a few moves from his days riding with the Dirty Birds.

He ducked off into his apartment to both check his wound and change his clothes. Stripped down in front of his bathroom mirror, he could see the cut on his side was even worse than he thought. Even when he got around to getting it stitched up, it was likely to leave a nasty scar. Didn't matter. It would be one more to add to the collection. He tossed his blazer and white shirt into a plastic bag to drop in the trash can on his way back out. From his closet he plucked a black turtleneck, before taking off the shoes he'd been wearing and swapping them out for a pair of black three-quarter Timberlands. Next, he popped open a trunk in the back of his closet, which held the last of the memories he had been able to preserve since going to prison. From among his timeline of adventures, he pulled a butter-soft black leather coat that stopped just above his knees. He slipped into the familiar garment and for the first time in a long time he didn't feel like the inmate who had just crawled out of a prison cell and could only think about doing his best not to go back. That was Toussaint. The man about to raise hell on the streets of Philadelphia was Trouble.

Toussaint was making his way to Blue Skies when his cell phone started buzzing. It was a series of texts from Aimee with links attached and instructions on how to access them. He'd promised himself when he started his investigation into why Jay-Jay had been arrested that he wouldn't involve the Weis if he could help it. Turned out he couldn't. He no longer had his contacts within the department to turn to when he needed to dig up dirt on someone, so he turned to the one place outside of the Philadelphia Police Department's database where he knew he could get what he needed. The internet. And who better to help him mine the things that he needed than someone the government felt was dangerous enough to ban from it?

Toussaint clicked the first link and with just a few

keystrokes Aimee had given him a window into Vickie Sparks's private life via her Facebook page. This was the first glimpse Toussaint had been allowed into who Vickie really was beyond what he had skimmed in the file that Leroy had given him a peek at. There wasn't much on her page but some pictures and a few random posts about school or life. She and her friends did have a few pictures of locations where they had checked in that might've been a little shady, but as near as he could tell, there was nothing that linked her to Fat Eddie or his gang. He was about to close the phone when he found the connection.

It was a picture she had posted on her Instagram three weeks before her body was found. There was Vickie, bright smile showing off two rows of teeth that spoke to a lifelong excellent dental plan, blue eyes twinkling in the light. With her face made up and blonde tresses spilling around her shoulders, she looked significantly older than her sixteen years. She also looked happy, glass raised in a toast with her companions. One of them was a Chinese girl; she was pretty and wore no makeup. She too was smiling, glass raised, but there was something in her eyes that didn't quite match the smile. He wouldn't call it fear, but there was definitely something lurking there. The third person in the picture was a man, also Chinese. He was covered in tattoos from his arms to his neck. He was in the life. Toussaint could almost smell it on him through the photo. Unlike the girls, the man wasn't smiling. He looked caught off guard, and none too happy about being photographed.

Seeing Vickie's smile in the picture wasn't what had made Toussaint pay attention to it, but what was in the background. He touched his thumb and index finger to the screen and pinched to zoom in. It was a neon sign. Though the wording wasn't very clear, Toussaint was pretty sure the sign spelled out BLUE SKIES.

No more than twenty minutes later, Toussaint was turning onto Adams Avenue off 10th Street. He found a parking spot in the lot of a twenty-four-hour laundromat. He put the Taser into his glove box but held on to the brass knuckles. Blue Skies likely required anyone entering to be patted down first. At least he hoped so. The last place he wanted to be was in a room full of armed and dangerous men with just his hands to defend himself. The brass knuckles wouldn't have done him much good against pistols, but it was a weapon he was pretty sure he could get past whoever was manning the door. No one was going find his treasure where he planned on hiding it—a little trick he had learned during his time in prison.

Blue Skies was maybe three or four doors down from the laundromat where he had parked. As he neared the place, he realized that he *had* been there before. Only it hadn't been a social club back then but a day care center. This was before Toussaint became a member of the Dirty Birds and was still just a young narcotics officer with delusions of ridding the city of drugs once and for all. That was exactly what he and his team found when they raided the place: drugs. The brother and sister team who had been running the day care were using it as a front to push large quantities of marijuana. The police had been tipped off by a concerned parent, who noticed that their child reeked of weed. The property had clearly changed hands several times since Toussaint had last been there, but it was still under the control of criminals.

Toussaint crossed the street and lingered in the doorway of a closed deli, observing Blue Skies from the darkness. There wasn't a lot of traffic going in and out, but it was constant. Scantily clad women hovered on the street, flagging down cars and accosting just about anyone walking by in an attempt to get them to spend a few dollars. The way the sex workers were pressing them reminded Toussaint of a fellas' trip he had taken years ago to the Dominican Republic. That was a week he would never forget, not just because he had laid with some of the baddest women he had ever seen, but because two weeks after their return, the wife of one of the guys had filed for divorce. Apparently, he had brought her home a special Santo Domingo case of the clap.

He continued his observation. Most of the guys ignored the girl's advances, but there were a few who entertained them. Those were the men who were ushered inside the club. The gatekeeper was a squat Chinese man who appeared to be sculpted entirely from muscle, with a shaved head and wearing dark glasses. As expected, each of the men were patted down before being allowed access to the spot, but the girls were not. At least not the working girls. They obviously had some type of arrangement.

Hearing the crunch of glass somewhere to his left, Toussaint turned to see a woman emerge from the shadows. She was a skinny girl, with long, stringy black hair that hung down to her shoulders. She was young, her face caked with makeup in an attempt to look older. Beneath it, you could see at one point she had been beautiful before life and whatever her vices were had started catching up to her. The tight skirt that hugged her bony hips was so short that you could see the beginnings of her pubic hairs peeking from beneath it. She shambled in Toussaint's direction, taking long pulls of the Newport pinched between her lips.

"You looking for some company?" the sex worker asked, blowing out a plume of smoke.

The question almost made Toussaint laugh out loud. Once upon a time in a galaxy far away, she might've been something he'd consider taking down on a drunk night, but there was no way he would risk sticking his dick in that walking petri dish. Not having been with a woman in five years had him thirsty, but not foolish. He was about to dismiss her when he realized that he knew her, or at least a more flattering version of her. "Maggie?"

PART II

STRANGE FRUIT

11

Toussaint had to stop his feet from moving when he walked in and heard the DJ playing Rose Royce's "Do Your Dance." That had been a hit cut when he was a kid, having always heard it playing in his mother's house. She and her friends would get tipsy on the weekends and pay him quarters to dance to the tune, so he knew it intimately. He fought the urge to cut a rug and shifted his concentration back to the business at hand.

Toussaint found himself standing under the very sign he had seen in Vickie's photo. Maggie had her arm hooked in his, ushering him inside the social club. He imagined that they made an odd couple to the people who saw them together; this well-built older Black man and the broken-down sex worker. One of the girls he had seen hustling outside was seated at a private table with one of the johns she had picked up. She let out a snicker when she saw Maggie. Maggie paused long enough to look the girl up and down and cap, "Hating is so childish," before flipping her wig and continuing inside with Toussaint. If nothing else, the girl was confident. That hadn't changed.

Getting Toussaint past the gatekeeper proved to be trickier than he had hoped. He had learned from Maggie that he was called Jin, and Jin took his job seriously. He and Maggie had history, so to speak, from back when Maggie had still been something to look at, when, she admitted, she had been part of the clique of girls who scouted potential customers, and in some cases victims. Sounded like she had been fairly good at it too, until she started using heavily and got greedy. Girls were allowed to bring in nonmembers and apply their trades, so long as they gave the people who owned the spot their cut. Maggie started rolling tricks without kicking up the agreed-upon tribute and got caught with her hand in the cookie jar. She had been cast out and now had to take whatever spillovers she could get on the outskirts of the club. None of the other gatekeepers would allow her inside anymore, but Jin would look the other way and let her slip inside. They had always been cool, and his soft spot for her remained even after the drugs had dragged her down. She said this was likely because she would sometimes treat him to free blow jobs in his car when he was on break.

Soft spot or not, Jin was suspicious of the Shaft-looking Black man Maggie showed up with. At first, he wanted to deny Toussaint entry. He claimed he smelled like a cop. But the fact that that reek was a few years old combined with Maggie's threadbare cred and a subtly delivered hundred-dollar bill got him a temporary pass. Jin greedily accepted the money, but made it clear that if Toussaint caused any trouble he was as good as dead. That was fine by Toussaint. He hadn't planned on staying inside the social club long enough to get into anything, let alone for Jin to realize the bill he just slipped him was a counterfeit.

The hundred was from the stash he'd found in his jacket earlier, a holdover from his days with the Dirty Birds. The bill was one of several thousand that hadn't made it into evidence when the unit busted up the ring that was printing them. Left-Shoe had divided them among the crew to fuck up at a massage parlor they were partying at that night. The guys had run through a half dozen girls by the time the madam who ran the spot wised up to the fact that the money was fake. Normally, a guy trying to pass off funny money in a spot like that would've received an ass whipping, at the very least. But they weren't regular guys. They were the Dirty Birds and protected by the badge, so all the madam could do was ask them to leave.

The odd couple found an empty table near where a stage was set up at the back of the club. Well, calling it a stage would've been a compliment. It looked more like a deck that had been salvaged from someone's backyard. There was barely enough room on it for the DJ and his equipment. Toussaint managed to get the attention of a passing waitress and placed a drink order: whiskey for him and a beer for the lady. He offered to buy her something stronger, but she preferred the suds over spirits.

Toussaint watched Maggie chug half her beer. He couldn't believe that of all the people in the city he could run into that night, he'd bump into Maggie. Seeing her was like some divine signal from the universe that he was either on the right path, or the wrong one. He wasn't sure which, but seeing her was definitely a sign. He observed as she downed the last of her beer and let out a deep belch before wiping her mouth with the back of her hand. The gesture reminded him of his mother back in the day. She was one of the few other women he had known who preferred a cold beer over liquor. He could remember summer days as a kid when his mother would send him to the store with a note. Back then store owners wouldn't hesitate to sell alcohol to minors, especially if they were locals. Toussaint would come back with six-packs of Olde English for his mother and her friends to sip while they sat on the porch and gossiped.

"Why are you looking at me like that?" Maggie asked, noticing that he was staring at her.

"No reason. Just remembering the last time I saw you," Toussaint told her.

"Not one of my finest moments," Maggie let out a weak chuckle. She was silent for a time, taking another drink from her beer. This time she sipped it, instead of chugging. "You know, for years I felt guilty about what I did to you."

"You didn't do anything, Maggie. That was on me," Toussaint assured her.

"No . . . it wasn't!" Maggie insisted. "Me being in that room cost you five years of your life!"

• • •

Toussaint had only been in Maggie's company twice. Both encounters had directly affected the trajectory of his life. The first time had been at a fundraiser in Wilmington, Delaware. The event was being held by a former mayor named Jacob Atwater, who had his sights set on the governor's mansion. Toussaint and a few of the guys from his unit were moonlighting as part of the security detail. He remembered being huddled in the parking lot out front of the banquet hall, trying to convince one of the girls who worked in the kitchen to sneak off to his car during her break to give him a blow job, when the limo carrying Atwater and his party arrived. They all watched as the politician emerged from the limo with his family, Atwater first, followed by his children, a girl of about sixteen and a boy who didn't appear to be older than ten or eleven. The children posed with their dad for a few quick pictures before Atwater turned his attention back to the limo, where one of his bodyguards was helping his wife out onto the red carpet. She was a caramel-colored sister wearing a sleek black evening gown that hugged her in all the right places. The slit up the side was enough to showcase her long legs, but not high enough to be considered distasteful. When Toussaint saw her, the caterer he'd been trying to get to pleasure him became an afterthought. His eyes followed Claire Atwater until she disappeared inside with her husband and family.

For the remainder of the night, Toussaint's attention remained focused on Claire. He damn near felt like a stalker for how intently he was watching her. At one point during the night she must've felt the heat coming from his gaze because she looked in his direction. When their eyes locked, something passed between them. It was more than a fleeting glance, but she didn't let her eyes linger long enough that anyone would notice. But Toussaint had. He waited until the night had started to wind down, and Atwater was occupied doing interviews. He found her tucked off in a quiet corner, sipping a glass of champagne and watching her husband charm the media. She didn't seem surprised by his presence. It was as if she had been expecting him.

"So, you planned on spending the entire night avoiding me?" Toussaint asked.

"I wasn't avoiding you, Toussaint. I just wasn't sure what there was to say," Claire answered honestly.

"You could've started with hello," Toussaint joked, but Claire didn't laugh. "Damn, I know it's been a minute, but I was hoping for a warmer reception."

"It's been almost two decades. I'd call that longer than a minute. Or are you still drinking and smoking so much that you can't keep your days straight?" Claire snapped in a sharp tone.

Toussaint didn't respond. Claire was the one woman who could call him on his bullshit, besides maybe Sue Wei. At one time he and Claire had been a *thing*. This was at the height of his Troubleman days, when he was still in the streets heavy, before joining the department and getting his shit together. They had spent a summer made up of stolen moments entertaining something that they both knew deep down in their hearts could never truly be. Toussaint had been the neighborhood thug and Claire the sweet church girl he was seeing behind her parents' backs. Claire was the first girl that Toussaint had ever loved, and he promised himself—and her—that he would one day marry her. But he would never have the chance. One day Claire and her family had just up and disappeared without a trace. Theirs was a secret, forbidden love, but a love no less, and it still stung that Claire hadn't even shown him the courtesy of saying goodbye.

"Nice to see that you landed on your feet." Toussaint motioned towards Atwater. He was in the middle of his interview but casting suspicious glances at the off-duty cop invading his wife's space. "He know about us?"

"What *us*, Toussaint? We were just a couple of kids who fooled around for a summer." Claire said it as if the time they spent together hadn't mattered.

"Damn, it's like that?" Toussaint tried to hide the hurt in his tone. He felt like he was eighteen again and trying to earn her favor.

"I'm sorry. I didn't mean it like it sounded," Claire said apologetically. "It's just that . . . I've been through a lot over the years since last we saw each other, and I'd rather let my past stay in the past. It was good seeing you again,

Toussaint." She started to walk off, but he stopped her by grabbing her wrist. Not aggressively, just enough to keep her from walking away from him . . . again.

"Claire, you left me wondering what happened to you, without an explanation! And now you're acting like I'm the one who did some bullshit!"

She noticed that people were watching and lowered her voice. "Now is *not* a good time, Toussaint. Give me a number to reach you and we can talk later."

The way she was brushing him off put Toussaint in his feelings. "You ain't gotta dismiss me like the help, baby. I can take a hint. Me approaching you tonight wasn't about trying to disrupt this new life you built for yourself. I just felt like maybe after all these years, maybe you owed me a little closure?"

"About what?" Claire appeared anxious.

"Why you left me without so much as a word? It might've been puppy love to you, but for me it was real. I just wanna know why?" Toussaint hadn't even realized until he posed the question how deeply Claire's departure still bothered him.

He was firing off questions that Claire wasn't prepared to answer, but her ex-lover wasn't going to let it go. She opened her mouth to speak at the same time as her children came streaking through the crowd of guests. The girl, who he would learn was named Maggie, was chasing her little brother, Jacob Jr. Maggie had fire in her eyes and looked like she intended to do little Jacob harm over whatever his offense had been had he not taken shelter behind his mother. Toussaint watched Maggie, chest heaving from running, nostrils flared, and long black hair a mess. The mask of anger she wore on her face reminded him of how his mother's features would contort right before she was about to whip his ass. When the realization finally hit Toussaint, it did so with the impact of a city bus.

The two years between that night and the next time he would hear from Claire Atwater again had been dark ones for the detective. He had thrown himself into his work and his vices. The night Claire had called him in a panic, Toussaint was so drunk and high that he barely remembered the particulars of the conversation, but he knew that she . . . *they*, needed his help. Maggie, who was about eighteen at the time, had taken up with some grown man and was last spotted somewhere in Philadelphia. The heiress to the Atwater legacy was out there lost in the woods, so Claire needed a wolf to hunt her down.

It took about a week for Toussaint to get a line on the teenager. Word on the streets was that Maggie had been keeping company with a cat named Roman, who was said to get his kicks and his paper off young girls who he had turned onto the life. Roman wasn't a local, so Toussaint didn't know a lot about him except where to find him on that particular night. He had set up shop in a hotel downtown and had some of his girls rolling tricks at the bar. For Toussaint this should've been a simple search-and-rescue mission, but when he walked into that hotel room and saw Maggie, beaten, naked, and high out of her mind, something in him just snapped. The next thing he knew, Roman was a stain on the sidewalk and he was in handcuffs.

At the time, Toussaint hadn't known that Roman had ties to law enforcement. This would come out at his trial. He was a Wilmington detective who worked as a part of the governor's personal security detail during his off time. Roman had been grooming and fucking Maggie right under their noses and neither of the Atwaters noticed. For killing a cop in cold blood, the state of Pennsylvania had been looking to put the death penalty on the table for Toussaint, and it seemed that there was nothing that anyone could do about it. This was when Jacob Atwater stepped in. He offered to use his influence to spin the story and get Toussaint a reduced sentence. In exchange, Toussaint had to keep their family secret. It was a raw deal, but it beat spending the rest of his life in prison or worse, so Toussaint took it. In hindsight, Atwater's offer had less to do with protecting Maggie than it did with protecting his own image. How would it look if it got out that the governor's daughter had been selling ass for a member of his own staff and he did nothing to stop it?

The day of his sentencing was the last time he'd seen Claire Atwater. She had shown up in court to wish him farewell. Two years into his bid, he got the word that Claire had lost a fight with breast cancer. The news of Claire's passing had hurt Toussaint. While he was serving time he would often think of Maggie, and what had become of her after her liberation from Roman and her mother's death. He wondered how she was doing. Did she ever manage to get her life back on track?

"I thought about you a lot while I was away. Especially after hearing about your mom passing. Wondered how you were holding up? Your brother too," Toussaint told her.

"Let's just say that my life didn't exactly go according to plan," Maggie half joked. She noticed that he didn't laugh. There was a question in Toussaint's eyes. "You're probably wondering how I got like this? It's okay, sometimes I ask myself the same question." She downed the last of her beer and stared absently into the bottom of the glass. Toussaint motioned for the bartender to give her a refill. Only when the beer was replenished did she begin speaking again. "I've tried to hold it together, ya know? To be strong for Jake's sake. Poor kid had always been a little on the soft side. I stayed clean for a little bit, but without anybody to lean on when things got hard for me, I slipped and kept slipping until I couldn't tell which way was up."

"What about your dad?"

"What about him? He was always more concerned about what was going on with his career than in his home. How do you think I was able to start sleeping with Roman in the first place? After mom died, it was like he didn't see us anymore. My last straw was when he brought home that blonde blow-up doll and announced that she would be our new stepmother. My mom hadn't been dead six months and he had already moved on. I just couldn't take it in that house anymore so I left and never looked back."

"Where'd you go?" Toussaint wanted to know.

"Here and there," she said with a shrug. "Worked a few odd jobs, but flipping burgers wasn't able to sustain my habit, so I started dancing. Hooked up with this older guy who owned one of the clubs I danced at and he picked up where Roman left off. I told myself that I wasn't gonna do more than dance, but the bigger that monkey on my back grew, the more I was willing to compromise my morals to get high. Realization set in when I found myself bent over in a cheap motel with a white man I had never met a day in my life plowing into me for fifty bucks."

"I know things were rough between you and your dad, but did you ever think about reaching out to him to try and help you get clean? I'm sure he had the resources to get you top-notch treatment."

"I did . . . once. Called the house one night when I was in bad shape. His wife answered and told me in no uncertain terms that I was no longer welcome there." Maggie let out a sad chuckle. "So, here I am." She parted her hands. "A junkie alone in the world."

"You ain't alone, Maggie. You got me," Toussaint told her.

"Toussaint, you've already sacrificed enough for me. What do I look like asking anything more of you?"

"Like a young woman who is going through a rough

patch and just needs a little help." He placed one of her smaller hands into his. "I'm here for you, Maggie, and I need you to know that. You understand me?"

Maggie nodded. "You're an honorable man, Toussaint."

"I wouldn't say all that. I'm just somebody who is trying to right his wrongs."

"I can respect that," Maggie said with a nod. "Enough about me," she changed the subject. "You never did tell me why you were itching to get into this place tonight?"

"I'm looking for somebody. A kid named Charlie Tang. You know him?"

"Sure, he's a regular here. He and that gang of Chinese punks he runs around with, Fat Eddie's crew. Why would *you* be looking for Charlie?"

"He might be able to help me get a friend of mine out of a jam," Toussaint told her.

"You must be talking about the dead white girl?"

"You know anything about it?"

"Enough to know this ain't the place you wanna be asking those kinds of questions. The walls got ears," Maggie said in a whisper.

"I ain't looking to stir up no shit. I just need to ask the boy a few questions. You seen him around lately?"

"Not in the last couple of days. He's gone underground, and if he's smart he'll stay there before somebody puts him there involuntarily," Maggie said seriously. "People are saying that Charlie is tied up in this some kind of way, which ain't no surprise. That boy stays in the mix, but I've never known him to be no killer. What's your stake in all this? Must be pretty high if you're in this place risking your ass by looking into it. You and the dead girl have something going?"

"Hell nah! I ain't got no appetite for babies. The man they locked up for this is the son of a friend of mine, Jay-Jay. Maybe you know him too? Hangs around with Charlie."

"Name doesn't ring a bell, but if he runs around with Charlie then I've likely seen his face before, but not recently. That whole little gaggle has been keeping a safe distance from this place since news broke about the killing."

Toussaint was about to press Maggie as to whether she thought maybe one of Charlie's crew had been capable of committing the crime when he noticed her eyes dart to something out of his line of vision. He turned to see what looked like a refrigerator with legs making his way across the room. He had to be at least six-seven and was built like an offensive lineman. A long ponytail swayed back and forth across his wide back as he disappeared through a door off to the side of the social club that was marked OUT OF SERVICE.

"What they got going on back there?" Toussaint asked Maggie. Since he'd been sitting there he had noticed quite a bit of traffic going in and out of wherever the door led.

"You don't want to know and you better pray that you never find out," she said, still in her serious voice. Near the bar area she noticed a man she sometimes did business with trying to get her attention. "Toussaint, it was good seeing you, but I gotta get this money," Maggie told him before downing the last of her beer and standing. "If you were smart, you'd find somewhere else to be too."

"I think I'm gonna hang around and have one more."

"Suit yourself." Maggie shrugged.

Toussaint scribbled his cell number on a napkin and handed it to Maggie. "Don't forget what I told you. If you need me, I'm a phone call away."

"Such a sweetheart." Maggie stuffed the napkin into her purse. "I wish the man my mother told me was my daddy cared about me as much as you do."

Toussaint suppressed the lump in his throat as he watched Maggie amble down to the other end of the bar to snuggle up next to the trick she had spotted. Maggie whispered something in his ear and the two of them headed towards the exit, off to execute whatever deal they had just negotiated. It took everything out of him not to get up and go after her in hopes of preventing yet another bad decision. But what advice could a father give to a daughter who didn't know he existed?

12

Toussaint sat at the table sipping on his second whiskey. He had been at Blue Skies for an hour, which was forty minutes longer than he intended on staying. His plan had been to come in and see if he could get a lead on Charlie, but it was proving to be a dead end. He was sitting there trying to figure out what his next move was when suddenly the houselights went out. Thinking something was about to go down, he reached into his underwear where he had hidden his brass knuckles and armed himself. With his other hand, he grabbed Maggie's abandoned beer bottle and stood, prepared for battle. A beat or so later, a spotlight came on overhead and illuminated the deck. A tune came from the speakers. He could hear grumblings coming from around the darkened room. The crowd was mostly made up of Asian men and women who were thirty and under, so he doubted many of them had ever heard the song. Toussaint, however, knew it quite well, as it had been in regular rotation in his house on those Sunday mornings when his mother would get up at the crack of dawn and start cleaning. "Strange Fruit" by Billie Holiday.

Toussaint had heard the song enough through the years that he didn't feel compelled to stick around for whatever watered-down karaoke version of it someone was about to perform onstage. He was making his way through the darkened social club, trying to find the exit, when he heard a voice that stopped him in his tracks. It was deep, yet soulful. Not quite Billie, of course, but damn close. He turned back to the stage, searching for the source of the sound. At the edge of the stage, the singer was draped in shadows; he was only able to catch a glimpse of the soft lights reflecting off the sequins covering her dress. Her voice was so powerful that Toussaint knew it just had to be a Black woman back there trying to give Ms. Holiday a run for her money. His jaw dropped when she finally stepped into the spotlight to reveal herself.

She had to be the tallest Asian woman Toussaint had ever seen, easily five-ten. Even taller in the rhinestone heels she wore. Her skin was the color of sunrise, sprinkled with gold dust that made her whole body shimmer like something magical. The singer's long black hair swayed with her as she rocked to the beat, becoming more engrossed in the song. Before Toussaint had even realized it, he found himself among a number of men who had moved closer to the stage to get a better look. Her eyes were closed, lost in the music. As she reached the part of the song about Black bodies swinging in the southern breeze, her eyes came open . . . enchanting dark eyes that stared directly at Toussaint. They were like two pools of sorrow that threatened to swallow him into their eternal blackness . . . and he would welcome it.

Toussaint had been so bewitched by the songstress that he hadn't even realized the performance was over until he was blinded by the houselights when they came back on. "Give it up for the lovely Ms. Butterfly," he heard the DJ say over the microphone. Thunder exploded in his ears from the dozens of hands that clapped loudly in honor of the brilliant performance. When the woman called Butterfly stepped from the stage, she was greeted with cheers and people invading her space. Two members of the club's security cleared a path for her to get through the mob. It wasn't until the crowd snapped closed behind and she was out of his view that whatever hold the Amazon had over him finally relinquished its grip. Toussaint had been in the presence of many women over the years, and very few were able to have that type of effect on him.

Toussaint was still standing at the foot of the stage, processing what he had just experienced, when he heard a voice come from behind that told him his night was about to turn for the worse.

"Since when did they start letting pigs in this muthafucka!" Spider was walking in Toussaint's direction. He wasn't alone either. With him was a Chinese dude with hair dyed green. And also the bald man from earlier in the day, his head now sporting fresh stitches where Toussaint had slammed it into the car door. The murderous look in his eyes said that he hadn't forgotten the beating he'd taken at the hands of the Black man and was spoiling for some get-back.

"I would say that it's good to see you again, Spider, but we both know that'd be a damn lie," Toussaint said with a smirk.

"You're out of bounds, nigger!" the bald man spat.

"And you're about to be back in the hospital, my man," Toussaint shot back. "Listen, boys, I didn't come here for any trouble. I just wanted to grab a quick drink and be on my way." He moved to leave, but Spider blocked his path.

"Or maybe you came looking for Charlie? I hear you visited his mother today."

"Yeah, I was looking to borrow a cup of sugar, but she was all out. You got any?"

The guy with the green hair laughed and Spider barked something at him in Chinese that wiped the smile from his face. He then turned back to Toussaint. "Always with the jokes, huh? You think you'll still be funny after me and my boys kick your ass?"

It was now Toussaint's turn to laugh. "Spider, I could bend over one of these chairs with my ass hiked in the air and your foot still couldn't find it. Now, I'm trying to be cordial because I already reached my two-beatdown-per-day limit with your crew here, but don't push me. I get the fact that you puffing up ain't got nothing to do with you actually wanting to lock ass with me. You're trying to put on a show for your boys, but if you don't get the fuck out of my face we gonna make a whole movie in here." He cracked his knuckles. "You got two choices: Get the fuck on and let me go about my way. Or I can show your guys what kind of bitch you really are."

There was uncertainty in Spider's eyes. He really didn't want any smoke, but he had overplayed his stroke when he laid down the gauntlet, obviously expecting Trouble to back down. He looked at his boys, who were waiting to see what the play was going to be. Was Spider going to go out like a bitch and shame their gang? Or would he answer the call to arms?

Spider telegraphed the punch before he threw it. It was the tensing in his shoulder before he swung, a mistake often made by dudes who were not fighters. Toussaint, however, was a fighter. Toussaint could've probably gone to the bar, ordered another drink, and been back by the time Spider's fist finally reached him. He blocked it with his forearm and countered with a punch that landed squarely in Spider's chest. You could see the wind leave the skinnier man as his body damn near folded in on itself before he left his feet and hit the floor. He lay on the floor, gasping like he was having an asthma attack.

"Like I said, straight bitch!" Toussaint spat, hovering over him. He caught a flicker of movement in his peripheral. The bald thug was coming for a second helping of what he'd gotten earlier. This time he was smart about it and brought a knife with him. Toussaint dipped and dodged as the blade whipped past him. In his maneuvering, Toussaint stumbled over a beer bottle on the floor and went down. The bald thug took this opportunity to close in.

Toussaint waited until he was right on top of him, knife raised for the kill strike, before shooting his foot out. When his heel connected with Bald Thug's knee, there was an audible crack, followed by him collapsing. Toussaint swung his legs in a circle like a helicopter and spun back to his feet, ready to take on the next challenge.

The man with the green hair stood a few feet from Toussaint, hands folded behind his back. He was slight of build, pretty about the face. You'd take him for the lead singer in a K-pop band before the kind of fella you'd expect to be hanging around a gangster like Spider. Yet here he was, ready to defend his boss's honor. Toussaint outweighed the green-haired man by so much that it almost felt like a crime to lay hands on him, but if it was an ass-whipping he wanted then it would be an ass-whipping he got.

Toussaint waited for him to advance, but he didn't. He just kept standing there, smirking like he was daring Toussaint to try him. A warning bell went off in Toussaint's head, but he couldn't hear it over his rage. He rushed at the green-haired man, launching a combination of punches, all of which the green-haired man avoided, hands never leaving their position clasped behind his back. Toussaint threw a roundhouse, which the green-haired man caught in midair. He let out an amused chuckle before pushing Toussaint's leg, causing the Black man to involuntarily spin, leaving his back exposed. Before Toussaint could turn back around, a foot connected with the back of his skull and damn near put his lights out. Toussaint found himself on all fours, looking back at the man, still smirking. One of his arms was still folded behind his back, and with his free hand he taunted Toussaint to come at him again. This one was no common thug.

"Oh, you know some shit about some shit?" Toussaint pushed himself to his feet. He took a boxer's stance. "Me too! Let's get to it."

A ring of spectators had gathered around the men as they circled each other. Toussaint danced on the balls of his feet, keeping his guard up so as not to get hit with another one of those kicks. His green-haired opponent spun his arms extravagantly before settling into a stance, fingers curled like a tiger about to pounce. Toussaint recognized the technique from his sparring sessions with John. Someone had trained the man. This much had been obvious even before he damn near kicked Toussaint's brain from his skull. Toussaint faked a high punch, and when the green-haired man moved to block it, Toussaint kicked him in the ribs. The green-haired man wasn't the only one who had some training.

They went back and forth, trading kicks and punches. Toussaint had to admit that the man was good. Possibly better than him, but Toussaint still had some tricks up his sleeve. They launched for each other at the same time, the green-haired man choosing to go high, while Toussaint went low. The green-haired man landed a chop to Toussaint's shoulder blade with so much force that Toussaint feared he had broken it. Ignoring the pain, Toussaint focused on his training. Curving his fingers like claws, he struck the green-haired man in his sides. When he felt the rib cage under the soft flesh, he dug in deeper, trying to grab the actual ribs. The green-haired man howled in pain. Once Toussaint had him off balance, he struck him in the chin with the top of his head. The green-haired man threw another blow, which Toussaint deflected. Now that his chest was exposed, it was time for the grand finale. Using only his index fingers, he struck the man with a rapid, complex series of blows from chest to left shoulder. With the final strike, he twisted his fingers as if turning a key in a lock.

When the green-haired man made to counter, he found his left arm paralyzed. He looked at Toussaint in wide-eyed shock, with a touch of admiration. "Crippled Boxer's Revenge?" He had immediately recognized the technique. It was a forbidden style of kung fu that few had ever heard of and even fewer had seen executed in real time. Fewer still had lived to tell the tale.

"With my own little twist!" Toussaint announced before kicking the green-haired man in the balls.

The fight was over but not the war. There was the familiar sound of a gun being cocked behind his head, followed by a voice he hadn't heard in quite some time.

"When I got the call telling me that there was *trouble* at my place, I didn't know she meant literally."

13

Toussaint sat in a not-so-comfortable leather armchair. His head was killing him from where he had been kicked. He was fairly certain that he had a concussion. He'd suffered enough of them over the years to know what one felt like. The throbbing in his head failed to bring him out of his state of semishock. The shock hadn't come from the fact that he hadn't been killed after the mess he had just made inside the notorious social club, but from who he had to credit for it.

There were six people crammed into the small office, including Toussaint. Spider was sitting on a folding chair, staring daggers at Toussaint. Toussaint had embarrassed him. Their organization was big on respect, and getting laid out had caused him to lose face. The loss was sure to lower his standing within his gang. Leaning against the door was the big man he had seen earlier, who had ducked off into the back room. He had looked bigger when Toussaint first saw him walking across the social club, but lingering over Toussaint like a shadow the man seemed like a giant. Jin was also in the room. He wore a look that you would see on a kid who had just been called into the principal's office for a meeting with his parents. The singer, Butterfly, lounged on a sofa in the corner. She took slow pulls off a joint of something that smelled like pure joy. She wore a disinterested expression, but her body carried a tension to it that said she was just as uncomfortable as Toussaint being in a room full of gangsters.

Sitting across from him, behind a large wooden desk and staring at him with cold, beady eyes was the man who had stayed Toussaint's execution. He was large, easily tipping the scales at three hundred or so pounds. A gold watch adorned one of his thick wrists and a pinky ring squeezed onto one of his chubby fingers. He looked like a parody of the Godfather with his bulk stuffed into a black tuxedo and a bad comb-over atop his balding head. But as comical as he appeared, this man was no joke. This was Fat Eddie, the new Don of Chinatown.

After an uncomfortable silence, Fat Eddie finally spoke. "You know from the way Trixie, my bartender, was going on about my spot being busted up, I rolled in heavy," he said, patting the long revolver that lay on the desk in front of him. "I was expecting one of my rivals had come to lay siege to my shit. I was a little disappointed when I got here and saw that it was one man who was kicking the shit out of my guys. But when I saw who that one-man wrecking crew was, it made sense. Troubleman, give me one reason why I shouldn't let Goliath snap your fucking neck?" He gestured to the mountain leaning against the door.

"C'mon, Eddie. Is that any way to talk to an old friend?" Toussaint asked with a knowing smirk.

Before becoming Fat Eddie, the Don of Chinatown, he had been Eddie Chong, low-level crook. Toussaint had first come to know Eddie about 120 pounds ago. Back then, Eddie was a part of a ring of car thieves who had come onto the radar of the Dirty Birds. Eddie and his crew had made the mistake of snatching a car that belonged to a schoolteacher who happened to be a part-time bedmate of Left-Shoe. To make matters worse, Eddie had slapped the woman around pretty good during the jacking. When they finally caught up with Eddie, Left-Shoe showed him how he had gotten the moniker, introducing Eddie's face to his left shoe about a half dozen times. He probably would've killed Eddie had Eddie not offered up the name and location of a man the police had been looking for in connection with the accidental murder of a kid during a gang shoot-out. The resulting arrest earned Left-Shoe a promotion and made him one of the most beloved cops in the city. It also made Eddie a bitch of the Dirty Birds. From time to time they would tap Eddie for information on cases they were working in exchange for cash and turning a blind eye to his petty crimes. From what Toussaint could see in the man sitting across from him, Eddie had come a long way from stealing cars.

"Fuck you, Troubleman! We ain't never been friends!" Eddie spat.

Toussaint leaned back in his chair and looked at Eddie. "We was sure friendly enough when I helped you get your little cousin out when the police busted him with that coke on him. Where was all this piss and vinegar then?"

Eddie glanced at Butterfly, who was now paying attention to the conversation. Had it been anyone but Toussaint speaking to him that way, Eddie would've had him killed. But a murdered cop in his club, even an ex-cop, would've brought down unnecessary heat on him and his spot. "What do you want, Troubleman?"

"Information," Toussaint said flatly. "I need to have a conversation with a guy named Charlie Tang." Eddie opened his mouth to speak, but Toussaint waved him silent. "Now before you go bullshitting me about how you've never heard of him, I know he works for you and is known to hang out in here. I'm not looking to cause you or your boys any grief. I just want to talk."

"About?" Eddie questioned.

"That's between me and Charlie. I'd owe you one for putting me in contact with him," Toussaint said.

"You owe me three for not letting my boys drag you out into the alley and stomp a hole in you, especially after what you did to Jade." Eddie was speaking about the man with the green hair. "They're saying that you used an old Wah Pei technique. That true?"

"I just landed a lucky hit is all."

"Lucky hit, my ass! You done turned ol' Jade into a gimp with just one touch." Fat Eddie wiggled his arm loosely, mimicking the condition he'd found Jade in. "Crippled

Boxer style is a myth, said to only be known to the disciples of the man who created it. You sure as hell don't look like no Chinaman, so you wanna tell me the real story of how you learned it?"

Toussaint leaned in to whisper. "If I tell you the story, are you gonna tuck me in afterward like a good little boy?"

The response made Fat Eddie livid. With rage in his eyes, Fat Eddie sprang to his feet. Toussaint rose with him, hands raised to defend himself. Eddie's boys surrounded Toussaint, ready to pounce when their boss did. It was up, and everybody in the room knew it. The only thing that stopped the pending violence from erupting was Butterfly's voice.

"My grandfather used to tell me and my sisters about the Crippled Boxer when we were kids," Butterfly began. "Many years ago, the province of Wah Pei was under the rule of a cruel warlord. His reign was bloody, one that saw him conquer many cities, making slaves of people. For sport, he would force men he had taken captive into combat matches against one of his generals, Lee Un. Un was said to possess the gift of invincibility, having survived several battles and never sustaining so much as a scratch. The warlord declared Lee Un the greatest fighter in all the lands and challenged anyone to prove him wrong. That was when the Crippled Boxer showed up in Wah Pei."

The whole room was silent, hanging on to Butterfly's every word. Toussaint had heard this story before, but there was something about the way Butterfly told it that made him feel like he was hearing it for the first time. The lovely Butterfly was as good a storyteller as she was a singer.

"No one knew the real name of this one-armed man or where he had come from. He made a wager with the general that he could defeat his champion with three blows. In return, the warlord would grant him one thing that his heart desired. Eager to make an example of the cripple for making such a fool's bet, the warlord accepted. The Crippled Boxer had been wrong about being able to defeat Lee Un with three blows . . . He did it with one. A single strike left Lee Un paralyzed and thus ended the match, much to the embarrassment of the warlord. When the one-armed man came to claim his prize, it was not gold nor silver that his heart desired, but the life of the man who had murdered his parents and cut off his arm when he was a small child . . . the warlord. The one-armed man managed to fell a half dozen of the warlord's guards before finally being subdued. The warlord had him placed in a gilded cage and put on display in the village square, until his scheduled execution at sunrise. As the sun crept over the mountains the next morning, the one-armed man prayed to the Gods for justice, but it would not be the Gods who answered."

"This is the good part!" Fat Eddie said with the anticipation of a kid waiting on Santa.

"The next morning the warlord was awakened by the frantic screams of his wife. He found her in the bedroom of their children. The guards posted outside their door had both been killed, and the children were in their beds, unable to move. They had all been paralyzed, just as Lee Un had been. The warlord didn't know how, but the Crippled Boxer had to be behind it. He ordered the prisoner brought before him, only to have his soldiers return and report that they found the cage empty. Some believe that it was disciples of the Crippled Boxer who aided in his escape, but there were others who speculated that there were darker forces at work."

"Personally, I've always thought that story was bullshit," Fat Eddie picked up. "No way you can convince me that a demon sprang that one-armed joker from his cage so he could get his lick back. If you'd asked me about it yesterday, I'd have told you that the style didn't really exist, but that was before you used it to make an invalid out of my best fighter. If I didn't hate you so much, I might be tempted to offer you a job."

"As if I'd ever work for you," Toussaint said with a chuckle.

"You'd be surprised what a man might be willing to do if properly motivated." Eddie scooped the gun from his desk and pointed it at Toussaint. "I could kill you just for what you did to Jade, and I wouldn't be wrong." He let his finger caress the trigger. "But I won't." He put the gun back down. "At least not yet. That guy you sent to the hospital is one of the most dangerous men I know, next to Goliath. At least he was. I've made a ton of money in the pit off Jade, but thanks to you, we don't know if he'll ever be able to use his arm again, let alone fight."

"He should be fine in a few days," Toussaint said, sounding more confident than he actually was. That was the first time he had used the style other than with the rats he and Chung would catch at night for him to practice on. Toussaint had failed with every rat he tried it on, so he was just as surprised as Jade that it had worked.

"Maybe you should have Mr. Troubleman take his place," Jin suggested.

"And maybe you should shut the fuck up?" Eddie whirled on Jin angrily. "I should throw your ass in the pit for being fool enough to let a cop in my place."

"A what?" the color drained from Jin's face. He'd thought that the Black man was just another one of Maggie's tricks.

"Oh, you didn't know? This is Detective Toussaint Batiste, pride of the Dirty Birds and one of the meanest and dirtiest sons of bitches to ever pin a badge to his chest."

"I ain't a cop no more, Eddie."

"I heard. You threw some poor bastard out a window and got a slap on the wrist for it. Word on the street is you turned into some kind of snitch," Eddie said with a smirk.

"If that ain't the pot . . ." Toussaint mumbled and the smirk melted from Eddie's face.

"You helped me out once upon a time and it's for that reason that I'm gonna let your disrespect slide . . . just this once. But don't test the limits of my hospitalities, Toussaint." Eddie fingered the revolver.

Toussaint was smart enough to know when to push and when to pull back. "So, back to Charlie . . ." Before he could go any further, Spider said something to Eddie in Chinese. Whatever he said didn't sit well with Eddie, but the fat man kept his game face.

"Yeah, I know him," Fat Eddie confirmed. "He isn't a part of my organization, just a young punk who likes to hang around and take up space." He cut his eyes at Spider when he said this. "I could throw a rock out into that club right now and hit ten Charlie Tangs. He's nobody special."

"Then why do you keep trying to blow smoke up my ass? We both know how much of a headache I can be when I put my mind to it. So, why not save yourself the trouble and let me talk to the boy and get out of your hair? Unless you think me talking to him is gonna jam you up in some kind of way?"

That struck a nerve.

"You are swimming in some very dangerous waters throwing around those types of accusations," Eddie said in an icy tone.

"I think I'm going to get a drink," Butterfly interrupted as she uncoiled herself from the couch and stubbed out her joint in the ashtray.

"This shouldn't take too long. I'll be out to join you in a few." Eddie cupped her ass, marking his territory. Butterfly leaned in and kissed him on the lips, which was a testament to either how strong her stomach was or how deep Eddie's pockets were. No way Toussaint could see any woman willingly kissing that slob unless there was something serious in it for her. Butterfly wisely excused herself but spared Toussaint a passing glance that said she was questioning his intelligence.

When Butterfly left, she took the air in the room out with her. The tension had become so thick that Toussaint was finding it difficult to breathe. From the corner of his eye he could see Goliath position himself so that he was in arm's reach if his boss gave the order to make good on the threat to have him snap Toussaint's neck. If he caught him off guard, Toussaint liked his odds against the behemoth. Not beating him, but getting through him and out the front door. That's if Eddie didn't shoot him in the back before he could make his escape. He had begun to realize that he just might've overplayed his hand.

Seeing some of Toussaint's defiance abandon him, Eddie struck: "Let me tell you something, Troubleman, and you might want to pay attention because I'm not a man who repeats himself. I could give a fuck what Charlie is into and why you're looking for him, but you won't find him here. So, let this be the last time I see your Black ass in my joint. We clear on that?"

"Crystal," Toussaint replied. He stood to leave, but Goliath stepped to block his path. Toussaint had to look up to meet his eyes and in them he saw cold, black emptiness.

"It's cool, Goliath. I think me and Mr. Batiste have an understanding now. We won't have any more trouble out of him. Will we?" Eddie asked.

Toussaint never took his eyes off Goliath when he replied. "Nope, no trouble at all. We done?"

"You better hope so," Eddie responded.

Goliath waited for a few beats before moving aside. As Toussaint made his way out, Eddie had some parting words. "Give my best to the Weis."

Toussaint didn't respond, but he had received the threat.

Fat Eddie waited until Toussaint was gone before dropping his mask of cool and giving into the rage that had been quietly building. "Muthafucka!" he slammed his meaty palms on the desk, shaking it. "With all that I got going on, the last thing I need is that damn bloodhound with his nose up my ass! That's what I get for surrounding myself with incompetent people." He looked to Spider.

"You want me to take care of him?" Spider offered.

"And bring more shame on my organization by getting your ass kicked again? No thanks," Eddie said with a snort. "I need you to get a line on Charlie Tang. Find whatever rock he's crawled under and make sure that he understands the importance of his silence."

"I will," Spider promised.

"You better. You made this mess and you better get it cleaned up," Fat Eddie warned.

"I don't think we've seen the last of that cop, Eddie," Goliath spoke up.

"Yeah, that Troubleman is like a dog on a damn bone when he gets an itch for something. He's not going to stop digging until he finds something. That's just in his nature," Fat Eddie said.

"You should let me deal with him. I'll make sure he dies real slow and real nasty," Goliath offered.

"Not yet, you're too important for me to have taken off the board, especially with Jade being a damn cripple. We'll throw Mr. Batiste a bone and hope it satisfies him enough to leave this shit alone."

"And if it doesn't?" Goliath asked.

"Then you make sure he finds a comfortable spot to lay in that grave he insists on digging."

A rare smile appeared on Goliath's face. He would never say this to Fat Eddie, but he hoped that the Black man would continue to pursue this. Jade was good, probably the best fighter they had in the crew. Next to him, of course. Yet Toussaint had defeated Jade. For the last few years that Goliath had been serving as Fat Eddie's muscle, his skills had been wasted on roughing up people who owed money or tossing the occasional unruly drunk out of the club. After seeing what Toussaint Batiste was capable of, Goliath deemed that he would be worthy of killing.

"If we're done? I'm going to get back to my post at the door," Jin said. He was eager to get out of the room.

"You let a cop come in here and you think I'm going to trust your dumb ass to guard my door?" Eddie said with a laugh. "Consider yourself fired."

Before Jin could even process what Eddie was implying, a massive pair of hands gripped both sides of his skull from behind. Goliath snapped Jin's neck with the ease of someone opening a jar of pickles. It was a quick, painless death.

Spider let out a small yelp when Jin's body landed at his feet. His head was twisted at an impossible angle, lifeless eyes staring up at him. He and Jin had come up together since chess club in middle school, and now he was gone.

"I don't take failure well, Spider. You keep that in mind when you catch up with Charlie."

Toussaint hadn't even realized that he had been holding his breath until he was standing outside Blue Skies, inhaling deeply of the night air. He had made a dire mistake that he wouldn't have made a few years prior, before prison had dulled his street sense. He peacocked his ass into that club like he still had the badge to protect him, and he was almost reminded the hard way that he didn't. In his search for a fish, he'd almost found himself devoured by a shark. He wanted to say that it was luck that allowed him to leave there on his feet instead of on his back, but that was only partially true. The real reason he was still standing and not being stuffed into a dumpster was because Eddie had counted on him stirring up less trouble for his business if he were alive rather than dead. Toussaint intended to prove him wrong on that.

Hands shoved into his pockets and head on a swivel, Toussaint walked briskly back to where he had left his car. He processed what he had learned from his trip to Blue

Skies. Two things in particular stuck out to him. The first was that Fat Eddie knew what Charlie knew, and probably knew how to find him. The little game he was playing in that office wasn't to protect Charlie, but himself. Toussaint knew that if he dug deep enough into this pile of shit, he would find a two-day-old kernel of corn with Eddie's tooth prints on it. The gangster's reaction confirmed what Toussaint had already suspected: Jay-Jay had been set up. But the question remained as to why.

He found his car just where he had left it in the laundromat parking lot, but as he neared it, he noticed something on his windshield. At first, he thought it was a parking ticket, but when he got closer he saw that it wasn't that. He gave a cautious look around before removing the folded piece of paper from under his windshield wiper and opened it up. He had to read it twice before he could make sense of it. It was a three-line note written in a delicate scrawl: *We need to talk*, followed by an address and a time. There was no signature on it, but it didn't need one. The butterflies printed on the paper told him exactly who had left it.

14

Toussaint woke up close to noon the next day. It took him almost a full fifteen minutes from the time he'd opened his eyes to muster up the strength it took to sit up straight. His body felt like he had just gone twelve rounds with Clubber Lang. He made to push himself from the bed when a pain shot through his shoulder that was so intense he had to plop back down. Memories of the green-haired man, Jade, and that brutal chop he'd caught Toussaint with came flooding back. Jade had given him more of a run than Toussaint had been expecting. He sat on the edge of the bed rolling his shoulder forward and backward. It clicked a few times, but that was more him showing signs of his age than it being broken. At least he hoped. Either way, self-care would have to wait. He had shit to do.

He pulled himself out of bed and into the shower. He turned the water as hot as he could stand it and stood under the spray for a time. The heat helped with his aching body but did nothing for his throbbing head. He grabbed a bottle of aspirin from the medicine cabinet and dry swallowed four of them before heading back to his bedroom. He snatched the phone from his nightstand and checked the screen to see what he had missed while he was asleep.

There was a missed call from Aimee and two from John. John had an appointment that morning to meet with a lawyer Toussaint had plugged him in with. It was an attorney who Toussaint trusted to play fair with the Weis. John was probably calling to deliver the play-by-play of how things had gone.

The way John had been acting had Toussaint concerned. John Wei was one of the most composed and easygoing men that Toussaint had ever known, but he seemed to be coming unglued. The fact that he was fool enough to walk into a precinct with a piece only added to Toussaint's concerns. There was something else, too, a remark that John had made in passing: *One way or another, the people responsible for what's happening to my boy will pay*. Was that just John venting, or was he thinking about doing something stupid? John was not a violent man, at least as far as Toussaint knew, but there was no telling how far a parent would be willing to go to protect their children.

He had two hours before he had to meet the author of his love letter. He dressed faster that day than he had the previous one, grabbing a black V-neck sweater from the hanger and slipping into black jeans. He wanted to look good for his meeting, but also not be so constricted by his clothes that he couldn't comfortably lock ass with the next ambitious punk who got it in his mind to try him. He pulled on his black suede Timberlands and tugged at the laces but didn't tie them. They were still new and hadn't been broken in yet, so they weren't the most comfortable boots, but the high ankle gave him a place to stash the stiletto he was bringing for protection. Standing in front of his mirror he gave his daily affirmation: "You will survive the day."

When he stepped outside, he found Tommy sweeping out front of Good 4 Yu. He had his headphones on and was humming along with whatever he was listening to while pushing his broom. Toussaint was about to go over and greet him when two kids from Jay-Jay's crew rounded the corner. One of them was eating a cheeseburger out of a Styrofoam container—they sold them at the deli around the corner. When the boy spotted Tommy outside sweeping, he tapped his friend and motioned for him to pay attention. He crossed in front of Tommy and tossed what was left of his burger into the path where Tommy was sweeping, before roaring with laughter.

This was obviously nothing new to Tommy. Jay-Jay's friends were always fucking with him because he was in a different way. Toussaint only swung one way, but this didn't make him look down on people who didn't. As far as he was concerned, it wasn't his business if a man lay down with a man, woman, or somewhere in between, so long as it was consensual. Unfortunately, there were certain pockets of society who were still stuck in a more antiquated way of thinking.

But Toussaint didn't step in on Tommy's behalf. Not because he didn't want to, but because he wanted to see how Tommy would handle it. The best way to handle a bully was to sit him on his pockets, or at least try to. Even if you lost the fight the bully would likely think twice about messing with you again if they knew you were willing to defend yourself. Tommy's face was calm, but his body language had tensed. Toussaint became hopeful when he spied Tommy stealthily unscrewing the stick from the broom. Toussaint prayed silently for Tommy to crack one of those smug sons of bitches over the head with that broomstick. All Tommy had to do was start it, and Toussaint would happily end it for him. He'd wipe the sidewalk with those punks. Alas, instead Tommy set the broom down and bent to pick up the burger scraps.

"You okay?" Toussaint waited until the boys had gone before approaching Tommy, who had just picked up the last of the burger bun and was tossing it into the trash.

"The cost of freedom," Tommy half joked, wiping his now-grease-stained hands on the red Good 4 Yu apron he was wearing.

"Ain't nothing funny about these dudes thinking you're some kind of hors d'oeuvre that they can take a bite out of whenever they got the munchies. I don't know what it was like for you back where you come from, but this is Philadelphia. The weak feed the strong here."

"I'm reminded of this every time I leave the safety of my family's restaurant," Tommy countered. "I'm also reminded that the childish games played by the closed-minded people in this country are far more tolerable than what happens to people like me where I come from. That being said, I'd much rather live under the threat of being talked to crazy from time to time or even being punched in the face by some homophobe rather than live with the fear of having my door kicked in and being dragged off to some camp or worse because of who I chose to love."

Toussaint wasn't ready for that: Tommy's perspective on his new life in America. This had been the longest conversation Toussaint had with Tommy since meeting him, and by far the most informative. It had nothing to do with what Tommy said, but how he'd said it. There was a conviction to him that reminded Toussaint that no matter how feminine Tommy might come across, he was still a young man. A young man struggling under not only the weight of being a minority in a country that loved him less than the one he had fled, but also being openly gay in a neighborhood that was still not quite as accepting as it could be.

"I just want you to be safe is all I'm saying," Toussaint offered. "Sometimes, I train on the roof of the brownstone. Nothing too intense, just keeping my skills sharp. You're welcome to join me any time you like. Maybe you might pick up a thing or two to help you to protect yourself?"

"What makes you think I don't know how to fight?" Tommy asked quizzically. He completed his task of unscrewing the broomstick, twirling it like a baton before driving it back into the broom head without missing a beat.

"You learn that from your uncle John?" Toussaint wondered. He'd seen John's pole work and it was impressive, but Tommy's was cleaner. More precise.

"No, I picked it up from someone who knew that the world would be twice as hard on me because of how I chose to love. They wanted to make sure that whenever small-minded people tried to make me a victim, I was always able to give as good as I got."

"That's gangsta." Toussaint nodded approvingly.

"No, that's my reality," Tommy said honestly. There was a small silence between them. Tommy was the first to break it when he spotted the bruise on Toussaint's cheek. "Long night?"

"Fell off the curb and landed on somebody's fist. Happens all the time." Toussaint winked playfully. He glanced through the front window of the restaurant and saw Sue Wei wiping down the tables. "Y'all plan on opening today with everything going on?"

"No, Auntie Sue is just trying to keep busy. I told her that she should be upstairs resting, but you know how she is," Tommy said.

"Indeed I do." Toussaint shook his head. Sue was a tough old bird who marched to the beat of her own drum. Nobody short of God could get her to do anything she didn't want to, and even with him it would be a negotiation. "I'll catch you in a few," he called as he slid inside the restaurant.

Sue was busy wiping down the small tables when he walked in, so she didn't notice him at first. This gave him some time to observe her. Her brows were knitted while she wiped vigorously at a stain on the last table. From the way she was going at it, you'd think the spill had done something to her personally. She must've felt Toussaint's presence in the room because she abruptly stopped her scrubbing and looked up at him. For as long as he had known Sue Wei, whenever she greeted him it had been with a smile. This time he could see nothing but worry etched on her face.

"Hey, lil mama . . . What you know no good?" Toussaint scooped Sue about the waist and leaned down to plant a kiss on her cheek.

"Careful that my husband doesn't see you and discover our secret love affair," Sue teased.

"I'd duel him for your love. And if I fell, I'd come back from the grave to take my revenge." Toussaint picked Sue up and gave her a playful twirl.

"Cut it out and put me down!" Sue laughed. Seeing her smile put Toussaint a bit more at ease. "You're up later than usual. I made you breakfast, but it's cold by now. Do you want me to put it in the microwave?"

"Don't put yourself out. I gotta hit the streets, so I'll grab something later. I just popped in to check on you. You good?" Toussaint asked.

"Honestly? No, but what can I do about it at this point other than hope justice exists in the state of Pennsylvania," Sue said with a sigh.

"Try not to stress over Jay-Jay. This will all get worked out," Toussaint assured her.

"So I keep hearing, but my son is still in jail." It wasn't an accusation, but it felt like it.

"I've been doing what I can on my end," Toussaint offered.

"I heard. I went across town to the market to grab some things for the kitchen and everywhere I went, people were talking about the Black man who pissed on the shoes of Fat Eddie and lived to tell about it."

"It wasn't even close to that serious," Toussaint downplayed it.

"Tell that to the bull's-eye you strapped to your back when you decided to poke that overweight bear," Sue said to him. "You need to stay away from that place, Toussaint. Nothing but criminals, deviants, and freaks destined to go to hell for the way they hang around that place."

"I don't know about all that. I just popped in to get a drink," Toussaint lied.

"I was born at night, not last night, Trouble." She called him by his nickname to let him know how serious she was. "Don't get me wrong, Toussaint, we love and appreciate everything you've been trying to do to help us with this, but we don't need you to make a martyr of yourself in the name of my son. The last thing this family needs is more blood on its hands."

"This ain't on you, Sue. I made my own conscious choice to help Jay-Jay. Whatever happens, I accept responsibility. No need for you to feel guilty."

"Yet I do. I can't help but feel like all of this is my fault,"

Sue said sadly. "I've never let the men in my family take accountability for their actions. From my brothers back when I was a girl in China, to my husband and my children, I've always made excuses for them when they did something wrong. I saw it as me loving them, when I was actually enabling them. My unwillingness to call out wrongdoings when I saw them has cost me my son."

"You say it like Jay-Jay has already been tried and convicted. Don't speak that over him, Sue," Toussaint warned.

"Nobody wants my son exonerated more than I do, but I'd be lying if I said that I was hopeful. If only I could trade places with my Jay-Jay, I would do it in a heartbeat. Let me burn for this, not him." A tear rolled down her cheek.

"Don't you go getting soft on me now." Toussaint wiped her tear away with his thumb. "Jay-Jay is not going to prison for this. If I gotta run up in the precinct guns blazing and pull a *Gunsmoke*-style bust out, Jay-Jay is coming home to you," Toussaint joked, making his fingers like two pistols firing. This made Sue smile again.

"Even in times as dark as these, you have the power to make an old woman smile. I appreciate you for all you do, Toussaint."

"I got you, baby girl." He pinched her cheek playfully. "John have any luck with the lawyer I connected him with?"

"I wouldn't know, I haven't really seen him today. I tried calling him, but he hasn't answered. I'm starting to get worried," Sue told him.

"John can handle himself," Toussaint assured her.

"Of this I am sure. But John hasn't been himself since all this began. He's hardly slept, and whenever I can get him to sit still long enough to ask about my son, I get one-word answers. He promises to keep me informed, yet still I'm in the dark. If this situation with my son is that bad, then rip the Band-Aid off and let me bleed freely."

"Don't take it like that, Sue. I'm sure John is just trying to protect you," Toussaint suggested.

"Protect me from what? I was mopping up blood long before grease. John and I haven't always been what you would call respectable." She chuckled.

"Is that why Betty Tang acts like she's spooked of him?" Toussaint asked. He could tell that the question caught Sue off guard.

"Has that old hag been talking crap about my husband?" Sue asked sharply.

"Nah, nothing like that. She just insisted that I be sure to tell John that she tried to help. Called him *dage*. That's something like a boss, right?" Toussaint questioned.

"Not exactly. It's just a term of endearment reserved for men who the neighborhood respects. John was always helping people out back home."

"Betty made it sound like John was some type of shot-caller back in China."

"Toussaint, you've known us long enough to know that the only shots John calls is when he's playing pool." Sue laughed it off. "That Betty is always embellishing things and trying to make trouble. It can be drizzling outside and she'll make it out like it's a tropical storm. She's been that way since back when we were all still trying to get out of the old country."

"I had no idea you guys had been friends that long?"

"I don't know if I'd call Betty Tang a *friend*, at least not anymore. We were friendly at one time, until I found out she had been making advances towards my husband behind my back," Sue revealed, much to Toussaint's surprise.

"Really? I've never known John to have a wandering eye."

"He doesn't anymore. Especially not after I punched him in it," Sue joked, waving her fist like she was reliving the moment. "To John's credit, he never entertained her advances, but I had to give him a sample of what playing with me would be like. Just in case. Was it Betty who sent you to Blue Skies to get your ass kicked?"

"I wouldn't say I got it *kicked*. Maybe lightly grazed. And no. In fact, she wasn't very forthcoming about Charlie at all."

"I'm not surprised. She babies that boy like he's still a child instead of making him stand up like a man and take accountability for the things he's into. Jay-Jay had never been in trouble before he started hanging around Charlie Tang. I know what kinds of things Charlie is into, which is why John and I were always so adamant about Jay-Jay not spending so much time around him. Hopefully, when this mess gets sorted out, Jay-Jay will turn his focus back to his studies and away from the streets."

Toussaint was silent while Sue spoke. Hearing Sue speak, you would think Jay-Jay was some kind of saint. With just how sloppy Toussaint had seen Jay-Jay move, he was surprised that he had been able to keep his parents in the dark about the kinds of things he was into for so long. Not that it was for him to snitch the kid out. Toussaint was about to attempt to change the subject when Aimee walked in.

"I'm glad you have so much confidence in your son." Aimee tossed her two cents to the conversation right away. She was coming out of the freezer, carrying two slabs of ribs on her shoulder. A stained white smock covered her green Nautica sweat suit and her hair was pulled back into a ponytail. She slammed the meat angrily onto one of the wooden countertops. Aimee never hid her contempt when she was asked to work in the restaurant.

"Everyone deserves the benefit of the doubt. Allow your brother the same grace we gave you after you brought the federal government to our doorstep," Sue checked her daughter.

"The difference between us is that I was trying to help a kid who was down on her luck and Jay-Jay only thinks of himself," Aimee shot back. Her response prompted Sue to spit something at her in Mandarin, and Aimee's response came just as sharp.

Toussaint's head whipped back and forth as if he were

watching two foreign countries negotiate peace terms and both had a problem with the fine print. Before things could boil over between the two Wei women, Toussaint jumped in: "Aimee, you got a smoke I can bum?" He was an occasional smoker and didn't currently have a craving for a cigarette, but the ask was the closest thing to water that he could find to throw on the fire building between mother and daughter.

Aimee's green eyes flashed to Toussaint, ready to take on another opponent until she realized his intentions. "Sure." She reached into the pocket of her smock and produced a fresh pack of Newports. "I think I could use a smoke break too."

Toussaint marched out of Good 4 Yu with Aimee on his heels. "What was that shit about? The way you were talking to your mom?" He cut right into her once they were outside. Jay-Jay was the Wei family's troubled child, while Aimee had always been the good one, so he wasn't used to hearing her use such a tone with her parents, especially Sue.

"You wouldn't understand," Aimee said, tapping one of the Newports out and putting it into her mouth. She lit it with a cheap corner-store lighter before offering the pack to Toussaint.

"Try me." Toussaint accepted the offer and slipped one of the cigarettes out. He placed it between his lips and sparked it.

Aimee didn't answer right away. Her eyes were turned heavenward, smoke billowing from the sides of her mouth as she tried to find the words to articulate what she was feeling. "It's unfair," she finally said, just above a whisper. "I get in trouble *one* time, while trying to do what I felt was good work and my mother and father treat me like I'm the chick from *The Scarlet Letter*, having brought the greatest of shame to this family. My brother has been a fuckup for his entire life and my parents constantly make excuses for him or find somebody else to blame for Jay-Jay's poor decisions. Don't think I didn't hear my mom trying to put all this on Charlie. We both know he and Jay-Jay were two rotten-ass peas in a pod!"

"Try not to take it personal, Aimee. Your mom and dad are old-school. The boys in the family always get more grace than the girls." Toussaint was trying to reason with her, but Aimee wasn't trying to hear it.

"So they get away with *murder*?"

"We still don't know that Jay-Jay is guilty of what they're charging him with. Have some faith in your brother."

"Jay-Jay is actually the only person in this family who I'm sure *isn't* capable of doing terrible things," Aimee let out in a moment of frustration, before catching herself and switching the subject. "I've spent my whole life trying to appease my parents and what do I get in return? Lectures about how I'm not doing enough? What more do they want from me?" Aimee tried to hold the tears back but couldn't stop a few loose ones from rolling down her cheeks.

Toussaint had never seen her like this. Aimee was the

rock of the family, the one who was emotionally removed. Seeing her cry wasn't something he was used to. He stood there awkwardly, not sure how to respond to the emotional outburst other than embracing her. Aimee sobbed into his chest while he rubbed her back. After a time, her sobs subsided. She looked up at him with those alluring jade eyes and he found himself entranced. Before he knew what was happening, Aimee pulled him in for a kiss. His mind told him to pull away, but his body wouldn't allow it. Before he knew it, their lips touched. Aimee's kiss was sweet. He suckled her bottom lip like a bee pulling nectar from a flower. For a moment he allowed himself to get lost in her touch, before Tommy appeared in the doorway of the brownstone and Toussaint quickly came back to his senses. The two of them put a respectable distance between each other.

"I'm sorry . . . I didn't mean to intrude," Tommy said apologetically, eyes cast to the ground as if he didn't want to see what he already had.

"You're not intruding on anything. Me and mom got into it and Toussaint was just comforting me. That's all."

If Tommy saw through the lie, he gave no indication. "She told me. Auntie Sue needs supplies from the Restaurant Depot and asks that you take me since . . . How did she phrase it? *You obviously would rather not be where you're needed.*"

"See what I mean about the guilt trip?" Aimee asked Toussaint with a suck of her teeth. "It's bad enough my hair smells like cleaning solution from helping her power wash the kitchen all morning and now she wants me to play Uber driver!"

Tommy and Toussaint stood there awkwardly while Aimee vented.

"I can take him," Toussaint finally volunteered. "I got a lead that I need to follow up on about your brother over in Passyunk."

"Restaurant Depot is going to take you out of your way. I don't want to put that on you," Aimee said.

"I told you, I got it." Toussaint insisted. "I don't know how long I'm going to be, so I can drop him off. You just pick him up when he's done getting your mom's stuff. In the meantime, you go and be where you're needed. Get me?"

"Got you." Aimee understood what he was hinting at. She hugged his neck. "You be safe out there."

"You know me." Toussaint gave her a playful wink before going to do the exact opposite.

15

It was warm outside. Not hot, but warm. The weather made it just stuffy enough inside the car to where Toussaint cracked the windows instead of relying on the half-working air conditioner. John had done a lot, but it was still a damn near forty-year-old car, a *classic*. Toussaint pushed the Monte Carlo up 24th Street. He watched the faces of the people who watched him and Tommy as they rode by, bumping Curtis Mayfield's "Little Child Runnin' Wild."

Tommy sat in the passenger's seat. He hadn't said too much, simply scrolling aimlessly on his phone. Occasionally Toussaint would catch Tommy watching him from the corner of his eye. Toussaint suspected that riding in such close proximity to a strange Black man put him on edge. When he reached for his cell phone in the center console and noticed Tommy flinch, it confirmed it. Tommy was reacting like a mouse who had been forced to have a play-date with a cat and asked to trust that he wouldn't end up getting eaten. Toussaint could only imagine what kinds of stories he'd heard about Toussaint while he was away. He decided to try at easing the tension.

"What you over there looking at that got you so quiet?

Some kind of porn site?" Toussaint opened the conversation with a joke.

"Pornography is illegal," Tommy said primly.

"Shit, maybe where you come from, but sex is what this country was built on. I started an Instagram account, and so far, all I've seen on it are asses clapping. Not that I'm complaining." Toussaint chuckled. Tommy mustered a weak smile and went back to his scrolling. "So, what's your story, Tommy?"

Tommy looked up from his phone. "I think you know my story, Toussaint," he said in a tone that let Toussaint know that he was approaching uncomfortable territory.

"Nah, man. I don't mean like what happened to you in China that brought you here. I mean like, who were you back home?"

"Ah." Tommy nodded, understanding that Toussaint wasn't trying to intrude, only get to know him. "Back home, I was a Nobody."

"C'mon, don't downplay yourself. Everybody is somebody," Toussaint told him.

"No, that was literally what they called us at my work . . . Nobodies," Tommy clarified. "I worked in the intelligence department at the Chinese consulate."

"Like some kind of spy?" Toussaint was interested in hearing more.

Tommy laughed, and when he did, it had the ring of sleigh bells. "Nothing quite that glamorous. We were a small group of nondescript people who were good at blending in with everyday folks. The government used us for small things, like investigating people who were applying for visas to see if they were who they said they were, or if they were hiding something. Occasionally we did process serving, but we had no real standing. Unless you worked at the consulate you probably didn't even know we existed. This is why they nicknamed us Nobodies. It's like a back-handed compliment."

"I can dig it," Toussaint said with a nod. He paused for a beat before asking a question. "If I ain't getting too deep into your business? Was there any kind of blow-back that came from you being attacked? Seeing how you worked for the government and all, I suspect it caused some waves?"

"A wave only strong enough to wash the crime away," Tommy said with a chuckle. "You have to understand something, Toussaint. China is not as tolerant of certain things as the U.S. My people are very big on pride and honor. There are some in power who would've frowned upon a gay man having access to their personal information. Rather than risk creating a scandal, it was easier to let me go."

"That's fucked up."

"Yes, it was. On the upside, I was presented with a handsome settlement package in exchange for not going to the press about what had been allowed to happen to me. I used part of it to help Auntie get me to the U.S., and Auntie Sue has been guiding me on how to invest what's left. I don't know what I would've done if it hadn't been for her."

"You love your auntie Sue, don't you?"

"More than you can possibly imagine. Everything that I am, I owe to her," Tommy declared.

Toussaint smiled at Tommy. He admired the boy's loyalty to his auntie. He didn't know the kid very well, but he liked him and hoped that America would be kinder to him than China had been. He wanted Tommy to win at his new life.

"Auntie Sue says that you are an honorable man," Tommy said quite randomly.

Toussaint gave him a quizzical look. "I'm not sure if I would go that far, but I'm trying to stay on the right path."

"My aunt and uncle are very fond of you."

"I'm fond of them too, but why do I feel like you're going somewhere with this?" Toussaint asked. Tommy remained silent. "Tommy, if you've got something to get off your chest, spit it out. I ain't gonna get mad at you over it."

After a moment of hesitation Tommy spoke. "I saw you two today. Outside the restaurant."

"It's not what you think, Tommy."

"No, Mr. Batiste. It's not what *you* think," Tommy informed him. "I think Aimee is a different girl than the one you remember. I haven't been in the country with the Weis for very long, but in my time here I've come to see Aimee for who she really is."

"And what is she?" Toussaint asked.

"Someone whose games you don't want to get caught up in," Tommy warned. Toussaint waited for him to expound on what he meant, but Tommy felt no such inclination. He went back to his scrolling, leaving Toussaint to read between the lines.

The rest of the ride was spent in silence. Not even the radio played anymore. Toussaint dropped Tommy off at Restaurant Depot and told him to give him a call in the event that Aimee didn't show up to give him a ride back. He would've doubled back for him, but truthfully, he hoped that the boy didn't call. On that thirty-minute ride Tommy had accomplished something that not even the toughest men he'd met in prison had been able to do. He made Toussaint uncomfortable. It wasn't anything Tommy had said, but in fact what he hadn't. Tommy was the fly on the wall who you might never notice but saw and heard everything. Tommy might not have posed a physical threat, but information used properly could be far more lethal than a pistol. He was one Toussaint would have to keep a close eye on.

It took him nearly another thirty minutes to make it to the other end of town, where he was to meet Butterfly. Ironically, the spot she had chosen was one of Toussaint's old haunts, a sandwich place located in a neighborhood said to be controlled by Philly's Armenian mafia, though this was never *officially* confirmed. There were ongoing debates about who had the best cheesesteaks in the city: Max's, Ishkabibble's, Geno's, et cetera . . . Toussaint had sampled them all, and though each establishment had their respective draws, Philip's had become his go-to. Not because they made the best sandwiches—though their roast pork hoagies with the soaked peppers were something special—but because they stayed open twenty-four hours and were off the grid. It was the perfect location for unsavory business to be conducted.

Toussaint looped the block twice, surveying the area. He'd been ambushed twice in the past thirty-six hours, and he wasn't trying to find out if the third time would be the charm. At the hoagie stand, a few stragglers lingered while waiting on their orders, but nothing appeared out of the ordinary. He parked the car across the street and let it idle for a while. It was dark, and the block was lousy with sketchy characters. A man passing his car let his gaze linger a little longer than Toussaint was comfortable with. Toussaint matched his gaze. There was a short staring contest between them before the man finally decided to move on. Toussaint had a bad feeling about being out there like that on the whim of a broad he didn't know.

Toussaint kept looking through his rearview for signs of the lounge singer but didn't see her. Maybe she had gotten cold feet about whatever she had invited him out after dark to discuss? Or maybe this was another setup? He was about to back out of the spot and head back to the restaurant when a tap on his window startled him. He was surprised to find a young girl, about thirteen, with short, cropped black hair and large dark eyes, staring at him from the other side. Toussaint cracked the window and waited for the girl to state her business.

"She's waiting."

16

Toussaint followed the little girl across the street, in the direction of Philip's. The whole time Toussaint followed her, the little girl was humming some weird song and it was starting to make Toussaint uncomfortable. She reminded him of those little twins from *The Shining*. Whenever they showed up, you knew that things were about to go left. There was a sprinkling of people standing around, waiting for their orders. Among them was Butterfly. She was standing at the condiment counter, squirting mustard onto a steak-stuffed hoagie. Toussaint almost didn't recognize her out of costume. With her face wiped free of the makeup, she looked different, less glamorous. Her skin was darker than he remembered, closer to the color of burnt sand. In the right light she might've been able to pass for Latina. She wore a pair of leggings with green Nikes, a black T-shirt, and a green Eagles baseball cap pulled low. Had it not been for the length of dark hair spilling from beneath the cap, you could've mistaken her for a young man. He guessed that had been her intention, to wrap herself back in her cocoon before coming to meet him. A caterpillar was harder to spot than a butterfly. When she spotted Toussaint and her envoy, she moved in their direction.

"You can't be Philly if you're putting mustard on a steak and cheese. You done fucked that all up," Toussaint remarked.

"I haven't eaten meat in years. She loves these things though. Especially drenched in mustard. For reasons she hasn't saw fit to share with me yet, but we'll get there," Butterfly handed the sandwich to the little girl, who tore into it like she hadn't eaten all day. "Thank you for coming out to meet me."

"Your note said that we needed to talk, so I'm here," Toussaint said with a shrug of his broad shoulders. "I figured what you have to say must be heavy, if you had me come all the way out here after sundown instead of just leaving me your number with the note."

"I don't trust phones. Never did, and especially not with sensitive information. You never know who's listening on the other line," Butterfly told him. "Do you mind if we walk and talk?"

Toussaint made a sweeping gesture. "Lead the way."

The trio walked for a half block, mostly in silence if you didn't count the chomping sounds from the girl destroying the sandwich a few paces behind them. She was halfway done by that point, fingers stained with mustard, which she paused to lick clean every so often. Toussaint was grateful for the sandwich because so long as her mouth was filled with food, it kept her from humming that damn creepy-ass tune.

"Your kid?" Toussaint asked Butterfly, nodding towards the little girl.

Butterfly looked over her shoulder, seeing the girl's mouth and fingers stained, and it made her smile a bit. "In a way, you could say that. Lucy is one of many children who I try to help out from time to time. I call them the children the world forgot about. Lucy lives with me in my apartment above Blue Skies. She's the closest thing I have or will likely ever have to a real daughter."

"A beautiful woman like you with no kids? I'm sure it's not for lack of suitors offering to plant their seeds." Toussaint looked her over. Even dressed down with no makeup, Butterfly was still fine as hell.

Butterfly chuckled. "I see you're one of those guys with no gray area, huh?"

"Damn, I didn't mean that like it sounded." Toussaint gave a nervous laugh at himself. It had been quite a while since he had held a conversation with a beautiful woman, and he was out of practice.

"Yes, you did. I respect your candor, Toussaint. I've had a few guys who wanted to play house and I've always wanted kids of my own one day, but unfortunately, God didn't design me to bear children," Butterfly said sadly.

This made Toussaint feel even worse. "I'm sorry. I didn't mean to offend you."

"Trust me, I don't offend easily. Not for lack of people trying. I've had all kinds of slurs and insults hurled at me and I learned to let them all roll off like water," Butterfly said as she gently traced a line over his chest with one of her manicured fingers. She felt Toussaint flinch from the contact. She gave him a sly smile before removing her hand. "Being with Eddie for the last few years has taught me to develop thick skin. He can get real disrespectful when he puts his mind to it."

"A common trait in small men. They disrespect other people to make themselves feel bigger," Toussaint said. "You don't strike me as the kind of woman who settles, so why stay shackled to a small man who disrespects you?"

"Because it's what's familiar to me," Butterfly said quickly, and honestly. "Men been dogging me my whole life, and Eddie ain't no different, but at least me and him got an understanding that keeps us both happy. Eddie is a piece of shit. We both know that, but he's *my* piece of shit."

"You love him?" Toussaint asked, uncertain why. It just felt like the proper response to her statement.

"Haven't you been listening to anything I've said?" Butterfly teased. "Honestly? I think I love the idea of Eddie more than the man. You ever experience that? Knowing somebody is bad for you, but you loved the idea of them so much that you'd rather suffer the familiarity than take a chance on something new?"

"I might know a thing or two about that." Toussaint thought of Tisha and how he had ignored all the red flags in their relationship until it was too late. "I guess in your line of work, faith is one of the few things you can hold on to to stay sane."

"And what kind of work might that be?" Butterfly asked.

The question caught Toussaint off guard. "I don't know. I just thought that seeing how you're a part of Fat Eddie's outfit, you were a player in the game same as the rest of them?"

"The only games I'm interested in playing are ones of survival. Contrary to what you seem to have assumed, my business with Eddie has nothing to do with the gang. I am my own woman, not one of his chess pieces," she informed him. "I hear you work for John Wei?"

"Something like that. John is an old friend and gave me a gig when I came home to meet my parole requirements," Toussaint explained.

"A *respectable* Chinese business owner opens his home to a random Black man fresh out of prison? Sounds like something John Wei would do. What better way to conquer a jungle than by helping uplift the natives?" Butterfly shook her head.

"I didn't realize you knew John."

"Mostly by reputation. It's more like a six-degrees-of-separation kind of thing. I once knew someone who had been touched by his *mercies*, but that was in another life," Butterfly said with a far-off look in her eyes. "If I'm to believe what I'm told, you're the Weis' avenging angel. The streets say that if you fuck with the Weis, Trouble will find you sooner than later."

"I do what I gotta do to protect the people I care about," Toussaint said with a shrug.

"Don't we all," Butterfly cracked. "I guess that's what's brought you and me together tonight. To help the people we care about." She was about to add to her statement when he noticed the little girl trailing them had finished her sandwich and was watching their exchange curiously. Butterfly said something to the girl in a language that Toussaint didn't understand—he could tell it wasn't Chinese, which he had assumed she was—before peeling off a twenty-dollar bill from her purse and handing it to her. The little girl nodded and went off to do whatever Butterfly had tasked her with. "Children who hear and see too much too soon grow up too fast. That one I'd like to keep a child for as long as possible."

"That's admirable, but it still doesn't explain why I'm here," Toussaint wanted to know.

"Because you are searching for answers."

"Answers that you have?"

"That remains to be seen. They say you're investigating the dead girls found in that apartment?"

"Not officially, but yes. I'm looking into it."

"About time that someone took a *real* interest in Sarah's death," Butterfly said with a sigh of relief.

"Sarah?" Toussaint was unfamiliar with the name.

"Yes, Sarah. Sarah was one of the two girls who was

killed that night," Butterfly added. Seeing the confused look on Toussaint's face, she frowned. "Why is it that two girls were found dead in that apartment, but only one makes headlines? Tell me, Toussaint, what makes a white life more valuable than a yellow one?"

"I didn't mean it like that, like the other's girl's life doesn't have any value. I just hadn't heard her name."

"Sarah," Butterfly informed him. "I'm so tired of hearing people speak of her as if she's just some kind of afterthought." Butterfly pulled out her cell phone and scrolled through her photo gallery until she came across the picture she was looking for. She thrust the phone in Toussaint's face.

There was a picture of Butterfly and another girl at the bar inside Blue Skies. From the glassy looks in their eyes they were both tipsy as hell, toasting with two champagne bottles in celebration of something. As Toussaint looked closer at the second girl in the picture, he realized that this wasn't his first time seeing her. She was the same young lady Toussaint had seen in the photograph Vickie had posted to her social media. The plot had officially thickened!

"She was your friend?" Toussaint asked.

"Not in the beginning. We initially clashed over, let's say . . . cultural differences," Butterfly said.

"Meaning?"

"An imaginary line in the sand drawn between our respective people. She being from Cambodia and me of Thai descent."

"I thought you were Chinese?"

"So, you think all Asian people look alike? Sounds kind of racist," Butterfly joked. "My family moved to Taipei when I was a baby, but I was born in Thailand. When I was about ten or so they sent me to live in Shanghai. That's where the *special school* was that my parents decided to hide me in when they realized that I wasn't quite like other girls," Butterfly said with more than a hint of disdain in her voice.

"You were a wild child?"

"That's putting it mildly." She laughed. "My behavior was part of the reason they sent me away, but the root of it was when it became obvious to them that I would never be the child they wanted me to be. To let my father tell it, I was an embarrassment to the family. He had me sent away to hide his shame. I hated that place . . . the school. They treated us kids there so poorly that it was almost a relief when I was sold."

"Wait, what do you mean *sold*?" He was certain he had heard her wrong.

"At your age, do I need to explain to you how commerce works?" Butterfly folded her arms. She watched him while he fumbled for a response before smiling. "The question was a joke, but I'm serious about having been *sold*. The headmaster of the school brokered my sale personally. I was one of many students who over the years had met with unexpected and unfortunate circumstances while enrolled at that school."

"How does something like that even happen? A kid

being sold by a place where they were sent to be safe?" Toussaint fumed.

"Unfortunately, where I'm from, things like that happen all the time. Especially to children who come from nothing, as I did. Why do you think so many people from impoverished countries are constantly trying to flood the U.S.? At least they were before this country started to employ tactics reminiscent of the Nazis. But that's another story entirely."

"Didn't your parents make a stink? I mean, their daughter was sold off right under their noses?" Hearing Butterfly's story made him think of Maggie and how things might've played out differently for her if her mother and husband hadn't taken their eyes off the ball.

"Why raise a stink over an arrangement you blessed?" Butterfly questioned, sounding more resigned than angry. "That bastard Andrew, my father, had no intentions of ever seeing me again when he sent me away. Being able to profit from my disappearance only served as a sweetener to the devil's bargain he struck. The official report written up for the authorities by the headmaster was that I had drowned during a fishing accident. Meanwhile, I was on an airplane headed to Kowloon to meet the man who had purchased me. I remember it like it was yesterday, meeting my new owner for the first time. He took me into the city proper, where we looked out over it from one of its highest points. I had never seen anything like Hong Kong at night.

That was the night he would place his hands on my shoulders and whisper three words in my ear that would change my life: *You are beautiful.* From that moment until he grew tired of me, I was his. He is the one responsible for making the woman you see before you today."

"Fat Eddie?" Toussaint asked, figuring that's how she had come into his possession.

"If only," Butterfly said with a chuckle. "The world would have to kick my ass a little more before Eddie's and my paths would finally cross. I had been with many men by then, but outside of the man who purchased me, Fat Eddie was the only one who was more concerned with my future than my past. I know you and Eddie have a history, and I know you're not a fan of his, but that man invested in a broken whore with half a voice and made her a star."

"Eddie has never struck me as the nurturing kind," Toussaint said honestly. The man she was speaking of sounded very little like the low-life snitch he remembered.

"No, he doesn't give that, but there is good in him. Sometimes you just have to be willing to dig deep enough to pull it out. But let's not go too far off topic."

"Right, Sarah." Toussaint nodded. He had been so engrossed in Butterfly's origin story that he had allowed himself to get sidetracked as to why he was there in the first place. "Tell me about her."

"She was much like me, a runaway from a foreign land who came here in search of the American dream. When she came into Eddie's . . . *possession,* he put her to work in the bar with the other girls. I happened to hear her singing in the bathroom one night and realized that the girl had a voice. Nothing like mine, but she could hold a note. I took her under my wing and convinced Eddie to put her to work on the entertainment side. She would sometimes open for me on nights when I was performing at the club."

"Is that how she met Vickie? Singing at the club?"

"No, I'm not sure where they met. Sarah brought her to the bar one night looking to score some coke, and Vickie made herself a regular. From the moment she pranced her prissy ass into Blue Skies, I knew that she was gonna be trouble."

"Because she was white?" Toussaint questioned.

"No, because I know her type: a privileged kid who comes down to the ghetto to watch the pot get stirred and dip back to the suburbs before it boils over. Sarah became like a groupie to Vickie, lusting after the lifestyle of the rich and famous. The life she saw getting close to Vickie would give her access too. She wasn't the only one either. Eddie became a fool for that alabaster skin and those golden locks. When I tried to warn him that letting that white girl hang around would bring trouble, he accused me of being jealous."

"Were you?"

"Hardly." Butterfly snorted. "That fast-ass young girl wasn't qualified to walk a mile in my heels. Besides, she wasn't Eddie's type. He was more interested in Vickie's pedigree than he was in her pussy. Eddie was using Vickie to backdoor his way into her father's circle of rich friends. He called her his *golden goose*."

"Until that goose got cooked," Toussaint thought aloud. "So, how exactly was he planning on using Vickie to get into her father's circle?"

"He never discussed that with me in detail and I never really asked. Sarah called me once and told me that she overheard Spider and Charlie talking about something big that Vickie was lining up for Fat Eddie. Something she didn't want to discuss on the phone. She was dead before I could find out who or what."

Toussaint weighed this new information. "Sounds to me like whatever Eddie had them into is what got the girls killed. Maybe they became a loose end and Eddie used Jay-Jay and Charlie to tie it up."

"Whatever happened to them, Jay-Jay wasn't a part of it. This I'm certain of." Butterfly argued with the conviction of a defense attorney trying to sway a jury.

"The evidence says otherwise. What makes you so sure he didn't do it?" Toussaint raised an eyebrow.

"Because he was with me on the night it happened," Butterfly admitted. Toussaint now knew why she had been so adamant about his innocence.

"How long you been fucking the help behind Fat Eddie's back?"

"You make it sound so dirty," Butterfly said with a frown. "Eddie fucks who he wants when he wants, and I'm not entitled to have a little fun?" She plucked an imaginary piece of lint from Toussaint's sweater.

"Can you prove that Jay-Jay was showing you his skills on the night those girls were murdered?"

"Unfortunately, no. We were always very careful. Whenever we met it would be at the Duffield. It's one of those long-term hotels. I've been renting a room there for the past few months. Not even Eddie knows about it. It's where I go when I want to get lost, like the nights Jay-Jay and I spend together."

"Maybe you weren't careful enough, and Eddie found out about your secret hideaway? Hanging those bodies on Jay-Jay might've been Eddie's way of teaching him a lesson for touching what was his?"

"I'm a woman, not a possession. My days of being someone's property are long behind me," Butterfly said confidently. "And no, I have no reason to believe that Eddie knew what we were up to. These days he's too busy chasing money and new pussy to worry about what I'm doing. Sadly, I've become little more than a showpiece for him. Like an accessory."

"So, the neglected queen starts keeping time with a pawn? Dangerous game you two were playing."

"It wasn't a game. I had my own reasons for sleeping with Jay-Jay when we started, but it had less to do with spiting Eddie than it did with me scratching an itch. I never expected to fall for him, but I did. He may not have

Eddie's money, or power, but Jay-Jay was able to give me something that Eddie never could and that was sincerity. Jay-Jay accepted me . . . *all* of me, without stipulations. Do you know what that's like? To be loved unconditionally?"

"Can't say that I do."

"Hearing you say that makes me sad. Everyone deserves to experience true love, if only once in a lifetime," Butterfly said sincerely. "I found that love once, but it was taken away from me. Jay-Jay was my second chance."

"If you love him so much, why let him sit on this bullshit charge and risk him going to prison for the rest of his life? You could always go to the cops and tell them what you told me," Toussaint suggested.

"And what do you think would happen to me when Eddie finds out that not only was I fucking around on him, but I snitched too?" Butterfly questioned. "I love Jay-Jay, but I love me more. Besides, just my word alone won't be enough to clear Jay-Jay."

"So, you need a scapegoat for when all this shit hits the fan." Toussaint finally understood why she had asked him to meet her.

"Not a scapegoat, but a champion," Butterfly clarified. "We share a common goal here, Toussaint, and that's to bring the real killer of these girls to justice. Why not work together to reach it?"

Toussaint considered Butterfly's offer. She had filled in quite a few of the blanks in the story, but he was certain that she still wasn't telling him everything. It was possible that Butterfly was telling the truth about her feelings towards Jay-Jay, but he suspected that her eagerness to help him was more about saving her own ass. "How do I know that this isn't a setup? For all I know you could be playing me for Eddie."

"I thought you might feel that way, so I brought you a good-faith gift." Butterfly reached into her purse and pulled out a book of matches, which she handed to Toussaint.

Toussaint looked at the matchbook suspiciously. Stamped on it was a black heart set against the silver cross. It looked just like the graffiti he'd noticed on the wall when Jay-Jay had picked him up. DHI was printed across the bottom of it. It was then that Toussaint recalled why the graffiti had looked so familiar. He had seen it on a billboard when he rolled into town on the bus from prison. What it was advertising, he still wasn't sure. He flipped it open and found an address written inside the flap in the same scrawl that had been on the note on his windshield. "What's this?"

"Where you'll find Charlie Tang."

17

For the first time in a long time, Toussaint drove in silence. Music was his muse when he needed to think, so it was always playing in the car, usually one of the DJs on Power 99 doing their thing. He always rode with a beat, but that night the radio was muted. The only sounds were the voices in his head and the rattling of the Monte Carlo's engine as it sped up 422 West. He'd been skeptical about the old and unkept car being able to make the hour-and-change drive to the address Butterfly had given him, and had considered asking John if he could borrow his, but that would've led to questions. Questions that Toussaint didn't have time to answer. He needed to get to Charlie Tang before the boy got in the wind again or, worse, before Eddie's people got to him first.

When Toussaint decided to show up at Blue Skies, he had only been trying to quietly get a lead on where he could find Charlie Tang. But Toussaint had never been good at quiet. Trouble followed him, even when he was trying to duck it, which is what had happened at the bar. The ruckus he had caused at Blue Skies was him unintentionally kicking a hornet's nest, and a lot of people were about to get stung.

From the conversation he'd had with Fat Eddie, he suspected that the new King in the North had a hand in what had happened to Vickie Sparks, and Butterfly all but confirmed it. For as fearless as Butterfly tried to present herself to Toussaint, she was spooked of Fat Eddie and rightfully so. Toussaint knew how Fat Eddie rocked. He was a predator and a piece of shit, and he would do whatever it took to ensure his own survival, including murder.

The Monte Carlo made it to Lancaster County without breaking down on him. For this, Toussaint was thankful. Butterfly's information had sent Toussaint to a place called Morgantown. Named after Colonel Jacob Morgan when it was established in 1770, according to the road sign. Older than the country but a blip on the radar of the Pennsylvania map that if you blinked you'd likely miss. It was small in size and population, boasting under two thousand residents. It was out towards Amish country, and really its only major draw was the Hollywood Casino. Toussaint had first become aware of Morgantown through Left-Shoe, back when he was still the budding young apprentice of the unit commander. He'd heard Left-Shoe remark to one of the guys how easily a man could get lost in a place like Morgantown. Judging by how small the town was, he didn't initially get Left-Shoe's meaning. This would come a few months later when Toussaint found himself standing guard in an empty field while Left-Shoe was digging a hole. That had been his first visit to Morgantown, and he had hoped that it would be his last. Yet here he was. Drawn once again to the place by yet another murder.

He pulled the Monte Carlo into the parking lot of a motel that sat just inside the town limits. It was one of those one-story joints frequented mostly by sex workers and drug addicts that looked more fit for demolition than habitation. He'd initially been suspicious of the information Butterfly had given him, fearing he was walking into a setup orchestrated by Fat Eddie, but he'd made a few calls, and to Butterfly's credit, it all checked out. Charlie had indeed been hiding out at the motel. It baffled Toussaint how a man on the run in connection with a murder wouldn't have the good sense to try and flee the country, or at the very least the state. His ignorance would be Toussaint's good fortune. Once he put the screws to him, he was sure he would be able to get the punk to talk and give him what he needed to exonerate Jay-Jay.

There was only one problem with this plan. Someone else had gotten to Charlie first.

When he showed up at the motel room scribbled on the matchbook, he found the door slightly ajar. It was pulled just enough to give the appearance of being closed, but a slight push and it swung open. When he stepped into the room he picked up the familiar, coppery scent of blood. Because the air conditioner had been shut off and it had been warm that day, the stink filled the tiny room. He found Charlie lying on his stomach on the twin-size bed, one arm hanging over the side. You might've mistaken him for being in a deep sleep, had it not been for the blood around his head on the stained pillow case. Charlie had crossed the rainbow bridge to the great beyond and taken the truth of what had really happened to Vickie Sparks with him.

The rational thing to do at that moment would've been to turn around, go back the way he had come, and inform the Weis that his best chance at saving Jay-Jay's life was no longer an option. But nothing Toussaint ever did could be considered rational, which is why he was always in some shit. The Weis had done a lot for him, and he didn't have the heart to go back and tell them that he had failed in his attempt to save their son without first exhausting all possibilities. So, instead of turning away from the trouble, he leaned into it.

Toussaint stepped inside the motel room and closed the door behind him. He crept around the bed and checked the bathroom to make sure no one was in there. He doubted that whoever had killed Charlie bothered to stick around, but with the way his luck had been lately he couldn't be too careful. Once he had cleared the room and was certain that they were alone, he turned his attention to the murder victim.

The first thing he did was touch his fingers to one of Charlie's wrists. He wasn't checking for a pulse; even a blind man could see that Charlie was as dead as a doornail. He found the skin on Charlie's wrist cold, yet still somewhat soft. Rigor hadn't fully set in yet, so he couldn't have been dead longer than a few hours, possibly a day at most. Careful not to disturb the body, he checked for wounds. Charlie had been killed by a single gunshot to the side of his head. Judging from the size of the hole, Toussaint deduced he'd been shot with a small-caliber pistol.

After he learned what he could from the corpse, he turned to the crime scene to see what it could tell him that the dead man could not. There were empty burger wrappers on the night table and a half-empty bottle of Hennessy. At least Charlie hadn't gone out sober. He combed through the room as much as he dared, for fear of leaving any traces of his passing by behind for the police when they finally showed up. The room was suddenly lit up by a pair of headlights shining through the motel room window. Toussaint dropped to his stomach, heart thudding in his chest and praying to God that it wasn't the police. He would be hard pressed to convince them that he hadn't been the killer, especially considering his record. The lights winked off and he heard people talking just outside. A few beats later, he heard one of the other motel room doors open before slamming shut, and the voices faded. That was close. Too close for his taste. It was time for him to leave.

Toussaint was pushing himself up off the floor when something caught his eye. A twinkle of something metallic sticking out from under the bed. It was just under where Charlie's arm hung from the bed, as if he had been pointing to it. Using the sleeve of his sweater to cover his hand, so as not to leave any prints behind, he retrieved the item. He smiled when he saw what it was: a shell casing that had been left behind by the killer. It was like old Charlie had been sending Toussaint a clue from beyond the grave as to who had murdered him. As he turned the shell over in his covered hand studying it, the smile melted away. The slug that had killed Charlie Tang had come from a .22.

By the time Toussaint spilled from the motel room, his head was spinning. He made hurried steps towards his car as if he had the devil on his heels instead of the other way around. He'd driven out to Morgantown in search of answers, but instead he left with even more questions. One of which he wasn't sure he really wanted the answer to, but no matter how painful it would be, he still had to ask.

His first order of business would be to call the police and alert them to the corpse that had been left in room 108. For all Charlie's flaws, he was still someone's child and didn't deserve to be left in some shitty motel room to rot. His family, Betty Tang and Coco Tang, deserved closure. He'd make the call once he was back in Philly. He might not be a cop anymore, but he had been on the force long enough to know that if his cell pinged from one of the towers anywhere near the murder scene, that would be enough to make him a suspect. He doubted that he could call on Governor Atwater to wave his political magic wand again, so Charlie would have to wait a while longer before he could properly be put to rest.

It was nearly 3:00 a.m. by the time Toussaint arrived back in the city. His initial intent had been to go straight back to the brownstone, but he wasn't quite ready yet. Not after what he had discovered. He drove around the city with no real direction. He just knew that he had to keep moving so as not to be consumed with his own thoughts. In the southwest part of the city, Toussaint found an after-hours spot, one of those joints that remained open after the regular liquor stores had closed where you could grab a bottle to go. He slapped a twenty on the counter in exchange for a bottle of cheap vodka. Toussaint had never been a fan of clear liquor, but it was either that or whatever rotgut rum they sold.

Toussaint drove to an isolated parking lot, where he parked the car and killed the engine. He took a seat on the hood and pulled the bottle from the brown paper bag he'd gotten from the carryout and stared at it for a time. It probably wasn't the best time for him to be drinking, especially in light of everything going on, but he needed something to numb the pain that he was feeling after his discovery. He cracked the bottle and took a small sip. The cheap booze tasted like old socks, but at least it got right to the point.

His thoughts then turned to Butterfly. How did she really play into all this? Had she known that Charlie Tang was already dead when she sent him to that motel? It wasn't likely. If Butterfly wanted to set him up to take a fall, she could've easily done it when she arranged for them to meet earlier that night. Butterfly's hands definitely weren't as clean in this as she would've liked for him to believe, but he didn't think she was aware of or involved in what had happened to Charlie Tang. This was the work of someone else. There were only two people he could think of who would want Charlie Tang dead, both for very different reasons. He wanted to believe that this had been on Fat Eddie, the gangster cleaning house to silence anyone who could connect him to the murder of Vickie Sparks, but his gut pointed him in another direction.

After taking another sip from the bottle, Toussaint's hand dipped into his pocket, and he pulled out the shell casing. It was now wrapped in the plastic label he had peeled from the bottle. It wasn't quite an evidence bag, but at least it would preserve whatever secrets the casing held. At least until he was sure. Turning the thing over in his hand, he thought on his old friend John Wei, and the warning he had issued when Toussaint dropped him off: *One way or another, the people responsible for what's happening to my boy will pay*. At the time he thought that John was just talking out of his ass because he was upset, but after finding Charlie Tang shot to death he was no longer so sure. He didn't want to believe that the sweet man who had taken him in was capable of doing such a thing, but he couldn't ignore the facts. He knew that at some point he would have to confront John, but he was afraid of where that confrontation might lead. If John was indeed guilty of killing Charlie Tang, would Toussaint have the heart to do what needed to be done?

Before Toussaint even realized it, he had killed half the bottle and was damn near three sheets to the wind. It had been years since Toussaint had been drunk, and he wasn't mad at the feeling. For the first time since his release from prison he felt like he wasn't weighed down by the problems of everyone else. It was liberating. A blonde call girl emerged from the darkness. She was wearing a red skirt that left very little to the imagination. She made eye contact with Toussaint, offering him a sample of her wares without words. He contemplated it for a second, but a trick riding up in an old Ford beat him to the punch. As he watched them ride away, it reminded him that being drunk wasn't the only thing he hadn't experienced in the last few years.

His drunken brain scrolled through his mental Rolodex but kept coming up blank. Had this been several years prior, there would've been no shortage of options who would be all too willing to scratch the itch he was feeling, but this wasn't then. It was now. He was a washed-up ex-con with nothing to offer but a hard dick and a sob story. The only way he was going to get laid would be if he paid for it, and at the moment he didn't have a pot to piss in. He had resigned himself to the fact that any release he would be given that night would come at his own pleasure. He had just pulled his car keys from his pocket, ready to call it a night, when something fluttered to the ground. When he bent down to see what he had dropped, he found a business card with a number scribbled on the back.

18

He woke up late the next morning. He had a headache that was out of this world. It was his own fault for downing the bottle of cheap liquor. It was the last time he would dance with anything white, or have a drink at all for that matter. As he tried to sit up and felt the room spin, he was reminded of the DJ Quik song "Tonite," when Quik promised that if God spared him, he'd never get that drunk again. At least until the next opportunity presented itself.

When he finally got his wits about him, he expected to find himself in the twin bed of the Weis' brownstone, but instead found himself wrapped in the silk sheets of a California King in an unfamiliar bedroom. It was painted soft pink, with picture windows that looked out over a leafy residential neighborhood. This was definitely not the brownstone. He untangled himself from the sheets and sat up. It was then that he discovered two things: the first being that he was as naked as the day he was born; the second, that he wasn't alone.

Lying in the bed next to him was a buxom brown-skinned beauty. She was on her stomach, hands folded under her chin, while she slept soundly. The bouquet of roses tattooed on her left shoulder rose and fell with her soft snoring. Toussaint, careful not to disturb the girl, leaned over to steal a glimpse of her face. When he saw who it was, fragments of the night before began to come back to him.

He wasn't sure how long he had sat in that parking lot before deciding to call the number on the business card. Even when he dialed it, he half expected her not to pick up. Especially considering that it was the middle of the night. He was about to hang up when her sleep-laced voice came over the line. He couldn't say for sure how their conversation started, but it ended with her texting him her address. Considering how drunk he was, it could only have been by the grace of God that he made it there without wrecking his car. She opened the door wearing only a T-shirt and boy shorts. He could only imagine how he must've appeared, blasted out of his mind and standing on her doorstep in the middle of the night. Still, she allowed him in.

Natasha led him into her home, through the living room into the kitchen. The whole time, his eyes were locked on her ass, just a bit of cheek peeking from beneath her shorts. They reminded him of two glazed hams, and he had to stop himself from dropping down and biting them. She invited him to take a seat on one of the stools at the kitchen island while she busied herself in the refrigerator.

Whatever she was looking for, she made it a point to bend over so he could get a good look. When Dobbs closed the door she was holding a pint of ice cream and a bottle of water. The chill from her time in the fridge caused her nipples to harden a bit, making them visible even through the bra under her T-shirt. So was the print from the small-caliber gun that she had tucked in her bosom. Dobbs might've been inviting, but she was no fool.

Natasha Dobbs sat on the stool opposite him and slid the bottle of water in his direction. "Looks like you could use this," she had said, popping the lid off her ice cream. She was right. Toussaint hadn't realized how dehydrated he was until he chugged the water down without stopping.

"I hope I didn't wake you?" he remembered asking her.

"Actually, I only just got in a little while ago. Me and some of the girls went out to this club," she told him, taking a scoop of the ice cream.

"When I met you on the job you didn't strike me as the nightclub type," Toussaint said, absently squeezing the empty water bottle, making a crackling sound.

"I'm Natasha at work, but just Tash when the badge and gun come off."

"Who are you now?" Toussaint asked, eyes on the gun in her bra.

"All depends on why you showed up on my doorstep in the middle of the night," Dobbs said. "What made you elect me as your drunken phone call tonight, Mr. Batiste?"

"Honestly? I don't know," Toussaint half lied. They

both knew just why he had called her on the late night after he'd had a few drinks. Toussaint had drawn a gun but was now acting shy about pulling the trigger. Luckily for him, Natasha Dobbs had no such hang-ups.

"Oh, but I think you do." She locked her predatory eyes on him while licking ice cream from the spoon. She made sure to exaggerate the act, letting the tip of her tongue swirl around the head of the utensil.

Whatever, if anything, was said between them after that, Toussaint couldn't remember. The next thing he knew, the two of them were rolling around on the tiles of her kitchen like they were the marquee matchup at WrestleMania. It had been a long time since Toussaint had been with a woman, so he was a bit out of touch. Some might even say awkward in his movements, but Dobbs was intentional with hers. She pinned him to the floor and pressed her thick lips to his. Whereas the kiss he'd shared with Aimee had been soft and sweet, Dobbs's kiss was electric. It was like she was trying to suck the breath from his body.

Dobbs raked her teeth across his throat before sucking at his neck and repeating the process. She almost popped his belt when she shoved her hand down his pants in search of his manhood. From the way she was on him you'd have thought she was the one fresh out of prison. Dobbs had heard stories from some of the veteran female officers about how gifted Troubleman was, and she was ready.

Toussaint's brain was firing signals to him, but because he was blitzed his body was reacting a half step behind. He felt more like a spectator than a participant when Dobbs straddled him and began trying to guide his dick inside her. She was moist but not quite wet, so there was some friction when she slid down on him. But once she got settled on top of him her juices began to flow and it changed the pain to pleasure. She rode him slowly at first, with him pumping his hips trying to find a rhythm. Once they got in sync it was on!

If Toussaint was ever given a quiz on all the women he had been with in his forty-plus years of life, he would likely fail. There were too many of them to count, but there were a few that he remembered vividly for the way they had put it down. That night Natasha Dobbs had joined that number. She fucked him on the kitchen floor and then he fucked her on the living room couch. She eventually managed to drag him into the bedroom, intent on a tiebreaker. Whether she had succeeded or not, Toussaint wasn't sure. By that point he was too tired and too drunk to do much more than let her continue to have her way with him while cheap vodka and good sex sucked him into the most peaceful sleep he'd had in years.

"The way you're staring is starting to creep me out." Natasha's voice cracked. She was still lying on her stomach and hadn't bothered to open her eyes when she said it.

"Just making sure you're still breathing." Toussaint laughed it off and scooted back a taste to give her some space.

"Yeah, I'm still among the living." Dobbs rolled over onto her side, facing him. "But it was touch and go for a while. I probably won't be able to walk straight for a week."

"Sorry, I didn't mean to be so rough. It's just been a while for me, ya know?"

"Oh, make no mistake. I'm not complaining at all. I haven't been fucked like that since . . . well, ever," Dobbs admitted. "Maybe you should've been a porn star instead of a cop."

"Well, considering that I'm currently unemployed, maybe it's something I should look into," Toussaint joked.

"Damn, sorry about that," Dobbs apologized, realizing she had touched on a sore subject.

"It is what it is," Toussaint said dismissively.

"Let me get myself together and I'll make us breakfast," Dobbs said, climbing out of bed, still naked, allowing him to admire her body. Her breasts were still full and sat up; her body curved in all the right places.

"You ain't gotta do all that. You already fed me," Toussaint said with a devilish grin, remembering the sweet taste of her pussy while she had rode his face a few hours prior. Dobbs's brown face turned a ruddy shade.

"That was dessert." Dobbs laughed. "I promised you a proper meal back at the station, so let me keep my word.

Hop in the shower and get dressed. The food should be done in twenty."

Thirty minutes later, Toussaint was showered, dressed, and back at the breakfast nook in Dobbs's kitchen. She had prepared fluffy scrambled eggs, wheat toast, and turkey bacon. Toussaint had never been a fan of turkey bacon, but Dobbs didn't eat pork. From his first scoop of the eggs Toussaint thought that he might be in love. They were like butter and melted in his mouth. Dobbs was the total package: fine, could throw down in the kitchen, and fucked like a porn star. He could get used to being in her company, but with the direction his life seemed to be going in, he didn't feel like he would have the opportunity to further explore their relationship.

"What's on your mind?" Dobbs asked, noticing the pensive look on his face.

"Nothing, just thinking about all the shit I have to do today."

"You still looking into the Chinese boy's case?" Dobbs asked.

"I promised his people I'd get to the bottom of it. If you don't mind me asking, how's he doing?"

"Scared. He cried the whole first night he was in there. Leroy found a single cell to put him in because some of the other inmates were giving him crap," Dobbs told him.

"When you see Left-Shoe next, please extend my thanks for looking out."

"You can do that on your own. I relay that message and he's gonna start asking questions I'm too grown to have to answer. I don't want Leroy's hating ass in my business."

"Right, I almost forgot that this is our little secret." Toussaint made a zipping motion across his lips.

"Unless you don't want it to be?" Dobbs took a bite of one of the bacon strips. An awkward look crossed Toussaint's face. "I'm sorry, am I doing too much too soon? I don't want you feeling like I have expectations."

"Nah, it ain't like that. I fucks with you, Tash. And not just because you fucked me into a coma. You seem like a great girl, and I would love to see where this could go."

"But?"

"What makes you think there's a *but*?" Toussaint asked.

"The fact that you looked like you wanted to swallow your tongue when I made the crack about us not being a secret. You don't have to worry about me turning into some stalker trying to press you into a relationship," Dobbs said defensively.

Toussaint put his fork down and placed his hand over hers. "Baby girl, I'd like nothing more than to wake up to that sweet ass and warm smile a few nights per week. Like I said, I fucks with you. It's just that I'm at a weird space in my life right now. I'm a disgraced cop, fresh out of prison without a pot to piss in. A woman like you deserves more than I have to offer right now. Can you dig that?"

"Yeah, I can dig that," Dobbs playfully mocked him. "And I respect you being straight up with me. Just know that I'm no stranger to men with baggage. Lord knows that's the only kind I seem to attract. You're just the first one to be honest about his bullshit. That says more about who you are than your current set of circumstances. Maybe once you get yourself settled a bit, we can revisit this conversation?"

"I'd like that. Well, if this thing I'm looking into doesn't get me killed or thrown back in prison first."

"You really don't believe he did it?" Dobbs questioned.

"Honestly? No. I've known Jay-Jay a long time and he's just not the type of kid capable of something like this."

"I talked to him a little bit while he was in lockup, and I don't disagree with you. I've come in contact with a lot of killers in my years on the force, and Jay-Jay doesn't fit that mold," Dobbs admitted. There was a pause, as if she had something more to add, but was uncertain. "I'd like to help you, if I can?"

"I appreciate that, Tash, but I can't have you put your job on the line behind this shit."

"My job is to serve the people of Philadelphia. Some years back, I stood by while a man was sent to prison who didn't deserve to be there. I've had to live with that for a long time. Maybe I see a chance to right that wrong."

Toussaint didn't respond right away. He just sat there, studying Sergeant Natasha Dobbs. He didn't know if she realized what she was volunteering to get herself tied up in, but he also didn't think she cared. Beneath that phat ass and pretty face beat the heart of a good cop. One who actually cared about justice. "This thing is likely to get very, very messy."

Dobbs leaned in and locked eyes with him. "If last night didn't teach you anything else, it should've taught you that I don't mind a little mess. Now, where do we start?"

19

It would be a good while before Toussaint left Natasha Dobbs's place. They spent an hour going over what he had learned so far about Jay-Jay's case and another hour enjoying each other. When he'd first showed up on Dobbs's doorstep it had been in drunken search of a sexual release, but instead he found an ally, and potentially something more. Natasha had agreed to help him in whatever way she could to prove Jay-Jay's innocence, but she had made it clear to him that she was not willing to break the law in order to do it. She was a good woman, but still a cop first, and that was a line that she wouldn't cross. Toussaint assured her that he would never ask her to compromise her badge, but he had no such obligations to the department. He would cross whatever lines necessary to exonerate John's son. Speaking of John, it was time for Toussaint to do something that he had been putting off.

When he arrived back on the block, he found Good 4 Yu already open for business. John stood outside, smoking a cigarette. The fact that he was no longer hiding the fact that he still smoked from his wife spoke to the amount of stress he had to have been under. Wanting to prolong the inevitable, Toussaint circled the block twice before finally parking half a block away from the restaurant, near the mouth of an alley. He sat in the car for a while, with the engine idling, thinking about what he would say to John. How did you accuse one of the only friends you had in the world of being a murderer? This was going to be a hard but necessary conversation.

After finally getting up the nerve, he killed the engine and got out of the car. His heart thudded loudly in his chest. He hadn't been this nervous since his first day of walking the beat. He was just turning the key in the lock of the car door to secure it when he heard the sound of a bottle being kicked. With instincts born of years of combat against the criminal element of Philadelphia, Toussaint hit the ground. It was a split second before the bullet aimed at his head had shattered the driver's side window of the Monte Carlo. Standing over him, holding a smoking gun, was Man-Man. "Remember me, muthafucka?" Man-Man snarled, aiming the gun at Toussaint. His foot, the one Toussaint had shot him in, was wrapped in a cast, and he was leaning on a single crutch.

"Would you believe me if I said that I didn't?" Toussaint quipped. Pain exploded in the side of his head as he was kicked from behind. After his world stopped spinning, he managed to roll himself into a sitting position. He could now see who had kicked him.

"Bet you never thought you'd see us again." Vic had joined them. He too was holding a gun.

"I'd hoped not, yet here we are."

"You got a real smart mouth. Maybe a bullet in it would help you to keep it closed," Man-Man said, with hatred for the ex-detective in his tone. From the way the gun trembled in his hand, you could tell he was itching to use it.

"Take it easy, boys. You got the drop on me, so now what?" Toussaint asked as calmly as he could. He already knew the answer, but hoped that chatting them up would buy him some time.

"We dead your punk ass for what you pulled at my spot earlier. The police got to Jay-Jay before we did, but your ass is new-mown grass. I'm going to enjoy killing you," Vic informed him.

"I know you boys are smarter than that. You gonna shoot me in the middle of a residential block? In broad daylight? How long you think it'll be before the police are beating down your door?" Toussaint questioned. Vic and Man-Man exchanged uncertain glances.

"Fuck it, I say we smoke him right here and take our chances," Man-Man said impatiently. Vic didn't look convinced. Unlike Man-Man, the prospect of going to prison for a homicide gave Vic pause.

"Give me your car keys!" Vic demanded, suddenly having an idea. He turned to Man-Man. "We can take him somewhere quiet then take his car to the spot. We can probably fetch a nice piece of change for this classic."

"You can take my life, if you got a mind to, but you ain't getting my wheel."

"You willing to die over a whip?" Man-Man questioned.

"If I'm gonna die anyhow, might as well be on my own terms," Toussaint said.

Man-Man shook his head. He was regarding Toussaint with almost a respect for standing on business, even in the face of his own death.

Tiring of the chatter, Vic cracked Toussaint in the mouth with his gun, busting his lip. "Don't make me ask you again."

"A'ight," Toussaint spat blood on the ground. "You got it." He leaned to one side, which prompted Vic to press his gun to the back of Toussaint's head.

"Don't go getting any bright ideas," Vic warned him.

"Take it easy, man. I'm not holding," Toussaint flipped his jacket back to show that he wasn't carrying a gun. "My keys are in my back pocket."

"Hand them over, but do it real slow," Vic instructed him.

Toussaint nodded. He continued his motion, slowly so as not to set either one of the gunmen off. He brought himself to one knee and measured the distance between the two men. He had one shot at surviving the morning, so he took it. Spinning on one knee like a breakdancer, Toussaint swept Vic's legs out from under him. Vic's feet went in the air before he came crashing down on his ass. His gun leaped from his hand and slid under the Monte Carlo.

Man-Man fired at Toussaint, but because he was on a crutch, he couldn't set his center of balance properly and missed, nearly hitting Vic in the nuts. Toussaint was on him immediately, delivering a sharp blow to his neck. Man-Man stumbled backward, sending his arms flailing and his crutch flying. He crashed to the ground on his back. Man-Man glared up at Toussaint, rage in his eyes.

"Be it today or another day, your ass is as good as dead, Troubleman!" Man-Man rasped.

"You know? I've been hearing that from men like you since I came home from prison, and frankly, I'm still not convinced," Toussaint told Man-Man before stomping him in the face.

After tucking Man-Man in for his nap, Toussaint turned his attention back to Vic. He found the man recovered and waiting for him. He didn't have a chance to dodge it when Vic swung Man-Man's discarded crutch. The walking aid struck Toussaint in the jaw and dazed him. He'd barely recovered before Vic hit him with the crutch again. This time across the top of his head. Toussaint hadn't even realized that he was falling until the ground made contact with his chin. A stinging sensation resonated through his face. Vic didn't let up; he cracked Toussaint over and over with the crutch. Apparently, he had decided to beat Toussaint to death instead of shooting him. He was doing a pretty good job of it too. Blood poured into Toussaint's eye, making it hard for him to see, but he could still feel. With every blow Vic landed he found himself slipping further and further down the rabbit hole leading to the hereafter. Of all the ways he had expected his life to end, being beaten to death with a crutch hadn't been one of them.

As he was succumbing to the darkness, he heard something. It was a wonder that he could hear anything over the loud whacking sound the crutch made every time it struck a different part of his body. He strained his ears, and if he hadn't known any better he could've sworn it was something shrieking. Just as suddenly as the beating had started, it stopped. He rolled over onto his back and saw Vic fighting with someone . . . no, *something*. Toussaint reasoned that he was either dead or had suffered some type of head trauma from the beating because he could've sworn when he looked up, he saw Vic going head up with a monkey. The small brown ball of fur was giving Vic hell as it clawed at his face, long brown and white-tipped tail wrapped around his neck. The sight of it was comical, but what would happen next was anything but.

Vic had finally managed to dislodge the monkey from his face and tossed it to the ground. His face was covered in bloody scratches and it looked like the tip of one of his ears was missing. He held the crutch in his hand like a sword, trying to fend off the monkey, who was gearing up for a second attack. Just behind him, someone appeared, as if out of thin air. He was dressed in a baggy blue Howard University hoodie, with the hood pulled over his head, making it near impossible to see his face. Vic was so preoccupied with the monkey that he didn't realize there was someone behind him until his head was snatched back. A hand reached around and grabbed his face and then he suddenly collapsed, dead on his feet.

The stranger then turned his attention to his next victim. Toussaint tried to will himself off the ground, but he didn't have the strength. Vic had really done a number on him. All he could do was lie there and watch as the man in the hoodie stalked in his direction. In his gloved hand he held a crescent-shaped blade, which left a trail of blood drops in his wake as he closed the distance. The stranger stopped just short of Toussaint and studied him from under his hood.

"If you're gonna do it, get on with it!" Toussaint spat.

The stranger knelt beside Toussaint and removed his hood, revealing his face. Not a *he*, but a *she*. The girl was about Aimee's age, possibly a few years older, with dark skin that was so smooth he doubted she had ever had a pimple in her life. Dusty brown dreadlocks hung over her shoulders and tickled his face when she leaned over him. Eyes the color of honey bore into his, and when she spoke he felt like he was hearing her voice in the back of his mind. "Sleep," she whispered. "Mr. Batiste, maybe you should sleep?"

Yes . . . sleep. Her words washed over him like a warm ocean, and his eyes suddenly felt heavy. He was so very tired. Tired of the world kicking his ass. Tired of people he thought he knew lying to him. He was tired of it all. At that moment he wanted nothing more than a good nap. With that in mind, he drifted off into a peaceful slumber, hoping that when he woke up it would be in heaven and not hell.

PART III

•

THE HEARTS OF MEN

20

Toussaint found himself in the middle of a beautiful dream. He was on a white sand beach, staring out at a turquoise ocean. He was shirtless, resting on a beach chair with his ankles crossed, sipping from a chilled glass of thirty-year-old Scotch. Angela Bassett was massaging his shoulders while Taraji P. Henson rubbed oil over his chest. Dream Taraji paused her oiling to plant a kiss on his lips.

"You taste like liquor," Dream Taraji told him.

"I wonder what you taste like?" Toussaint said with a devilish grin.

"You're about to find out," Dream Taraji told him before removing her bikini top, exposing her full breasts and dark nipples. She straddled Toussaint and leaned in to kiss him again.

Toussaint closed his eyes and enjoyed the sensation of Dream Taraji suckling his bottom lip like a starved infant. At that moment, all was right with the world . . . until it wasn't. "The fuck!" He jerked away when Dream Taraji bit his bottom lip. When he opened his eyes, Dream Taraji was gone, and sitting atop his chest was a monkey. "Wake up, Mr. Batiste," the monkey said in Dream Taraji's voice. And that's what he did.

Toussaint came out of his dream like a drowning man who had just cracked the surface of the water. He found himself disoriented. He looked around and found that he was no longer on the beach, but in a bedroom. The sand had been replaced by a thick red carpet, and his beach chair a quilted queen-size bed. Sitting on his chest, staring at him curiously, was that damn monkey. "Off!" he managed to croak before swatting at the monkey. The monkey squawked and scurried off into a corner of the room.

"That was rude," a voice said softly. Sitting in the corner was the girl who had killed Vic. She had traded in her Howard hoodie for a black silk blouse and jeans. Resting on her lap was the novel she had been reading: *Song of Solomon* by Toni Morrison. "Azuma likes you, and that bitter primate doesn't like anyone. That says a lot about your character, Mr. Batiste."

"Who are you?" Toussaint asked.

"Someone who sees the value in keeping you alive," she replied.

"You know, I'm getting tired of asking questions and getting riddles in response. It's been happening since I came home, and frankly, I'm over it." When Toussaint made to sit up, the room began to spin and forced him to lie back down. Vic had probably given him a concussion when he cracked him over the head with that crutch.

"You've been through a lot. You should take it slow. Let the juju bag do its work," the girl suggested.

"Juju?" It was then that he noticed the IV in his arm.

The IV bag hung from a tall pole near his bed, pumping green liquid into him. Panicked, he reached to rip the tube from his arm.

"I wouldn't do that if I were you. Those sheets cost a lot and you'll ruin them if you bleed on them." She got up from the chair and placed the book on it, then approached Toussaint's bedside. "It's not poison, if that's what you're thinking."

"What is it then?"

"Old family remedy. It'll help speed up the healing process," she told him, before slipping on a pair of latex gloves. With the skill of a trained nurse, she removed the IV from his arm and put a bandage over the entry point. "How are you feeling?"

"Better than I expected after what I've been through," Toussaint said, flexing his arm. He was sore from the fight and a bandage covered the wound on his head, but he wasn't in half as much pain as he would expect to be. Maybe there was something to that old family remedy. "Whatever that stuff is, you should bottle it and sell it."

"That would be against the house rules. Last time I broke the rules, it didn't go so well for me," the girl told him.

"What is all this? Why did you save me from those guys back there?" Toussaint wanted to know.

"I realize that you've probably got a lot of questions, but it's not my place to answer them. I'll let him fill in the blanks. If you're feeling well enough to get out of bed, you'll find a shower and some fresh clothes through there."

She pointed at a door that led to the bathroom. "Don't be too long; we've already fallen behind schedule waiting for you to recover."

Toussaint sat up on the bed and planted his feet on the floor. He was still a bit woozy, but the vertigo had passed. "How long have I been out?"

"About a day and a half."

"*What?*" Toussaint was shocked. He felt like he had just taken a nap, not been in a damn coma. "Where's my phone? I gotta make a call." He patted his pockets. He didn't find it on his person, but on a night table next to the bed. He snatched it up and tapped the screen, but the phone was dead. "Shit!"

"I'll get you a charger, but first we have business to discuss. Get yourself cleaned up and join us in the Hive. Azuma can show you the way. There's a lot to talk about, and he doesn't like to be kept waiting," the girl told him before leaving the room.

Toussaint continued to sit there for a while, trying to make heads or tails of what was going on. And who was this *he* that the girl kept referring to? He looked to the monkey—Azuma—who was now perched on the dresser. "I don't suppose you can tell me what's going on?" Azuma shrugged. It was an eerily human gesture. "Didn't think so."

Ten minutes later, Toussaint emerged looking like a different person. The bathroom he'd been directed to was small, maybe a little larger than the one in his apartment at the Weis' but with more modern fixtures. He showered and dressed in a set of clothes that had been left for him: fresh socks, underwear, and a gray sweat suit. The pants fit him almost perfectly, as if whoever had provided them knew his exact size. When he held up the sweatshirt to slip it over his head, he paused. There was a small logo at the breast of the shirt: the same black heart and crucifix that he had been seeing all over the place since he returned to the city. Toussaint wasn't a man who believed in coincidences. The universe had steered him to this place. Whether it was for divine or sinister purposes, he would soon find out.

Azuma was waiting for him when he stepped out of the bathroom. Toussaint followed him out into a carpeted hallway that seemed to go on forever. He passed several doors on each side of the hall. Outside of each room door there were abstract paintings, framed in glass with small lights illuminating them. Judging by the distance from the room he just exited to the stairs, he gathered that it was a large house. Larger than any he had ever been in. This made him wonder if he was still even within the city? Or even the state for that matter. If the girl was to be believed that he had been unconscious for a day and a half, he could be damn near anywhere.

Azuma led him down a spiral staircase, which let out into a huge living room. A chandelier hung twenty feet above, illuminating the room in soft light. Every few feet, the monkey would spare a glance over his shoulder to make sure that Toussaint was still following. The fact that he was in a strange house in an unknown place with a monkey as his tour guide made Toussaint feel like he was trapped in the pages of *Alice in Wonderland.* They passed through the living room and into another hall. At the end, there was a wooden door. Azuma stood on his hind legs and fumbled with the knob until the door clicked open. He then looked at Toussaint.

"You first," Toussaint insisted. He had no clue what was behind that door and the fact that it was a monkey who had led him to it made him even more suspicious. Azuma folded his arms and continued to stand there. He wasn't budging, but neither was Toussaint.

"We don't have all night, Mr. Batiste," the familiar voice of the girl called from the other side of the door.

Toussaint looked at Azuma, who was grinning at him triumphantly. "Smug little bastard," he grumbled before stepping through the doorway.

21

Toussaint wasn't sure what to expect when he entered, but he certainly wasn't prepared for what he walked into. It was a spacious room, larger than the living room he had passed through. The entire space was white, from the carpet to the furniture. The pretty Brown girl sat on a white sectional that was so plush it almost swallowed her, novel resting on her lap while she tapped her fingers impatiently.

Azuma scurried past Toussaint, purposely whacking the leg of his sweatpants with his tail. Toussaint barely noticed. He was too in awe of the world he had just stepped into. On every wall in the room there were monitors mounted, each showing a different image from around the city. On one screen there was a live feed from the traffic camera at the intersection of Broad and Erie, and on another a man and woman had a muted argument in the luxury suite of a hotel. They were all like that, each showing some intrusive moments of people that didn't realize they were being watched. It was all like something out of a spy movie.

"What is all this?" Toussaint asked. The question was directed at the girl, but it was someone else who answered.

"The future." A masculine voice filled the room as if being broadcast through a surround-sound system. Toussaint hadn't noticed him at first. He was standing on the far side of the room, his back to Toussaint and eyes locked on one of the larger screens. It was one of the few that weren't broadcasting from somewhere in the city. It was tuned to CNN, where a talk show host whose name he couldn't remember was interviewing a ginger-haired white man in a pin-striped suit. The sound was muted, so he couldn't hear what they were saying, but the caption at the bottom of the screen read: Mayoral Candidate Atticus Gallagher. "You into politics at all, Mr. Batiste?" he asked over his shoulder.

"Not really, unless I got a dog in the fight," Toussaint answered.

"Let me guess: Your first time voting was for Obama?" the man asked. Toussaint didn't respond. "No shame in that, Mr. Batiste. We all secretly prefer someone who looks like *us* making critical decisions that will affect our lives and livelihoods." He finally turned to face Toussaint. Racially ambiguous, which roughly meant that Toussaint found it hard to place him. His skin was deeply tanned, like he could've been Latino or Middle Eastern, but his silver-blue eyes made him look closer to European. His hair was wavy and with streaks of gray going up the sides, that put Toussaint in mind of Paulie Walnuts from *The Sopranos*. "They say that Sparks is a lock to win this election, but I like to think for myself, and what I think is that if the right dominoes fall, Gallagher will come out of this as the dark-horse winner."

"Sounds like you got the inside track," Toussaint suggested.

"Or I'm just a man who likes to stay informed. But I guess I don't have to tell you that." The man motioned around at the cameras. He pulled himself away from the CNN interview and approached Toussaint. He wore a black turtleneck and black slacks that stopped just short of his ankles, showing that he wasn't wearing socks. His black loafers carried him across the carpet to the former detective. "You promised to call, but you never did. My mother always warned my sisters about boys like you." A mock sad expression fell over his face.

"Come again?" Toussaint was lost, feeling like Alice having her first conversation with the Mad Hatter.

"Mrs. Gould assured me that you would reach out," the man explained.

"You're Ezekiel Darkhart?" It finally clicked.

"I am," Darkhart confirmed with a nod. "At least these days. Ask me again in a few years, and I can't guarantee you that the answer will be the same. You'll excuse me if I don't shake your hand. I've heard what those mitts of yours are capable of. I don't suppose you'd be willing to let me take a peek at that little book of yours?"

"What book?" Toussaint faked ignorance, but he knew exactly what Darkhart was talking about—but how did he know about it? Still, Toussaint wasn't about to break the promise he'd made to Chung to protect the secrets of Wah Pei for a complete stranger. Letting John see the book was one thing, but he didn't know Darkhart from a hole in the wall.

"Understood." Darkhart read his body language. "Trust is earned. I meant no disrespect, and certainly wouldn't ask you to break the promise you made to the old man on his death bed. It's just that, as I'm sure you've noticed, I'm a junkie for information. I'd give anything just to get a glimpse of what's in those pages. They say there aren't too many of you left. Meaning: disciples of the one-armed boxer. And you're certainly the first Black student on record. At least that I've heard of."

What *didn't* this guy know?

"You seem to know an awful lot about me, yet I don't know shit about you or what you want with me."

"I'm sorry. Am I rambling?" Darkhart looked concerned that he might've offended Toussaint. "I do that sometimes. Especially when I'm excited about something. It's not every day that I find myself in the presence of a living legend. Thank you for coming too, by the way."

"Like I had a choice."

"Mr. Batiste, the only things that we have no say over are when we are born and when we die. Everything that happens in between is a choice that leads to an outcome. Take Asha for example." He motioned towards the girl. So, that was her name? She never looked up from her novel. "She could've made the choice of letting Vic continue trying to crack your skull open instead of saving your life, but allowing you to be killed wouldn't produce the desired outcome. At least not as it benefits us in this moment in time. Tomorrow may be a different story."

"What's today's story?" Toussaint asked.

"Whatever you write it to be," Darkhart said. When he spoke, several of the screens shifted and became a reel of photos. There was a picture of Toussaint being sworn in when he graduated the academy. Another showed when he had made detective. The reel fast-forwarded to the day he had been released from prison and picked up by Jay-Jay at the station. There was even a photo of him meeting with Butterfly outside Philip's. "If you haven't figured it out already, Mr. Batiste, I've been monitoring you for some time. You came to my attention during your prison bid. I initially didn't think much of you, another dirty Philadelphia cop who got himself thrown in jail. Then I did some digging and was able to unearth the circumstances surrounding your arrest. It was after processing that information that I came to truly understand the nature of your beast, Toussaint."

"And what kind of beast might that be?" Toussaint questioned.

"One that will run through a brick wall for what he believes in," Darkhart said seriously. "You and I are more alike than we are different, Toussaint. Two kids who came up through the mud and proved that we were better than the world said we would be. We beat the odds."

"Says the rich Peeping Tom to the recently released convict," Toussaint said.

"See, that's the problem with men like you, Toussaint . . . respectfully. You see what's on the surface and get an idea in your head about how it came to be, but everything is not always what it seems. Sure, I've done well for myself, but I had to literally dig through a river of shit to find the brass ring. I've sacrificed a great deal to build Darkhart Industries. I grew up in a dirt-poor country that you probably don't even know exists. Stole, lied, cheated, and some other shit that I won't mention, to finally get out. I was street, but also very smart and curious about the inner workings of things. I was one of those kids who was always taking shit apart, figuring out how it worked, and putting it back together. This is how I discovered how to turn shit into sugar."

Toussaint cocked a quizzical eyebrow. That was a new one to him.

"Quite literally. While salvaging some parts at an abandoned waste plant, I developed a way to turn waste into clean energy. That was enough to get me into an exchange program at an American university. By the time I turned twenty, I had already received my degree in engineering and was halfway into my first year of grad school at MIT. Learned a lot from those eggheads, including the *true* value of knowledge. There I was, living off meal plans and taking the bus back and forth when there were people out there willing to pay good money for the tech I was helping to develop. So I stopped depending on grants that wouldn't benefit me in the long run and found alternative means to fund my research." A dark expression fell over his face.

"Drug money?" Toussaint questioned.

"I never asked where the money came from, but I wasn't naïve about it either. Back in those days, I was young, and incredibly ambitious. The consequences of my actions meant less to me than achieving my goals. I never considered the costs of the decisions I made until it came time to pay the piper." He rubbed his chest absently. "Sadly, how to turn back time is the one trick I haven't learned how to pull off . . . at least not yet. Even if I could, I can't say that I'd have done anything differently. The pound of flesh I sacrificed was a small price in exchange for knowing what imprint I will leave on the world when I'm gone."

"A very interesting story, Mr. Darkhart. It still doesn't explain why you wanted to meet with me?"

"Because I owe you a boon and intend to honor it."

"A boon? For what? I ain't never met you a day in my life, let alone done anything for you to feel obligated to look out for me," Toussaint pointed out.

"Not directly, no," Darkhart confirmed. "On the streets they call you Troubleman, someone who looks out for poor souls who can't look out for themselves. One of those souls happened to be my wife's son, Milton."

It caught Toussaint by surprise to hear the name of his old cellie, Milton Hodges. The kid he had gotten stabbed for trying to defend. Milton would always tell Toussaint stories about his rich stepdaddy, but he never mentioned his name. Toussaint would half listen to the stories but never put much stock in them. Reason being that, during his incarceration, maybe the first thing he had learned was that a lot of those dudes were liars. Cats made up fantastic stories about who they were on the outside and what would be waiting for them when they touched back down on the world. Toussaint peeped the bullshit but never judged the guys who were on it like that because he understood that they needed something to hold on to to get them through their bids. He had no reason to believe that Milton was any different, just another con telling a story in search of trying to seem like he was more than what he was. Apparently, he had been on the level.

"Old Milton? Sure, I remember him. Decent kid, though maybe not the sharpest knife in the drawer. How's he doing these days?" Toussaint asked.

"Dead," Darkhart said flatly. "Overdosed some time ago. As I'm told, a dealer he ran afoul of arranged for him to get hold of some bad drugs."

"I'm sorry to hear that," Toussaint said sincerely.

"Thank you, but I think we both knew enough about Milton to see the inevitable. Long before I married his mother, Milton had been afforded opportunities that men like you and I could've only dreamed of. He could've been anything he wanted in life, but he chose to be an addict. Milton is gone, but that doesn't change the fact that a debt is owed to you."

"I respect that, but you can keep your money. I was only trying to do the right thing by the boy," Toussaint told him.

"That I can respect, but this isn't about money. At least not solely. This is about an opportunity that could benefit the both of us." Darkhart made a gesture with his hand, and the monitors switched again.

Over a dozen pictures appeared on the screens, depicting the Wei family at various points in time. There was the family photo they'd taken in front of Good 4 Yu when they'd first opened. Back then Jay-Jay and Aimee were kids, Aimee still a chubby little girl. Another photo depicted John Wei. He was a much younger man with a head full of black hair and dressed in a tailored suit. He was flanked by several hard-looking men, also wearing suits. It looked like a poster for a Chinese gangster flick. From the background he could tell that the picture was taken at the Hong Kong Observation Deck. There was a young boy in the picture with them, standing just in front of John. He was barely in his teens but had the eyes of a child who had seen far too much far too soon. Toussaint didn't recognize him as being one of the Wei children, but from the tender way John's hand rested on his shoulder, he could tell that the boy was dear to him. In the center was a black-and-white mugshot of a boy who Toussaint did know to be one of John's, Jay-Jay Wei.

"Tell me something, do you believe in generational curses?" Darkhart continued.

"What kind of question is that?" Toussaint asked, still focused on the photo of John and the sad boy.

"A serious one. There are some who believe that the actions of those who came before us can affect certain events in our lives. I personally believe that we create our own fates, but that's just my humble opinion," Darkhart said with a shrug. "So the baby boy of the Wei clan is the latest soul you're out there trying to save? Very selfless of you to put yourself in harm's way for people you don't share blood with."

"Blood don't always make you family. The Weis have done more for me than people I actually share DNA with. I'm always gonna look out for them when I can," Toussaint said proudly.

"And while you're looking out for them, who is going to look out for you?" Darkhart asked. Toussaint opened his mouth to speak, but Darkhart continued. "It was rhetorical. All I'm saying to you is don't put your sense of honor above your sense of self-preservation. Judging by the fact that Asha found you getting your ass kicked and still no closer to freeing Jay-Jay, I think it's safe to say that none of this has gone how you thought it would when you agreed to help the Weis."

"My investigation has been less than fruitful," Toussaint admitted.

"More like stalled," Darkhart suggested. "There are some very powerful forces at work behind the scenes. Didn't you find it strange that two girls are viciously murdered, but only one makes headlines?"

"I figured it was because of her high profile, being the daughter of a district attorney and all."

"So you have been led to believe. Vickie Sparks was but one string dangling from a ball of yarn. A ball that some would rather not see unraveled," Darkhart said.

"You being one of them?"

"To the contrary. I'm one of the few people in this whole city who is actually hoping that you do blow the lid off this shit and expose it for what it really is," Darkhart informed him. "Darkhart Industries was established by the strides we've made in the clean energy space, but we've built quite a diverse portfolio. We've established a few lucrative companies under the DHI umbrella. One of my less-than-talked-about endeavors specializes in, let's say . . . fixing broken things. We have a small yet exclusive list of people who we provide services to. One of these clients has a vested interest in Jay-Jay going free and the people really behind this being exposed."

"Seems like with all this surveillance equipment you have planted around the city it would be pretty easy for you to find out who really killed the girl. What do you need me for?"

"That part is a little more complicated. My direct

involvement becoming public would cause more harm than good. Considering the delicate nature of this thing, it's best if I outsource."

"So, you use me as a hired gun?" Toussaint saw where this was going.

"Oh, not at all! It's as Mrs. Gould told you, I have need of a man with your skill set. This is a legitimate employment opportunity I'm offering. Our paths being linked by this murder was purely coincidence, of this I can assure you, but in it I see a way where both you and Darkhart Industries can benefit from this partnership. You're already investigating the case, so why not be compensated for it? Think of it as on-the-job training. I can make it worth your while."

Toussaint weighed what Darkhart was offering. It was tempting, but there was something about the man that didn't sit right with him. Who was this client of his and what interests did he have in Jay-Jay Wei? His mother would always warn him that something that sounded too good to be true usually was. "I appreciate the offer, Mr. Darkhart, but I'm gonna have to pass. I'll take my chances on my own. Now if somebody can just show me the way to the nearest bus station?" Toussaint turned to leave, but Darkhart had a few parting words.

"Fifty thousand."

Toussaint stopped walking.

"I thought that would get your attention. A one-time retainer fee for your services. You'll also have the full resources of Darkhart Industries at your disposal. When it's all said and done, if you're still not convinced to take the position I'm offering, you'll never hear from me again." Darkhart extended his hand.

What Darkhart was offering was life changing to a down-on-his-luck ex-con like Toussaint. He stared into Darkhart's silver-blue eyes, the lights from the monitors dancing in them. It made him feel like Jabez Stone must've felt when he met Mr. Scratch. Only he wouldn't have Daniel Webster to argue his case for the return of what he was about to wager. None of this stopped him from shaking Ezekiel Darkhart's hand and sealing the deal. He knew that if his mother could see him, she would be ashamed. But his mother had never had fifty thousand dollars.

22

The sun was coming up when Toussaint emerged from Ezekiel Darkhart's Hive. Darkhart had offered Toussaint the chance to rest and replenish before continuing his investigation, but he declined. He had already lost enough time and needed to get back to it. But he wouldn't be going alone. Asha would be accompanying him, along with her pet, Azuma. Toussaint didn't too much mind Asha accompanying him, especially after seeing what she was capable of. The girl was deadly, and he needed someone to watch his back if this thing ended up going where he suspected it might. Azuma was a different story. The too-smart monkey creeped Toussaint out, and he didn't need it getting in the way. Besides that, he didn't want to run the risk of the animal having an accident on his seats. But Asha assured him that when the time came, having Azuma there would come in handy.

Toussaint had changed out of the sweat suit and into a pair of jeans and a black button-up shirt that was a little short at the sleeves for him. They were the only clothes in the house that came remotely close to fitting him that didn't have the Darkhart logo on them. After dressing, he was given a knapsack full of items that Darkhart had said would assist him in his investigation. Inside the pack were burner phones, a pistol, a tablet, and some other odds and ends, including two-way transmitters that could be worn discreetly in their ears. They reminded Toussaint of the ones worn by the Secret Service, only these were wireless.

In the garage, among several luxury cars, he found his baby, the Monte Carlo. At some point Asha must've retrieved it from the block where he left it. When he examined the car to assess the damage from the bullet, he found that the window had been repaired. The dent he had put in the car several years prior had also been hammered out. An average mechanic would've taken at least a week to do the work, but Darkhart's people had taken care of it in less than two days. Maybe this partnership with Darkhart was going to work out after all?

When Vic had demanded the keys to Toussaint's car under the threat of death, the ex-detective had been prepared to die rather than give them over. That car was his baby. It broke his heart when he had to sell it off to pay attorney fees, and once John Wei had miraculously brought her back to him, he had vowed to never part with the car. Once she had come back into his possession, he promised that he would never let another living soul touch her again. So he couldn't understand for the life of him why he had handed the keys over without protest when Asha asked for them.

Asha was a woman that Toussaint's late grandmother would have said *had a way about her*. She reserved this phrase for people who had something in them spiritually that separated them from regular folks. He'd noticed that being in her presence gave him the same feeling one might get when you met somebody for the first time but felt like you knew them from somewhere else. Like you were old friends. It was that spirit that allowed him to trust her to steer his prized possession back towards the city.

While Asha drove, Toussaint fished out the tablet he had been provided with the knapsack. Well, he wasn't sure if he could even call it that, as it looked nothing like any tablet or iPad he had ever seen. It was slightly larger than a cell phone and completely transparent, like a sheet of ice that had formed on the curb on a cold winter day. The thing was so advanced that Asha had to show him how to turn it on. She informed him that it had been created by Darkhart Industries, and that Apple and Samsung were currently in a bidding war for the rights to the design. He couldn't wait to show it to Aimee. The girl would have a field day with this kind of advanced tech.

Thinking of the youngest Wei made him remember his dead cell phone. He plugged it into the charging wire and waited a few moments until it had enough juice to power on. No sooner had it come to life than notifications from missed calls and texts began going off like a digital symphony. There was a missed call and a text from Dobbs, asking if he had made it home safe. Most of the other notifications were from members of the Wei family. Sue had called him twice, and Aimee at least three times. Noticeably absent were any calls from John. Toussaint didn't feel like talking to anyone, so he shot Dobbs a text letting her know that he was good and would hit her later. Poor girl probably thought he had ghosted her after not hearing from him after he left. He then shot Aimee a text letting her know that he had a new lead on the case and would follow up with the family when he knew more. He thought about calling John but decided against it. If he was guilty of what Toussaint suspected then he didn't want to tip him off. This was a conversation that would be had face-to-face.

He busied himself poring over the files that had been loaded onto the tablet. Darkhart had certainly done his homework on this case. He had compiled names, locations, and other tidbits of information that spread out like a spider's web. At first, they seemed random—until he realized that they were all connected to Davis Sparks in one way or another. He decided to start from the middle and work his way out, double tapping on Sparks's file. Inside he found a biography of the district attorney, who was now running for mayor. He was a native of Philadelphia, having attended Julia R. Masterman Laboratory and Demonstration School, from where he graduated with honors. Then he headed west and studied criminal justice at UCLA. This is where the story got interesting. Six months short of receiving his degree, he had gotten himself into some legal trouble, named as a person of interest in an attack on a man outside a bar in West Hollywood. He was never formally charged, but it did get him expelled from school. He came home and enrolled at Villanova and shortly thereafter received his degree in criminal justice. It took him three tries, but he eventually passed the bar exam and spent a few years working as a public defender. He then switched sides and became a prosecutor. The rest of his professional history Toussaint already knew, so he started digging into his personal life.

Davis Sparks had been married to Violet Sparks, Vickie's mother, until she passed after a bout with breast cancer, leaving Davis to raise their daughter on his own. This was public information, but what Toussaint found that wasn't so public was that it hadn't been Sparks's first marriage. When he was still living in Los Angeles, he and his college sweetheart, Susan Parker, had been married in a spur-of-the-moment Vegas wedding. The marriage lasted six months before being annulled for reasons that weren't specified. For as public as most of Davis Sparks's life was, how was it that his first marriage had flown under the radar? Interesting indeed.

Toussaint's reading was interrupted when something plunked him in the side of the head. He looked down and saw a lone grape on the floor of the Monte Carlo. Behind him, Azuma sat in the back seat, holding a plastic container full of the grapes he had been snacking on. He flashed Toussaint a fanged smile before taking out another grape and extending it to him. "You got one more time to throw something in my ride before I turn you into a hood ornament." The monkey's grin faded, and he hissed at Toussaint.

"Azuma doesn't take kindly to threats," Asha warned.

"And I don't take kindly to food being tossed around my ride." Toussaint picked the loose grape up from the floor and plucked it out the window.

"Relax, he was only trying to share his snack with you."

"What is it with you and that monkey? Why not have a regular pet like a dog or cats. You got some type of weird fetish that you wanna tell me about?"

"Azuma isn't a pet, he's family," Asha corrected him. "And he has been since I was a little girl."

"I didn't realize monkeys lived that long. What's their average lifespan?" Toussaint asked.

"Depends on the species, some of them ten years, some of them more than forty. But Azuma is not your average monkey. He's my totem."

"Your what?"

"My *totem*. It's like . . ." Asha searched for a word that might translate better. "A familiar."

"You mean like a witch's cat?" he questioned.

Asha let out a chuckle. "Something like that, but not quite. Totems have been kind of a thing in my family for generations. When the female children of my bloodline come of age, we're gifted totems to form a bond with. They stay with us throughout our lives and serve as spiritual companions. In certain cases, a totem can be passed on from mother to daughter, as was the case with Azuma when my mother was killed."

"Oh . . . I'm sorry," Toussaint offered condolences.

"Thank you, Toussaint. Azuma had been a guide to my

mother from the time they first bonded up until her death. And now he serves me."

Toussaint was about to change the subject when something suddenly occurred to him. "If I'm not being too personal, you don't look to be more than twentysomething."

"Twenty-seven next month." Asha told him.

"So, if Azuma first came to serve your mother when she was a girl and you've had him since you were little . . ." Toussaint did the math in his head. "How freaking old is that monkey?"

"You wouldn't believe me if I told you," Asha said with a sly smile and left it at that.

A feeling of unease settled over Toussaint when Asha pulled into the parking lot of the Montgomery County Correctional Facility. After spending the last few years of his life surviving Rockview, the last thing he wanted was to be near any kind of lockup, voluntarily or otherwise. Unfortunately, the answers that Toussaint needed were inside that building. At least according to what he'd read in Darkhart's files.

Asha parked the car and got out, followed by Toussaint. Azuma wasn't pleased when he realized that he would have to wait in the car. It would be hard enough to get them to let in a convicted felon, but getting the guards to turn a blind eye to a monkey wasn't happening. Toussaint was happy to get away from the primate, if only for a little while. The monkey had been making Toussaint uncomfortable since meeting him, and Asha's tale made him even more leery.

It was just shy of 8:00 a.m. when they arrived. The building wasn't technically open yet, except to the staff and the guards. This didn't deter Asha. She marched up to the front doors and passed through them with the confidence of someone who worked there. The lobby was empty, save for one female corrections officer manning the front desk and an orange-clad trustee who was pushing a rank-looking mop across the floor. The man never looked up from his task as they passed, even when Toussaint offered an apology for stepping across his freshly mopped floor. They may as well have been invisible.

Asha told Toussaint to hang back while she approached the guard sitting behind the front desk and had a conversation. A few minutes later another corrections officer came through one of the doors. He was a tall white man, whose uniform was so wrinkled it was a good bet that he had slept in it. He stopped and exchanged a few words with the CO behind the desk. From the look on the wrinkled man's face, he clearly didn't agree with whatever he was being asked to do but complied anyhow.

After conducting the necessary screening for weapons and contraband, the wrinkled CO led them towards the visiting area. When the metal door slammed shut behind Toussaint, he reflexively jumped. As they walked, he took in his surroundings. The yellowing walls, chipped iron bars of the cells—most of them occupied by inmates—the constant hum of the ventilation system, and the scent . . . dear God! It smelled like misery and depression masked by cheap cleaning chemicals. These things all felt too familiar to him. Everything in that place was a grim reminder of what he had been forced to endure over the past several years. The temperature in the hall felt like it went up twenty degrees and he was finding it hard to breathe.

"You okay?" Asha asked, noticing the flushed look on his face.

"I'm good," Toussaint lied. Asha's expression said that she clearly didn't believe him, but she didn't press the issue.

They were escorted into the visiting room, which was empty—inmate visits wouldn't officially start for another hour or so. The wrinkled CO directed them to a small table ringed by hard plastic chairs, then he disappeared through another door. Toussaint opted to sit in the chair closest to the window. This gave him a view of the entire room. His foot tapped nervously under the table, and his shoulders were stiff. Asha could tell that he was uncomfortable. She placed her hand on top of his, and a feeling of warmth washed over him.

"You're just full of nifty tricks, huh?" Toussaint asked with a playful smile.

"No trick. Biology. Human touch releases oxytocin, the bonding hormone. It's like when a kid falls and scrapes their knee, the first thing their mother does is hug them and it suddenly doesn't hurt as much anymore," Asha explained.

"When I hurt myself, all my mother would do was tell me to drink a glass of ginger ale and go sit my ass down somewhere," Toussaint half joked. It was the truth though. "So, you think this trip will bear fruit?"

"I don't think Ezekiel would've steered us in this direction if it wouldn't. Something that I've learned in my time with him is that he isn't a man who does anything without thinking it through. He explores all possible outcomes and acts accordingly."

"You been working for Darkhart long?" Toussaint asked.

"A few years. Had some family troubles back home in New York, and I felt like I needed a fresh start. Floated around for a while when I first got here, trying to find work and a landlord willing to rent to me and my companion."

"I don't suppose too many places in the city were monkey friendly," Toussaint said with a chuckle. "As far as work, I would think a girl with your skill set would be in high demand. Especially in a city like Philadelphia."

"I left my criminal past in New York. I came to Philly to go legit."

"You call what Darkhart has you doing *going legit*?" Toussaint gave her a look.

"Compared to what I used to do? Yes."

Toussaint couldn't help but think about how they had first met and just let her answer lie, and then changed the subject, sensing that Asha's past was sensitive terrain. "So, anything you can tell me about this guy that wasn't in the files?" From what Toussaint had read, the person in custody had been an associate of Davis Sparks, but it didn't say much beyond that. The only other information the file contained on him were the charges he was currently fighting, which were assault and attempted murder.

"Only that he's said to be a very interesting character."

23

The first thing Toussaint noticed about Bobby Edwards was that he was a strikingly handsome man. He was tall, with dirty blond hair that hung down his back and the clearest blue eyes that Toussaint had ever seen. With his pale smooth white skin, Bobby Edwards looked like the perfect porcelain doll, save for an old scar just under his right eye. He was dressed in a blue jumpsuit and orange slides and still looked more like a model than a man capable of bludgeoning someone to death, which is what he stood accused of. But the one thing Toussaint had learned since beginning his investigation was that nothing connected to this case was as it seemed.

Wrinkled CO walked Edwards to the table where Toussaint and Asha sat and shoved him into one of the plastic chairs with enough force to make it clear that he was not fond of the inmate. "Five minutes," Wrinkled CO told them, before going to sit in a chair near the door he had just come through and flipping open a magazine.

"I declare, that man is as sour as an underripe lemon," Bobby said in a Southern twang, before rolling his eyes. He then turned his attention to the duo sitting across from him. "When they told me that I had a visit at the crack of dawn, I had assumed it was from that shitty-ass public defender that I've been assigned, but I'm pretty sure that neither of you are lawyers. Especially you, handsome," he addressed Toussaint. "I've either done something very right or very wrong to warrant a visit from Troubleman."

"I see my reputation precedes me."

"I may have read an article or two. I pride myself on being a man in the know. Last I heard you were rotting away in Rockview until the end of time, yet here you are." Bobby spread his hands. "I don't suppose you're here to refer me to the lawyer who got you off?"

"No, but I can do you one better. The man I work for is prepared to float your legal fees so that you get proper representation on these charges you're fighting," Toussaint informed him.

"Charges that I shouldn't be locked up for in the first place. I was attacked and defending myself!" Bobby shouted.

"By hitting a man over the head with a lamp ten times?" Asha added.

"What can I say? I'm passionate about life, especially my own," Bobby said. "So what do you want from me in exchange for this goodwill you're offering?"

"A bit of information about an old friend of yours, Davis Sparks," Toussaint said. At the mention of Sparks's name, Bobby's face darkened.

"That rattlesnake ain't got no friends. He's the reason I'm in here!" Bobby spat.

"How you figure?"

"Who do you think sent the man after me that I'm accused of trying to kill?"

"Bullshit," Asha spoke up. "What reason would Sparks have for wanting you dead?"

"To keep me quiet," Bobby informed her. "Me and Davis go way back. We were introduced through a mutual friend back in California. He was the ambitious young law student and I was the beautiful grifter, hustling on the Hollywood strip. I was the guy the college kids came to see when they needed party favors, girls, and other illicit things. I was their one-stop service provider." Bobby winked.

"You provide these services for Sparks too?" Toussaint asked.

"Absolutely! Davis was one of my regulars, but his thing wasn't drugs or girls."

"Then what was it?" Asha wanted to know.

"Take a guess," Bobby challenged.

It took a second for it to click in Toussaint's brain what Bobby Edwards was implying. "You're trying to tell us that Davis Sparks is—"

"Not according to him. 'A passing curiosity,' he would always say. Said it once every two weeks or so. He was in denial, if you ask me. Even married that dingbat Susan Parker to try and prove to himself that he wasn't what we all knew he was. Even she saw through his mask and left him."

That would explain why the marriage flew under the

radar, Toussaint thought to himself. "So, the beard wife finds out Davis is gay and leaves him?"

"Something like that," Bobby confirmed. "See, Davis had a type. He was into boys who liked to play dress-up. We called them the Beautiful People back then. He didn't have a taste for those of us who were comfortable in the skin we were born in. I learned that the hard way. It's how I got this." He pointed to the scar under his eyes. "We were out drinking one night at a bar in Hollywood, and I pushed up on him. I was only fishing a little to see if he would bite, but instead he beat me damn near to death."

"So, you were the guy he got arrested for fighting with?" Toussaint remembered what he had read in the file. "How come Davis didn't go to jail for it?"

"Because he has a rich family. They paid me to recant my statement, so I did. I needed the money more than I needed the headache. Not too long after, he left school, and that was the last time I saw him until I came to Philadelphia."

"Man does a number like that on my face, I'd do my best to avoid running into him again and not follow him across the country," Toussaint said. "Unless, of course, I had a motive."

"Guilty as charged," Bobby admitted. "I saw him on television one day, preaching about his war on drugs in Philadelphia. He looked like he was doing well for himself, meanwhile I'm living on the streets and sucking dick in bus station bathrooms for twenty dollars a pop. I figure if I tracked my old friend down I might be able to convince him to spread a little bit of that good fortune he had come into."

"You mean blackmail him," Toussaint corrected.

"I don't look at it like that. It was more like protecting his investment. The truth about who he really was could've done some serious damage to this new clean image of his. Besides, I figured he owed me. If I had let his ass sit in jail, he'd have probably ended up a janitor instead of a big-time lawyer."

"So did Davis agree to pay you off again?" Toussaint asked.

"Yes, he did." Bobby shook his head. "And like a damn fool I believed him. I gave him the address to the motel that I was staying in. He said he would send someone by from his office with the cash. Instead, he sent that thug who tried to kill me. The rest you already know."

Toussaint sat processing what Bobby Edwards had just told him. So, Davis Sparks was a closeted homosexual, and he was willing to kill to protect his secret. It made sense, considering what was at stake. He was in the middle of a mayoral campaign and that kind of information coming out would've destroyed his chances at winning the race. They lived in a progressive city, but there were plenty of voters who would refuse to put their support behind a man who didn't embody their idea of what America should look like. A thought came to Toussaint. He remembered what Butterfly had told him about Sarah and Fat Eddie having something lined up that had to do with Davis Sparks. "If

Sparks was willing to have you killed to protect his secret, is it possible that the girl they found dead with his daughter could've ended up in his crosshairs the same way?"

Bobby Edwards thought on it. "Anything is possible, but I don't think so. Davis did what he did to me because I threatened him. Davis Sparks is a piece-of-shit snake, but he's also very big on family. Always has been. Had it just been that other girl who got killed, then maybe that could've been the case, but I can't see him having put his own daughter in harm's way like that. If I had to guess? I'd say she was just in the wrong place at the wrong time."

"Time's up!" Wrinkled CO appeared, hovering over the table.

"Thank you for your time, Mr. Edwards." Toussaint and Asha stood to leave.

"Please, call me Bobby. And feel free to come see me some time, handsome." Bobby looked Toussaint up and down. Toussaint ignored the remark and turned to leave, but Bobby called after him. "What about that lawyer you promised me? I need to get out of here!"

Toussaint looked to Asha.

"Someone will be in touch with you shortly," Asha confirmed.

"So, what did you make of what he had to say?" Toussaint asked when they were back inside the Monte Carlo. This time Toussaint was driving and it wasn't up for debate.

"Edwards was telling the truth. I'd have known if he wasn't," Asha told him.

"So, you got a built-in lie detector to go along with your pet monkey fetish?" Toussaint asked with dripping sarcasm. Azuma shrieked at him from the back seat.

"No, I'm just very good at reading people. The same way I read you and convinced Ezekiel that you were worth saving," Asha shot back. "The story he told us was way too crazy to be anything but the truth. And it fills in some of the blanks from the file we have on him. Maybe we should go and talk to Sparks."

"After what happened to his daughter, the security detail around him has probably doubled. I doubt even your boss and all his resources could get us close to Davis Sparks right now."

"So, what are we supposed to do now?"

"Pray we get another break," Toussaint said. No sooner had the words left his mouth than his phone rang.

24

Toussaint didn't even wait for Asha's Uber to arrive before peeling off from the corner where he had dropped her off. He apologized and promised to hit her up later with an update. He didn't even give her a chance to argue before he got in the wind. It was kind of shitty for him to leave her like that, but he had an emergency to attend to. A family emergency, and she wasn't family. At least not yet.

He tore through the streets of Philadelphia like he was in the final lap of the Indy 500, weaving in and out of traffic at breakneck speeds. He'd nearly flipped the car while rounding the corner coming off the highway. He had no thoughts for his own safety, and none for the other people on the road. The tires of the Monte Carlo screeched when he slammed on the brakes in front of the brownstone. A few yards away, a crowd had gathered around Good 4 Yu. There was a heavy police presence at the restaurant, with several of the officers standing outside doing their best to keep the curious onlookers at a respectable distance while they did their work. The restaurant was now a crime scene.

Toussaint jumped out of the car and stormed towards the restaurant, blood pumping anger through his veins. The first thing he noticed was the front door, or what was left of it. The glass had been shattered and the metal frame was left barely hanging on. Toussaint ducked under the line of yellow police tape and approached Good 4 Yu. Halfway to the entrance he was stopped by an officer in uniform.

"Sir, I'm going to need you to step back. This is a crime scene," the officer told Toussaint and extended his hand as if he could stop the six-six tide of anger.

"No shit, Sherlock. I live here," Toussaint snapped. He hadn't indented to come off as short with the man, but someone had violated his home.

"*You* live in a Chinese restaurant?" The officer looked him up and down in disbelief. "Yeah, right. I'm gonna need you to step back behind the tape with everyone else until we're done."

"Let him pass," he heard a familiar voice call out. It was Sergeant Dobbs. She was dressed in street clothes, with her badge clipped to her belt. The officer wanted to argue, but she outranked him so he complied and stepped out of Toussaint's way.

"That's what the fuck I thought," Toussaint spat, making it a point to bump the officer as he passed him. "Thanks for that."

"No problem."

"And for calling me. I thought you worked a desk? How did you end up at the crime scene?"

"I was on my way to clock in for my shift when I got the call over the radio. I knew that you stayed here with the Weis, so I hit your line before coming over to see if I could help out. From what I've been told, the place got robbed and the older couple who own it roughed up."

Hearing this got Toussaint even more heated. "Anybody see anything?"

Dobbs shrugged. "Even if they did, nobody's saying anything. You know how that goes around here."

"Yeah, bullshit-ass code of the streets." Toussaint shook his head. "Give me a second." He excused himself and stepped inside the restaurant. The place had been torn up pretty bad. Windows were busted, tables overturned, and the paintings the Weis had hanging on the walls were slashed. In the middle of all the chaos he found John Wei. He was sitting on a chair and being attended to by a paramedic.

"I told you, I'm fine. I need to be with my wife!" John was arguing when Toussaint walked up. He had a black eye and a knot on his head. A young redheaded EMT was shining a light in his eyes checking him for signs of a concussion.

"You okay, John?" Toussaint asked.

"Yes, which is what I keep trying to tell them but all they want to do is poke at me and ask stupid questions. I need to get out of here so I can go check on Sue." John was borderline frantic. The incident had clearly shaken him up. "Those bastards robbed us and hurt my Sue!"

"Wait, what? What happened to her? Is she okay?" Toussaint was concerned.

"I don't know. The lady cop I saw you talking to told me that Sue was rushed to the hospital. Tommy and Aimee rode with her. We were getting ready to open when some guys in masks came in demanding money. We hadn't done any business yet, so there wasn't much in the register. I told Sue to let them have what they wanted, but you know how that woman can be sometimes. They got into a tussle and one of the guys hit her with a gun. She fell and hit her head. When I jumped in to try to defend her, I got knocked out. When I woke up, two police officers were helping me off the floor and my place was destroyed," he told him, sounding like he was fighting back tears.

"Damn" was all Toussaint could say.

"This is all my fault." John's shoulders sagged.

"You can't blame yourself for getting robbed, John," Toussaint told him.

"I'm not just talking about the robbery. I mean all of it. Everything I have done to get here. I did some things that I am not real proud of to escape Hong Kong, Toussaint. Always in the name of survival. And now I fear these things that are befalling my family are direct fallout from the decisions I've made."

"What you trying to say, John?" Toussaint felt like he was on the verge of a confession.

John looked at him, eyes tired. "That maybe fate doesn't let us change who we are, even when we try."

Toussaint studied his friend for a time. He searched for the words he needed. Words that would properly articulate where Toussaint was about to take the conversation without offending him. "John, we gotta talk."

"Toussaint, if it's more of this sit-and-wait business you've been preaching about Jay-Jay, I really don't want to hear it right now. Whatever you have to say can wait until I make sure Sue is okay," John insisted.

"Actually, it can't wait," Toussaint told him. He looked around to make sure no one was within earshot. "I found Charlie Tang."

"Really?" John looked surprised, and visibly brightened. "That's great news! He can tell what happened and they can let my son go!"

"Afraid that's not going to happen."

"And why the hell not?" John wanted to know.

"Because he's dead."

John's mouth fell open. "I . . . I don't understand."

"John, I gotta ask you something. Know that I mean you no disrespect, but I need a straight answer. Did you kill Charlie Tang?"

John's eyes went wide. "I tell you that my place has been destroyed and my wife assaulted and you respond with a joke?" He was angry.

"I ain't joking, John. I'm serious. Did you kill Charlie Tang?"

"Jesus, no! I mean, I'd be lying if I said the thought hadn't crossed my mind, being that he's to blame for my son being locked up, but I didn't kill him," he said with what sounded like genuine bewilderment. "Why would you even ask me something like that?" Now he sounded offended.

"Because he was murdered with a .22. The same as your pistol. John, you know me. If something happened, I need you to tell me so we can figure it out. Better you come clean with me than wait until the police start putting it together. By then I won't be able to help you."

John looked at Toussaint with disappointment filling his eyes. "For as long as you and I have known each other, I would've thought you of all people would know better than that. I haven't always been a good man, Toussaint, but I'm no monster. I would never kill a child, even one as rotten as Charlie Tang."

Seeing the hurt look on John's face made Toussaint feel like shit. He didn't want to believe the man who had taken him in would be capable of such a thing, but he couldn't ignore the evidence. "I'm sorry, John. It's just that I thought—"

"Save your apology, Toussaint. I thought I knew where we stood, but I guess I was wrong. Go ahead and check the gun for yourself. You'll see it hasn't been fired." He walked around the counter and dragged a lockbox from beneath it as he pulled his keys from his pocket. John turned the key in the lock and flipped the lid open—there was Chung's precious book, locked away as promised, but no gun. "I don't understand. I locked it in here after you dropped me off the other day. I'm sure of it. This is where I always keep it."

"Who else besides you has access to that box?"

"No one, only me. No one else could access that box without this key." He held up the small brass key.

"Then we have a serious problem. If we don't find that gun, Jay-Jay isn't going to be the only one the city puts away," Toussaint said seriously.

"Mr. Wei, we have a few more questions for the police report." A detective came over and interrupted their conversation. John looked to Toussaint, unsure what to do.

"You finish filling out the police report and then get to the hospital to be with Sue. I'll look into that other thing then meet you at the hospital," Toussaint told him. John nodded and walked off with the detective to finish filling out necessary paperwork.

Toussaint stepped back through the broken entrance of Good 4 Yu. He had been dreading that conversation since finding the shell casing. John Wei's .22 wasn't the only one in the city, but the whole situation hit too close to home to be a coincidence. Toussaint didn't believe in those. He was willing to bet good money that the bullet that killed Charlie Tang had been fired from that .22. John had said that he hadn't killed the boy, and Toussaint believed him. But if he hadn't, who had?

Toussaint stood there, arms folded and trying to keep his composure. The crowd of people who had been standing around when he pulled up had thinned, but there were still a good number of people gathered, gawking and anticipating news of the worst. The hood loved a good shit show that they could sit around and gossip about half the night when it was over.

"You okay?" Dobbs eased up on him.

"Honestly? Fuck no! The Weis are good people. All they're trying to do is make an honest living and fucked-up shit keeps happening to them. It ain't right." He was angry. Angry because the Weis got robbed, but even more so at himself because he still hadn't been able to keep his promise to bring their boy home.

Dobbs went to place a calming hand on his shoulder but caught herself. She could only imagine what some of her fellow officers would think if they noticed the gesture. He was, after all, a convicted cop killer, and she was a cop. So, instead, she placed her hand in her pocket and offered him words instead. "We're gonna find out who did this."

"No disrespect, Natasha, but we both know that's bullshit. The police don't give a fuck about what happens in the hood."

"Hold on, now. I know some cops could do better, but don't go grouping us all into that same barrel," Dobbs checked him.

"I know, but not enough cops think like you to really make a difference. And we as a community ain't making this shit no easier. I swear, we gotta be the only muthafuckas dumb enough to be more worried about standing on some G-code than speaking up when one of our own gets done wrong!" He was emotional, his voice raised now. Toussaint wanted to make sure the people from the neighborhood who were still watching could hear him loud and clear. Some of the cops were even paying attention now, as he addressed his neighbors. "Half you people spend more time out on these stoops than you do in your own homes and you mean to say not one of you know who did this bullshit?" His eyes landed on a cluster of young corner boys who he knew hustled in the area. "Y'all think you're keeping it gangsta by refusing to help the police, but really keeping it gangsta is being willing to do whatever you have to in order to look after your own. And the Weis are *our* own!"

Murmurs began to spread through the crowd. Some nodded and called out in agreement, while there were others who just silently, stoically listened. And of course you had those who dismissed the man and his plea for them to do better as a community as just another nigga shouting from atop a soapbox. Whatever their opinions were, they all heard him. Some even felt him, and it was showing. This made the police visibly start to tense, prepared to respond if this became a situation.

Dobbs felt the tension collecting in the air. She reached for Toussaint, and this time she did touch his arm. She didn't care who saw the gesture or what they thought about it. At that moment all she was concerned about was letting this man—this *Black* man—who was clearly in pain, know that he was not invisible. If nobody else did, she saw him. "C'mon, you've made your point." She tugged his arm gently. After a few beats he allowed her to lead him away, but not before his angry glare swept over the face of every person gathered there.

"Fucking cowards!" he spat at the crowd before turning back to Dobbs. "I'm sorry, Natasha. I'm just frustrated with all this shit," Toussaint apologized as he sat back on the hood of his car, running his hands down his face.

"And you have every right to be. But standing on a corner shouting at people who are either too scared to talk or just don't give a fuck ain't gonna do nothing but run your pressure up. Don't convince me to believe in you then you start crashing out. Stick to the script," Dobbs told him.

As they were talking, a young man walked up on them. He was short, wearing a baseball cap and jeans that fit a little too tight for Toussaint's liking. He wasn't sure, thought that he might've been a part of Jay-Jay's little crew. He looked from one side to the other, face twisted into a scowl that looked like he was born wearing it. Yeah, this was a tough kid. You could tell. This is why what he was about to say made Toussaint smile.

"Not everyone is a coward."

25

Reggie never saw it coming. Even if he had, he wasn't sure if he would've been able to do much to stop it. One minute he was sitting on a stool near the front door of Blue Skies, sipping a beer and listening to the guys talk shit. And the next, he was choking on one of his own back teeth. This is how it happened . . .

Blue Skies didn't jump off until it got dark. Unlike most regular bars, Blue Skies didn't cater to day drinkers or even the happy-hour crowd. Their patrons were the types of people who didn't stir out of bed until after 5:00 p.m. So during the days it was usually quiet as a cemetery, unless Butterfly called early rehearsals for her sets. Other than that, Blue Skies was dead during daylight hours. Except for days when they were receiving deliveries. Days like that one when Reggie lost his tooth.

Reggie had been Jin's replacement. His sole job was to sit in front of that door and keep his eyes open. So far he had proved pretty competent at it. That morning was his third day on the job. He had been asked to come in because Spider and some of the guys needed a few extra bodies to help with a shipment that had just come in. Reggie was at his usual post near the door, while a few of the guys sat around the table playing cards and drinking. It wasn't even noon, a little too early to be drinking, but what else were they supposed to do in a bar?

A light tapping at the front door drew Reggie's attention. This was followed by the door jiggling as if someone was trying to come in. He was sure that he had flipped the closed sign and the door was locked. The only people who were even aware that there was anyone inside at that hour were the people who were already inside. So who the hell could it be? When Reggie went to the door to tell them to fuck off, he found out. The door came crashing in, hitting Reggie in the face, knocking one of his molars into his throat and causing him to start choking. He was still doubled over, trying to dislodge the tooth from his throat, when Toussaint socked him in the back of the head, knocking him unconscious. The guys who had been playing cards and drinking had ceased their game and all became stone sober at the sight of it.

Toussaint stepped over Reggie's prone body and into Blue Skies. There was a baseball bat in his hand, which he slapped against his palm in a slow, rhythmic motion. "I'm looking for the bitch who calls himself Spider, bitch who thinks it's cool to be beating up on old people. Any of y'all seen him?" The men around the table exchanged confused glances. "Don't worry about it. I'll find him on my own." He entered their lair.

"Get his ass!" someone shouted, ringing the bell for the opening round.

Toussaint didn't panic when he found himself surrounded. He let the bat swing low, back and forth like a pendulum, while making sure to keep as many of them in his line of vision as possible. The men took turns fake lunging at him before retreating again, like they were about to jump double Dutch. They outnumbered Toussaint, but nobody wanted to be the first one to taste the wooden bat. One of them finally felt brazen enough to volunteer. He tried to go for Toussaint's legs. Toussaint swung the bat with enough force to have made Ryan Howard proud. The bat connected with the man's arm and broke it at the forearm. He followed up by bringing the bat around and hitting the man in the side, hard enough to crack a rib.

The next one to try his luck against the slugger found slightly greater success. He was smart enough not to come at Toussaint empty-handed, having selected a barstool as his weapon of choice. When the stool collided with the bat, the stool won out. Toussaint lost his grip and the bat skidded across the barroom floor. The man jabbed the stool at Toussaint, seat end first. Toussaint focused his energy, and when he shot his fist out to meet the stool it went clean through the wood. With his arm shoulder deep through the stool, Toussaint grabbed the man by his shirt and began yanking him against the legs of the chair, striking him repeatedly in the face. Toussaint finished him off by throwing him through one of the dirty glass windows. The last time Toussaint had gotten into a scuffle inside

Blue Skies, he was just trying to keep from getting his ass kicked. This time, he was out for blood.

"What the hell is going on out here?" Spider came out of Fat Eddie's office. When he saw his boys laid out and Toussaint standing over them with a crazed look in his eyes, Spider did the sensible thing and ran back the way he came. Toussaint was on his ass. He yelped as he was lifted off his feet by the back of his pants and tossed headfirst into a rack of pots.

"It's bad enough that y'all framed Jay-Jay, but now you fucking with his people? You should've never crossed that line, Spider." Toussaint stalked towards him.

"Hold on, man! I'm just a soldier following orders!" Spider pleaded, pushing himself backward to try and stay out of Toussaint's reach.

"And I'm just a man who is tired of people like you," Toussaint snatched him up and began pummeling him. Spider was almost out on his feet, but Toussaint shook him violently to keep him from passing out. He still had use for Spider. "Who killed those girls? Was it you? You the one who framed Jay-Jay?" All he got in response was a series of gurgled rasps and wheezes.

"Boy can't tell you something he doesn't know," someone spoke up behind Toussaint. Goliath stepped up through a side door, leading to what Toussaint assumed was the basement of the club.

"Then maybe it's a question I should be directing at your boss. Where is he?" Toussaint asked.

"That ain't none of your concern, Troubleman. Eddie tried to give you an out. Why didn't you take it?" Goliath asked, while he and Toussaint circled each other in the small kitchen. He cracked his knuckles menacingly.

"I guess that's just me being hardheaded." Toussaint rolled his neck to loosen up. They both knew what was coming.

"And now you'll just be dead!" Goliath struck first, sending a punch at Toussaint that would've likely put him in a coma had it smashed into his chin, instead of the frying pan Toussaint snatched up to place between them. "That was cute," Goliath observed and shook his hand. He threw another punch, and when Toussaint went to try his little trick a second time, Goliath surprised him and planted one of his size sixteen shoes into Toussaint's chest.

Toussaint flew over the counter that separated the kitchen from the bar area. He felt the wind flee his body as he fell through one of the tables. Goliath lumbered in his direction, murder in his eyes. Toussaint had just forced himself back to his feet when Goliath reached him. Goliath grabbed at Toussaint, but instead ended up taking two quick rabbit punches to the kidneys. This pushed Goliath up enough to give him some room. He threw a jump kick, but Goliath blocked it. Toussaint dropped down and tried to sweep his legs, but Goliath was rooted.

Goliath grabbed Toussaint by the back of his shirt and pulled it over his head, temporarily blinding him. The bigger man took full advantage by raining blows on Toussaint's sides and back. He tried to grab hold of Toussaint's neck, intent on breaking it, but Toussaint slipped out of his shirt and out of reach.

Toussaint staggered backward while the big man advanced on him. He couldn't keep going toe to toe with a man who outweighed him so much. He needed to put this fight to bed. Focusing his energy, he prepared for his signature strike. Goliath charged in, seeking to press his advantage. Toussaint let him get close before releasing the energy and striking with his two fingers. He had planned on crippling Goliath as he had done Jade, but the large man had other ideas. Toussaint howled as Goliath grabbed his finger before it could make contact and snapped it.

"I pride myself on learning from the mistakes of others." Goliath laughed before wrapping his massive hands around Toussaint's neck and lifting him off his feet. "I'm going to break you, Troubleman."

Toussaint kicked, punched, and did everything else he could think of to try and break Goliath's grip, but it wasn't happening. The joints in his neck sounded like milk being poured into a bowl of Rice Krispies as they began to make snapping and crackling noises. His vision was getting hazy. Just as he felt himself slipping away, something caught his eye that made him smile.

"Fuck are you smiling at?" Goliath wanted to know. Toussaint didn't respond. He just kept wearing that dopey-ass smile while watching an old friend descend from the ceiling like a tiny, furry ninja. The giant shrieked, released his grip on Toussaint as Azuma's claws raked at his eyes. He lumbered around the bar, knocking over furniture while trying to get the monkey off him.

"You good?" Asha appeared beside Toussaint, who was on his hands and knees, gasping.

"I will be," Toussaint coughed. "What are you doing here? You been following me?"

"Ezekiel asked me to keep you alive, so that's what I'm trying to do. But your ass isn't making it easy." Asha helped him to his feet. "Can you stand?"

"Yeah."

"Good, then that means that you can fight. Let's finish this," Asha said and went to aid her totem.

The trio of Asha, Toussaint, and Azuma moved like tightly choreographed dance partners, moving in and out of Goliath's space. Whenever he blocked one, the other two would strike: Asha with her blades, Azuma with claws and teeth, and Toussaint with his fists. Goliath was a mess of open wounds and covered in blood, but he still had some fight left in him.

"I'm gonna kill all three of you," Goliath threatened. He teetered from side to side like his legs were having trouble supporting him.

"Not before you bleed to death," Asha told him.

Goliath looked at her like she was crazy. He was cut up pretty bad, but he had endured worse. He was about to tell the smug girl as much, when he felt something splash on his shoe. When he looked down he realized that it was blood. It dripped from his nose, followed shortly after by one of his ears. Before Goliath knew what was happening, he was bleeding from damn near every hole in his body. "Witchcraft!" he spat at Asha.

"No, my own special anticoagulant that I treat my blades with. Faster and more efficient than general poisons, and it won't show up in your toxicology report . . . Not that you'll have one," Asha explained to Goliath.

Goliath did not die quickly, or pleasantly. It took him roughly five minutes to die. Five minutes may not seem like a long time, but it feels like an eternity when you're watching them bleed out. Neither member of the trio relaxed until the giant had stopped moving and they were sure that he was dead.

Toussaint pulled himself up to the bar, breathing heavily. His eyes landed on an unopened bottle of Scotch. One of the few that hadn't gotten broken when he came in and started kicking ass. He twisted off the cap and took a deep swig. "I guess I owe you two now?" he said to Asha and extended the bottle.

"I guess so," she said, taking a swig.

Hearing Azuma squawk got Toussaint's attention. It was coming from somewhere behind the door marked OUT OF SERVICE that Toussaint had asked Maggie about. Behind the door was a long corridor that seemed to stretch the length of the building. Toussaint, followed by Asha, ventured down it, following the sound of Azuma's calls. When they came out on the other side of the tunnel, Toussaint staggered back in utter shock and disgust.

Roughly an hour later, Blue Skies was crawling with cops and EMTs. What Toussaint and Asha had discovered, hidden behind a false wall at the end of that corridor, was literally a shop of horrors. Locked into wire cages were eight girls, ranging in ages from fourteen to twenty. A few were local, but for the most part they were from different ports outside the U.S. All were girls who had run away and ended up in the care of Fat Eddie—to be brokered and sold like used cars. But finding these girls was only the tip of the iceberg. It wasn't enough that he was kidnapping and selling them, but Fat Eddie was also recording them. The police confiscated two dozen boxes of tapes that Toussaint had no desire to see. Just the thought of it made him queasy.

Toussaint sat on the edge of the desk in Fat Eddie's office while one of the EMTs tended to his injuries. Two detectives were also in the room, taking his statement for the third time. "It's like I told you guys. I came in here to get a drink. These guys all started fighting and I ran off to hide in the bathroom, but took a wrong turn. That's how I found the girls. I hid in the back with them until it sounded like it was over. Then I called you guys."

In fact, immediately after the death of Goliath, Asha called Darkhart, who sent in a cleaning crew. Whatever she had poisoned Goliath with wouldn't likely show up in any blood work they ran at any Philadelphia PD lab, but why take unnecessary chances? Darkhart's people took the entire body and cleaned up any trace that might've been left behind. This is why she had made Toussaint wait to call the cops.

It was a bullshit story. Everyone in the room knew it, but did it matter? A sex trafficking ring happening in the middle of the city had just been blown wide open, thanks to Troubleman. Of course, Toussaint knew that Asha and Azuma had more than played a role, but he couldn't very well tell the cops that a witch and a monkey had helped him out. They were likely to lock him up in a rubber room.

While Toussaint was being bandaged up, he looked around Fat Eddie's office. There was a picture on the wall that he hadn't noticed during his first visit. It was a picture of Butterfly. She was leaning against a railing with the Hong Kong skyline in the background. Her dark eyes stared at him invitingly. It was then that the revelation hit him like someone had just dumped cold water down his back. "You have got to be shitting me."

26

Butterfly didn't seem too surprised when Toussaint showed up at her room at the Duffield. She opened the door and turned back the way she had come, without even looking back to see if he would follow. It was a nice room, with a small kitchen and a balcony. She curled one leg under herself on the couch and plucked a joint from the ashtray, which she fired up. "How did you find me?"

"Good memory"—Toussaint tapped his temple—"and nose"—he tapped his nostril. "I remembered you telling me that this is the place you come to when you're looking to get lost. All I had to do was sniff around for whoever was smoking the best weed. It really wasn't that hard."

"Well done, detective." Butterfly nodded in approval.

"Thank you, Butterfly . . . or should I call you Andrew Junior." Before coming over, Toussaint had put in a request to Ezekiel Darkhart, to find out the identity of the boy in the picture with John. Whether Darkhart knew his reasons for asking or not, he never said. He simply had his people provide Toussaint with the information.

Butterfly bristled. "It's been a very, very long time since I've been called that. I always hated my name because it was forever a reminder of that piece of shit."

"Your dad, the man who sold you." Toussaint understood her resentment.

"What gave me away?" she wanted to know.

"Your eyes," Toussaint said honestly. "I remember the first time I saw you on stage and saw those eyes I was struck by them. They were so unique. I've met a lot of women with dark eyes, but not like yours. They're like tar pits. It took me a minute to recognize them when I saw them again, but I eventually did. You lied to me about knowing John Wei."

"Technically I didn't. My dealings with John were in another life. When I was still Andrew. Besides, what was I supposed to tell you, that this sweet old man who you have such love and respect for is the one who turned me out?"

"What else have you been lying to me about? The story of how you came to be? You being in love with Jay-Jay and wanting to save him? How much of it is real and how much is part of the illusion?"

"I guess that all depends on who you ask."

Toussaint closed the distance between them. He was tired of playing games and people trying to spin him. He grabbed Butterfly by the wrist and jerked her to her feet. He had almost forgotten how tall she was until they were standing nose to nose. "Cut the shit and shoot straight. It's all in the open, so you might as well. Were you down with that shit Fat Eddie had going on?"

Butterfly jerked away from him. "After what I've gone

through, why would I be? I hated what Fat Eddie had allowed himself to become. I wanted to burn that whole vile operation to the ground, but I couldn't do it on my own. I could prime the charge, but I needed someone else to push the detonator. You should be thanking me for pointing you in the right direction. When the story of what you did back there hits the news, you'll be back in as darling of the city. I did you a favor."

"Don't try to play me, Butterfly. You wasn't trying to help nobody but yourself in this," Toussaint told her. "You've been pulling the strings from behind the scenes the whole time. It wouldn't surprise me if it was you who whacked those girls and left Jay-Jay to hang for it!"

"I would never. Admittedly, I started sleeping with the boy as a way to get back at his father. I wanted to build Jay-Jay up before I broke him into pieces, just like John Wei did to me all those years ago. Then I ended up liking the little fucker. That much about this story is true. Believe me, if I could tell you who really killed those girls I would, but it's the one thing I was never able to discover."

"Maybe I can shed some light on that front." A third voice joined the conversation. The pink balcony curtains fluttered and from behind them stepped Tommy.

"Tommy? What the hell are you . . ." Toussaint's words trailed off when he saw what was in his hand: John Wei's missing .22. "So you killed Charlie Tang?"

"He deserved it. He was trying to help set Jay-Jay up for the murder of that girl. That's how the earring got into

Jay-Jay's room. Charlie planted it," Tommy explained. "I'd kill Charlie twice more if I could. But the two girls . . . It's complicated," Tommy said.

"Murder usually isn't. What did them girls ever do to you, Tommy? Why'd you kill them?" Toussaint wanted to know.

"It's this bitch's fault!" Tommy pointed the gun at Butterfly, causing her to jump. "If you'd never come to this city then those girls would still be alive."

"Tommy, what are you babbling about?" Toussaint demanded.

"Don't you get it? She was going to ruin it all! I heard Auntie Sue and John arguing about it one night, after finding one of her flyers in Jay-Jay's room. Auntie said that the trans girl who sings at the club could ruin things for us here in America. If it ever got out who John used to be, we could all be thrown in prison or, worse, sent back. I had to protect Auntie Sue, so I got rid of the trans girl for her. Only thing is, I killed the wrong girl."

"Sarah was trans, too?" Toussaint looked at Butterfly, who nodded. This story was getting crazier by the minute. "I know Sue didn't put you up to this?"

"No, she would never condone what I've done. I'm doing what I have to do to protect us all." Tommy sneered at Butterfly.

"Don't do this, Tommy!" Toussaint stepped between him and Butterfly.

"I have to. We won't be safe until she's dead. I don't

want to shoot you, Toussaint, but I will to get to her," Tommy warned.

"Then that's what you're going to have to do," Toussaint told him. Tommy looked hesitant and Toussaint figured that he could reason with the boy. This thought died when the gun went off and Toussaint found himself on the carpet, bleeding from a hole in his thigh. "You fucking shot me!" he howled.

"I warned you." Tommy shrugged. "Now for you," he said, his attention was back on Butterfly. "You should've never come—"

The door to the hotel room flew in and the room was suddenly flooded with members of the Philadelphia PD, Sergeant Dobbs leading the charge. "Hands, muthafucka! Hands!" she ordered. Tommy wisely dropped the gun and lay down on his stomach.

"Jesus, it took you long enough," Toussaint said, clutching his injured leg.

"You told us not to come in until we got the full confession. Just wasn't expecting it to come from him. Where did he even come from?" Dobbs motioned towards Tommy, who was being placed in cuffs by another officer. "Thank God for technology." She pulled one of the earpieces Toussaint had gotten from Darkhart out of her ear.

"Thank God, indeed. Now can somebody get me to a hospital before I bleed to death!" Toussaint pleaded.

EPILOGUE

The whole ordeal made both local and national news: Ex-cop busts sex trafficking ring and exonerates innocent man. The press was all over it and Toussaint's name was ringing again, but this time for the right reasons. It felt good to be a hero.

Jay-Jay was a free man, and Tommy had taken his place in a cage. As it turned out, Tommy hadn't been especially truthful about his job back in China. The Nobodies weren't the glorified paper pushers he downplayed them to be. They were a shadow unit that specialized in espionage. Tommy didn't take it to trial. He confessed that he had killed Sarah thinking she was Butterfly, and Vickie Sparks had ended up as collateral damage. He was currently in a federal holding facility awaiting extradition back to China. The whole process was tied up in a shit show of red tape because of Tommy's affiliation with the Nobodies and the potentially damning information he possessed about their organization. If China got hold of him, Tommy likely wouldn't make it to trial, but Toussaint was quietly rooting for the loyal young boy.

Toussaint had been following the media coverage on

his phone. At the press conference outside the prison when Jay-Jay was released, Toussaint expected him to cap some gangster shit about being wrongfully accused, but to his surprise the boy spoke like he had some sense and was just grateful to be home. The few days he had spent in a cell, wondering if he would end up in the gas chamber, had done what his parents couldn't, and that was convince him to grow up.

Jay-Jay wasn't the only one in the news. Davis Sparks had finally been granted closure on what had really happened to his daughter, and he was thankful that the people who had been involved got what was coming to them. Butterfly was brought up on trafficking, prostitution, and extortion charges along with the rest of Fat Eddie's crew. As it turned out, the play Fat Eddie had put into motion was indeed blackmailing Davis Sparks. Unbeknown to any except those who had been involved in the twisted scandal was that Davis Sparks had been carrying on a relationship with Sarah, and Vickie had made secret recordings of them at her house. It was a damn shame that Sparks's own flesh and blood was willing to cross him for a few bucks. What made matters worse was that Eddie's fat ass had the audacity to attempt to blackmail someone for the same thing he was up to: having a taboo lover. Had some of the men Eddie was in business with realized that Butterfly was trans, Eddie would've likely been cut out a long time ago. It was the nature of the game they played. Butterfly had plans to cut a deal with the prosecutor for a lesser sentence, but

Fat Eddie beat her to it. He snitched on the entire crew, including Goliath, who was said to be a fugitive in hiding. Toussaint knew that they would never find him, but who was he to tell them to quit looking?

Not all stories had happy endings though. There had been losses on both sides of this case's coin. One that had the most impact was the passing of Sue Wei. She had succumbed to the injuries inflicted on her during the assault at the restaurant and passed from blunt-force trauma to the head. Because of his involvement, Spider had managed to turn what would've been an assault charge into a murder.

Toussaint was sad about Sue's passing, but after what he had learned about John Wei and his wife, it was hard for him to look at them as he had—the sweet family who had taken him in. Toussaint had always looked at the Weis as needing protecting, but in truth they were apex predators. There was no way he could ever look at them the same. Toussaint never revealed the truth about the Weis to Jay-Jay or Aimee. When he told them he was moving out of the brownstone, he downplayed it as him just needing his own space. They were innocent in it all, and after they lost their mother he decided to spare them further heartache.

After the loss of his wife, John became a shell of himself. His former friend was down bad, and it took a lot out of Toussaint not to try and comfort John as he and Sue had always done for him, but finding out what John had been involved in had drawn a line in the sand that Toussaint wasn't willing to cross. During the last conversation he had with John Wei, the former sex trafficker had asked Toussaint why he didn't turn him in to the authorities. In truth, Toussaint had considered it, but decided that him having to look into the faces of his children every day, living with the knowledge that his actions were responsible for the death of their mother, would be a heavy enough load for him to carry for however many years he had left on earth. Guilt was a far better prison than whatever concrete walls the state would put around him.

Toussaint stayed in the hospital a few days after being shot. The bullet had gone straight through and hadn't caused any damage. They were just keeping him for observation. On the last day of his stay, Ezekiel Darkhart had come to visit. He showed up at Toussaint's hospital room with his signature winged hair, wearing dark glasses and an overcoat, though it was nearly eighty degrees outside. "Have you seen this?" he asked, tossing a newspaper onto Toussaint's bed so that he could read the headline. It was about Davis Sparks withdrawing his name from the mayoral race. "Claims he had to drop out for health reasons."

"I don't suppose those health reasons have anything to do with the tapes Asha plucked from Eddie's place before I called the cops?" Toussaint eyed him. He was far from naïve, but Darkhart knew that by then.

"I told you Gallagher was the dark horse," Darkhart smirked. "This shit show you created was worth the price of admission, Mr. Batiste."

"Is that supposed to be some kind of compliment?" Toussaint asked.

"No, just an observation. Oh, and before I forget." Darkhart reached into his trench coat and produced something wrapped in a silk sack and placed it on Toussaint's bed.

Toussaint cautiously opened the sack and looked inside. It was the Book of Wah Pei that he had left with John. "How the fuck you get your hands on this?"

"By this point in our relationship, do you really need to ask?"

No, he didn't. "For as big of a hard-on as you've had for this thing, why give it back instead of adding it to your collection of information?"

"Because it was the honorable thing to do," Darkhart told him. "So what do you have planned for yourself when you get out?"

"I don't know, maybe think how I want to spend my fifty grand," Toussaint told him.

"That's a lot of frog skins." He whistled. "Maybe you take that nice girl of yours out on a real date. Or even better, help your baby girl get back on her feet? You know at Darkhart Industries we offer excellent health benefits. I'm more than willing to help you get that monkey off her back."

"Watch your mouth," Toussaint warned.

Darkhart raised his hands in surrender. "I'm just trying to look out for my people."

"I do one job and that makes me your people?"

"No, but this next one might. You up for some more work, Troubleman?" Darkhart asked.

"What kind of job?"

"I need you to recover something that was taken away from me a long time ago."

"And what would that be?" Toussaint asked suspiciously.

Ezekiel Darkhart undid the buttons on his shirt and showed Toussaint the long surgical scar stretching down his chest. "My heart."

ACKNOWLEDGMENTS

It has been many moons since I've done acknowledgments. Truth be told? I almost passed on adding them to this novel. Then I got a random message on Facebook from my sixth-grade teacher Mrs. Skeados of P.S. 84. She shared with me some of my writing that she had been holding on to all these years. Those pages are older than some of you who are reading this. That was a dark period in my life. I'll spare you the particulars, but if you grew up in the eighties then you have an idea of what some of us kids had to endure. Reading those tattered yellow pages that spoke in the voice of an old man who was tired of living rather than that of a child, I was reminded of who I am and who I am destined to be . . . A survivor in both cases. Now let's get to it.

First and foremost I have to thank God. You have resurrected me more times than Lazarus. We lost touch for a while, but I have been consciously working to rebuild our relationship. Thanks for hanging in there with me.

My mother, Brenda M. Foye, who passed this amazing gift on to me at the time of her passing. This was never my dream, but yours. Reluctantly, I have accepted the mantle and am running with it. It is in your name that I push myself to be the most well-remembered writer of this generation. When it's all said and done, achieving anything less than greatness means I have failed you, and that is not an option.

My wife, Charlotte, who has been my biggest supporter and given me grace while I continue to chase this elusive dream. I know this ride has been rougher than we'd imagined and you've given a lot of yourself to keep me propped up when I feel like falling down. You are loved and appreciated more than you know.

My children, Nijaa and Alexandria, who are the lights in my life. My reason for not crashing out when slipping into madness feels like an easier route than fighting to maintain my sanity. You both have grown into beautiful, educated, and powerful young women. Yours will be the voices that will help to change the world. Never forget that.

Young Star. Your mother gave you a name of power. Step into that and claim what the world owes you. It's taking you a minute to figure it out, but we'll still be here rooting for you until you do and beyond.

The Foye clan. As the years go by our numbers are dwindling. We are the last of a proud and magical bloodline. We've had our struggles individually and as a family, especially when we lost the glue, Tee-Tee. The blessing is that at ninety-something years old, the matriarch of our family, Nana, is still here and still raising hell. We've got more days behind us than we do ahead of us, let's make the most of them. If not for us, for her.

Marc Gerald and the Europa team. I am fairly certain that I am one of your more challenging clients to work with because I see the world a little differently than most. Yet you guys continue to have my back and I appreciate that.

Sean McDonald, for giving me the opportunity to prove that I am more than just a one-trick pony. This project was very challenging to me because it took me longer than usual to find my comfort zone. Thank you for your patience. I'm looking forward to seeing where this new journey takes us.

And where would I be without my readers? Shout-out to all my cousins in KRG (K'wan's Readers Group). I am so grateful for the love and support you guys have shown me over these last couple of decades. It trips me out when some of you guys tell me how you started reading me in school and have now turned your own children on to my work. God willing, I'll give you another two decades of heat to pass on to future generations.

That being said, on with the show . . . Let's get into some Trouble.